From: Farrell, Tam (t.farrell@tne.global.net)

Time: 17:22

To: hrrrpenny@rainandfire.co.uk

Subject: David Rain

Dear hrrrpenny,

Thanks for the feedback on David Rain. Appreciate you taking time to reply, but you've told me nothing more than I can find on your website already. Feature needs a definite angle. Some history. Circumstances of his disappearance, perhaps? If you can't supply, will look elsewhere.

Regards,

Tam Farrell

Features Editor

The National Endeavour

883 Wellington High Road

London N1

ORCHARD BOOKS
338 Euston Road
London NW1 3BH
Orchard Books Australia
Level 17-207 Kent Street, Sydney, NSW 2000, Australia

ISBN 978 1 84616 425 5 (hardback)
ISBN 978 1 84616 426 2 (paperback)

First published in Great Britain in 2007
First published in paperback 2008
Text © Chris d'Lacey 2007

10 9 8 7 6 5 4 3 2 1 (hardback)
10 9   (paperback)
Printed in Great Britain

Orchard Books is a division of Hachette Children's Books,
an Hachette UK company.

www.hachette.co.uk

The
Fire Eternal

Chris d'Lacey

ORCHARD BOOKS

for Owen and Denise

Thanks to everyone at Orchard who's been involved with this project, and for all your continuing enthusiasm and support. Also Andrew and Merel at J&A, one of whom is now delivering babies (mwah). I'd like to say a special thanks to Jo Williams of the Aldbourne CBG for wagging a stern finger and making me a lovely stew, and to Karen & Dennis at the Well Wisher Bookshop for looking after me and making sure I never got lost in Wiltshire! The same appreciation is extended to Ros and Julie over in the West Midlands, who've been there for me from day one. Also to Sam, who deserves a big hrrr for making the breakthrough and yet is still humble enough to lay some praise at my door. And last but not least to Jay . . . that polar bear sure was worth it.

. . . the eye altering, alters all.
William Blake

Part One

Arctic ice cap, unrecorded time

It began with a wind from another world. A fury unlike any other kind of blizzard. It tore a hole in the sky and screamed at the ice, forcing them together with an elemental charge. The eddy drew a death song out of the night and with it beat a storm all the way up to the clouds. The sea shook and the tablet of ice it supported broke in a random starburst of cracks.

And when all this had passed, what was left was a bear.

He was lying with his paws outstretched and straight, his snout pushed down between the hump of his knees. The wind at first refused to die. It ripped at his fur, making shallow angry waves across the curves of his back. It tugged again, and again and again, but on the fourth gust his great head rose in defiance and he breathed and held in the cold, sharp air. The wind grew tame in an instant and dropped. It fell to a whimper as he opened his eyes.

Lumbering slightly, he rose to his feet. The wind made apologetic circles around him. He ignored it and plugged ten claws into the ice. The auma of the north poured into his heart. With it came power and a terrifying knowledge, of a world disappearing too fast, too soon. He opened his jaws then and roared at the sky, until his voice became water droplets melting in the atmosphere. Snow fell on the crest of the planet.

This was the beginning.

And this would be the end.

But the Earth would not know it for another year yet.

A very special gift

Sunday. February 14th. St Valentine's Day. The words spiralled round Suzanna Martindale's head as she walked hand in hand with her daughter, Alexa, along the deserted High Street in Scrubbley. It had been five years to this day since her partner, David Rain, had disappeared during a student field trip into the ice cold waters of the Arctic Ocean – and still the memory would not settle. In her mind, she replayed that dreadful moment, holding him, willing him to keep on breathing, remembering his head falling into her arms before surrendering his body to the breaking ice and the awesome power of four guardian polar bears. Tears burned her eyes, fuzzing out the street lamps. She whispered his name. *David.* A gust of air as sharp as a blade replied, landing a crystal of ice on her face. She touched it, rubbing it into her tears. David, she said again, and squeezed Alexa's hand. *David. My one true love. David.*

"Mummy, are we going to see Santa Claus?"

The sheer sweetness of the question made Zanna chuckle. Such innocence could almost make her choke on joy. "No, darling, we did that at Christmas."

The little girl lifted her feet into a skip. The antlers of her reindeer hat flapped to the beat. "Are we going to see Snigger?"

Snigger. The 'hero' of David's squirrel story. Now a bestseller and family favourite. Zanna turned her head to one side. They were passing the precinct that branched off the High Street and led towards the library and the gardens beyond. Among those trees and twisting paths, David had first been inspired to write. "No, baby. Just to the shop."

"Mmm," went the child. And it wasn't really clear if she was satisfied by this answer or not. She changed her legs, almost stumbling for a pace or two.

"Careful," Zanna said, and swung her to a stop.

They were looking at a small bay window, with slightly rotting frames and gaps in the putty. It was a shop, Zanna's shop, and it was closed for the evening. The interior was locked and dark. But in one corner of the window, on a candlestick as gothic as a vampire's finger, a candle spilling lava trails was burning freely. Beside it was a card. A Valentine's card. A single red heart on a tall white background. It was open, but the words were difficult to read. Next to the card sat a small clay dragon.

"Ruffen!" cried Alexa, pointing to it.

"Guh-ruffen," said her mother. "Don't forget the 'guh'."

"Guh!" went Alexa and put her hand on the glass with just enough force to make it rattle.

To no one's amazement, the dragon rolled his eyes in recognition. He lifted a paw and dibbled his slightly stubby little fingers.

Alexa responded with a happy wave. "What's Gruffen doing?" she asked, pronouncing his name correctly this time.

"Just guarding," said Zanna, and feeling overwhelmed added quietly to herself, "Just guarding Daddy's flame." A gallery of pictures flashed through her mind. They gathered in a spear of ice in David Rain's heart. She took a tissue from her pocket and dabbed her eye. "Lexie, I've got something for you."

The little girl turned on her heels.

"Hold out your hands, together, in a cup."

No stranger to presents, Alexa adopted the pose right away.

"Listen carefully," said Zanna, dropping down on one knee. She brushed a curl of black hair off Alexa's forehead. "You know we talked about polar bears and the icy place they live?"

"Yes," said Alexa (possibly hopeful of receiving one).

Zanna looked at her a moment and tried to frame the

words. Those eyes. His eyes. That rich dark blue. Unsettling and comforting, all in one glance. "Your daddy gave me a dragon there once. I want you to have him, because . . . because Mummy can't look after him any more."

The little girl frowned and tilted her head. "Why are you crying?" she asked.

Zanna bracketed her hands as if she was holding an invisible piece of rock. "You have to look very, very hard to see him. But he's there. He's real. His name is G'lant and his is a flame that will never die out." She opened her hands – as if she was scattering the ashes of her grief – and set G'lant down on Alexa's palms.

The girl looked thoughtfully at the space above her gloves. "I like him," she said.

Zanna sobbed and reaching out, hugged her daughter tight. "I like *you*," she said. "And I love you so much." Her pale lips tremored against the child's head.

A second went by, then Alexa gasped.

"What? What is it?" Zanna drew back to look at her.

Alexa turned her face to the open sky.

And from out of the darkness came fairy lights: snow.

What Zanna wrote

At the same time that Zanna was out with Alexa, something odd was going on in the house at 42 Wayward Crescent where they lived with Elizabeth and Lucy Pennykettle, and Elizabeth's partner, Arthur.

Another dragon called Gwendolen was preparing for a mission.

Gwendolen belonged to Lucy. She was a special dragon made by Lucy's mother, Liz. Liz was a potter by trade and well known in the town of Scrubbley for her extraordinary dragon sculptures, though none that reached the market place there were quite as extraordinary as the ones that inhabited the Pennykettle household.

Gwendolen was just such a dragon. For years she had sat quietly on Lucy's bedside table, going almost unnoticed in the shadows by the lamp. Unlike the other special dragons in the house she had never shown any kind of magical ability. But on Lucy's eleventh birthday, when the girl's hair had begun to turn a deep shade of red (just like her mother's and her distant, dragon ancestor Guinevere's) Gwendolen began to show an interest in something.

Computers.

It was a pursuit which mirrored Lucy's ambitions, but one which left the other dragons wary and suspicious. For they had seen Gwendolen rise from obscurity to become the kind of dragon that understood *data* and *symbols* and *code*. It was unnatural, they thought. A little bit . . . *progressive*. But Lucy was Lucy, she had dragon in her blood. So no one ever questioned it and Gwendolen was left to her own devices. No one bothered her or enquired about what she was doing, and this was certainly the case on the day that she stole Suzanna Martindale's letter.

Some people go to church. Some people lay flowers. And some mark the anniversary of a loved one's death by writing to them, bizarre as that might seem. Every Valentine's Day, Zanna did just that. She would sit at her desk and compose a long letter telling David all that had happened that year. It was beautiful and romantic and healing and cathartic – and it annoyed Lucy Pennykettle all to hell. For she was never allowed to read them (Zanna burned them afterwards) and she knew that with every word Zanna wrote she became more and more accepting of David's death. That was wrong in Lucy's mind. David wasn't gone. He couldn't be dead. He was just . . . well, he was just not *here*.

So Gwendolen was sent to assess the state of play. It was a good time, the only opportunity in fact. Zanna and Alexa were out somewhere. Arthur was meditating quietly in Liz's pottery workshop, the Dragon's Den, where he'd been joined by the dragons Gadzooks and G'reth who were normally a fixture on the windowsill in Zanna's room. Bonnington, the Pennykettles' dippy cat, was asleep on Lucy's bed. And Liz was in the kitchen; she was always in the kitchen.

The house was quiet. The time was *now*.

Gwendolen zipped downstairs. The door to Zanna's room was usually ajar and was again as the little dragon flew down the hall. In a moment she was inside and on Zanna's desk. There was the letter, a fountain pen resting soulfully beside it. Four pale blue, neatly-written pages. Too long for Lucy to sneak in and read without fear of being disturbed; but a mere blink in the eye of an IT dragon.

Gwendolen made her eyes into slits and gathered her focus on the first page. A bar of violet light scanned it swiftly from top to bottom. In one flowing, nimble-clawed movement she flipped to page two and scanned that as well. It took her less than twenty seconds to raster the lot. She arranged the pages neatly and flew back upstairs.

Lucy was already at the computer. "Did you get it?" she hissed, as Gwendolen landed beside the keyboard.

Hrrr, went the dragon. She pushed her tail into a port on the back of the machine. The computer beeped and reported it had found new 'dragonware' then immediately downloaded Zanna's letter.

Lucy clicked her mouse and saved it in conventional bits and bytes. "Nice work," she said. "Now, let's see what slush she wrote. Oh, yuk. What a start. 'My darling David'."

Gwendolen swished her tail. She rather liked that, actually. Maybe Lucy did too, but didn't care to admit it. She turned her eyes to the screen and read along:

For once, St Valentine's Day has fallen on a weekend and I'm able to write from the quiet of home. I always promised myself I would begin these letters at the same time each year, the closest I could calculate to the moment you left me, the moment my heart froze with yours, in ice. I'm sitting at your desk in what was your room, with memories of you all about me: the wardrobe door that still doesn't quite close, cat hairs (of various shades) on the bed, a slightly threadbare Winston pining at me from the armchair opposite, Gadzooks firmly on the windowsill, studying the shape of a spider's web, G'reth right next to him lost in thought. These days, the room has a slightly more feminine touch, floral curtains, lace pillows, scents. A yellow hot water bottle (shaped like a flounder) sits upon the bed with a woolly mammoth called Bronson and a clutch of toys. Five years and a daughter do bring change. Yet, when I look up and peer into the garden, I still expect to see you out there with Lucy, rescuing squirrels or tripping over ice blocks, just being you, being frantic, being David. The man I love. I miss you so much.

Hrrr, went Gwendolen, moved by the sentiment.

"Don't," said Lucy. "Look at this. I can't believe she's written about the *weather!*"

. . . it's become such an issue. A conscience-nagging puzzle. There's a conference about climate change at Stavanger, in Norway, next week. Lucy's following it for a project for school. At Christmas (heat wave, daffodils in bloom), I had my seasonal email from Russ. Despite all that happened, he still talks fondly of our field trip to Canada. Until a few months ago he was still air-lifting polar bears away from Chamberlain, but they are closing down the Manitoba polar research station now because conditions have become so wild around Chamberlain. Some Inuit have evacuated their homes, he says. Everything is in such turmoil there, as if someone's turned the ring from simmer to boil. Here, in the not so wild suburbs of Kent, global warming is more of a soap opera than an issue. Each week we have

special news reports debating the changes taking place in the Arctic. One day they're warning us that polar bears are going to die out within twenty years, not fifty, because the ice is dwindling at such a devastating, unpredicted rate, the next it's all just a lot of hokum, part of the planet's natural cycle. And we all seem to care but we don't know what to do. So we build an ark of optimism and hope we'll be ok. We go shopping, watch movies, clean our teeth, go to bed. I do it. Liz does it. Henry, Arthur, Lucy. We drop ice into our squash while the north melts away. It's bizarre and frightening and very confusing, and even we, the daughters of Guinevere and Gwendolen, with dragons in our bloodline and magic in our fingertips, can do little more than sit back and watch it all happen.

"Wrong!" said Lucy, falling back into her chair. "If David was here, he'd know what to do."

Gwendolen raised a doubtful eye ridge.

"Well, he would," Lucy snapped, and carried on reading.

One unforeseen consequence of these crazy days of weather is the increase in book sales of all things Arctic. You've become a best-selling author, my love. The other day, I saw someone reading a copy of White Fire *on the train – a girl, not much younger than Lucy. I could see her eyes just above the pages, panning back and forth as she* devoured the text, one hand feeding her hair into her mouth. Suddenly, she turned to her mother and said, "This is really, really good, Mum. It's as if the author knows what it's like to be a polar bear." I had to move seats. That kind of stuff confuses me and fills me up with hurt. If only they knew what you and I had seen . . . Last year, Apple Tree brought out a special edition of White Fire with an 'adult' cover. It's typographical, you'd hate it, not a bear in sight. I don't approve, but contractually I can't argue. I just let myself be guided by Dilys's editorial experience (actually, she's risen to publisher now). We talk regularly on the phone, sometimes twice a month. She still holds you in great reverence. I honestly think she believes I've got you chained up in Henry's attic and that one day you'll surprise the world with another book. Talking of Henry, he's been such a star. Who could ask for a better neighbour? When the sales began to rise and the paperwork piled in, I couldn't cope with all the admin at home. So he gave me his study to use as an office. For the last few months I've split my time between managing your estate, running the shop and bringing up Alexa. It's exhausting, but not a day goes by when I'm not grateful for the legacy you left to me. Every birthday, whether she understands it or not, I read Snigger and the Nutbeast aloud to Alexa. We even had a session in the library gardens – with squirrels in attendance. She so enjoyed that.

She's too young, of course, for the drama of White Fire. *But she knows what Daddy does. And she knows that Daddy's clever. One day she will be so proud of you.*

Liz and Arthur love her to bits. I swear they get soppier the older she gets. BIG news on this front. Would you believe that Arthur popped the question? Liz announced it in true Liz fashion. She was grilling cheese on toast one night and rapping at Lucy for some minor misdemeanour when she suddenly said, 'Oh, I thought you'd all like to know that Arthur and I decided to get married. Does anyone want Worcester sauce?' Of course, we made a huge fuss – well, Alexa and I did anyway. Lucy was quite reserved, but took it well enough. She and Liz have had a few heart-to-hearts since. I think Lucy's primary concern is not the domestic arrangement, but the biological one, especially when Liz openly told her that she and Arthur might try for a child. Liz assures me it can happen, that even though she was birthed in the way of a dragon child, she still has the necessary human physiology to deliver a child as any 'normal' woman would, though the genetic situation might be . . . interesting.

"I'll say," muttered Lucy, clicking her tongue.

Anyway, they haven't set an exact date yet. Liz doesn't want to rush it. She's an old-fashioned dragon-girl, she says. We think the autumn, perhaps. Maybe even Christmas. I don't think Lucy will complain too much. Given the circumstances, she could do a lot worse for a step-dad. Arthur bought her a top of the range iPod last September to celebrate his promotion to Professor of Physics at the now upgraded Scrubbley University. (Scrubbley Uni. Doesn't that sound weird? Me and you were just lowly 'college' kids, struggling to understand basic geography; Lucy's planning to take a degree in 'Medieval and Mythological History' there when she's ready.)

Arthur works so hard. Despite near blindness, he gets through any number of meetings, lectures and tutorials. He employs two full time secretaries, dictates papers, marks essays (that Liz reads out to him) and still finds the time to meditate with me. He's such a steadying influence. His time as a monk at Farlowe Abbey wasn't wasted. I'm very fortunate to have two great 'teachers' around me. When I'm frazzled by income tax forms and the like, I turn to Henry. But it's Arthur, always Arthur, I take my woes to when I'm in need of spiritual comfort. Lately, we've been talking more and more about his days as a monk on Farlowe Island. He's still awed and moved by what took place there. I wish I could say that the Fain have become a forgotten subject, but I'm sure Arthur broods about them all the time. I think their absence worries him as much as their presence ever did. They're like a shadow he can't escape. It seems bizarre to think that we were ever attacked by alien 'thought forms',

23

even though you gave your life protecting us from them. I suppose, like anything else, our perception of that danger has altered with time. Even when Bonnington is wowing us daily with his shape-shifting tricks (he turned into a small black panther yesterday and nearly gave the postman a heart attack) we tend to overlook the fact that the benign Fain-being trapped inside him is responsible. But I know they're out there, in some peculiar parallel universe, hovering on the edge of human consciousness and doing . . . who knows what? Which is why in our sessions I try to steer Arthur clear of that subject and back onto peace, love, humanity and Gaia. He cares deeply about the soul of the planet. His take on global warming is a little more 'mystical' than the mechanisms proposed by most of his scientific contemporaries, but that's the subject of another letter perhaps.

Lucy is the one member of the family I still worry about . . .

"Oh, here we go," Lucy said with a humph.

. . . she's sixteen now and a real stunner. Flowing red hair, sweet green eyes (now turned completely from blue) and the attitude of a teenage warrior queen.

"Cheek!"

(*But true*, thought Gwendolen.)

She fascinates boys, but terrifies them too. One glance from her and they turn to mush. Yet she doesn't seem to show

24

a lot of interest in reverse. Most days she will come in from school, go straight to her room and disappear for several hours. We hear her tapping away at her computer, usually through a wall of soft rock music, but no one seems to know quite what she's doing. She's a genius at IT and even created a Pennykettle website so that Liz could go on selling the dragons after she gave up her market stall. (The school gave her an enterprise award and a certificate for her stunning 'lifelike' animations, lol.) It's such a shame that she's become so introspective. Every now and then she and Liz have a taut exchange about 'anti-social behaviour'. That goes down well (she said, with irony). I used to worry that this was a problem with Alexa stealing all of Liz's attention these days, but if anything, Lexie is the one person Lucy bonds with the most. She plays with her, talks to her, baby-sits her sometimes and generally seems happy to have her around. I think Lucy misses you terribly and Alexa is the closest link she has, possibly more so than Gadzooks or G'reth. She point blank refuses to believe that you are dead and cites your dragons as proof of this. Therein, I think, lies the fundamental problem between her and her mum. As the years go by and you show no sign of returning to us, Liz has become more accepting of the theory that a dragon created for whatever special reason can live a life independent of its owner. The fact that Gadzooks has not written on his *notepad since he left me with the name 'G'lant' so long ago is proof enough to Liz that you are gone. So she's settled to a life of pipe and slippers with Arthur, leaving her daughter angry and confused.*

"Too right," said Lucy.

A few weeks ago they had a real humdinger and I heard Lucy shout, "Have you forgotten who you are?" I think Liz has. She and Arthur are more in love than any couple I've ever met, but I do think they're guilty of neglecting Lucy's heritage. I mean, look at us. We live in a house of flying dragons, with a cat that has an alien life form sharing its psyche. We're the product of a time when dragons roamed the earth and bears ruled the Arctic. We're the kooks on the block. The real Addams Family. And all we seem to concern ourselves with is paying the bills and watching the telly. Lucy has a lot to fight for, I think.

"And she's going to," said Lucy, bashing her fist down right beside the keyboard and making Gwendolen jump a few centimetres.

How? the dragon hurred, concerned to see Lucy's eyes swimming with tears.

"We've got to do *something*," she said, almost sobbing. "We can't let bears die and . . ." She flapped her hands to fill in the gaps. "If David was here, he'd be out there saving them. And I don't care what Mum says or what

26

Zanna thinks: David's *not dead*. Arthur always says that the more people who believe something, the more likely it is to happen, right?"

Gwendolen nodded. She was expected to, she thought.

"So we ought to make sure that *everybody* knows who David is, right?"

Gwendolen glanced at the screen again. *There are still some words about Alexa*, she hurred.

"Later," Lucy sighed and tapped a few keys. Her email inbox quickly unwrapped. Top of the list was the message she'd been dwelling on for several days, the enquiry from the journalist, Tam Farrell.

Thanks for the feedback on David Rain. Appreciate you taking time to reply, but you've told me nothing more than I can find on your website already. Feature needs a definite angle. Some history. Circumstances of his disappearance, perhaps? If you can't supply, will look elsewhere.

"I can supply," Lucy muttered grimly. And she wrote back a short, twice-edited reply:

u don't kno what ur getting into

do this rgt, you get more info

do this wrg, you burn

The Healing Touch. Shop on Scrubbley High St.

ask 4 suzanna J

xhrrrpennyx

www.rainandfire.co.uk

the official website of David Rain

"There," she said defiantly, and clicked on 'send'. "Time to wake the world up."

Sea ice, northwest of Nordaustlandet
Svalbard archipelago, unrecorded time

It was many years since Thoran had watched the winter die. But there was little else a bear could do in these months, except shelter, rest, and wait for the long night to reach its end. Four days ago it had. He had seen the sun returning like a distant bird, its solar wings reaching out far across the north, setting the sea ice alight for miles. Each morning thereafter he had watched it rise a little higher in the sky, tinting the horizon with its pale shades of orange. Warmth. Spring. The promise of life.

But it was not in a moment like this when they came.

The sky was still half-lit. Moody. Grey. A blizzard was stirring up in restless circles, half-heartedly sighing as it ripped through his fur. Those parts of his body given mortal senses – the ears, the eyes, even the black-tipped snout – were all beginning to fail him now, so he did not hear the bears or scent them or see, but rather *knew*, in the ways of the shaman, they were close. He was dying naturally, growing weak, yet his instincts warned him there was something out there, something worth clinging to these shreds of life for. Not for him the heart stopping on a long bed of ice, nor the frosted eye staring at an unchanging sky. He was Thoran, creature of legend. Something wonderful was coming. Something strange.

There were three of them, approaching from the permanent ice to the north. The two bears on the outer came slugging through first, flanking nothing but a cloud of swirling ice. One was a fighting bear, heavy, in his prime. The other was younger, slender, thoughtful. A Teller's son if ever there was. That singular expression of awe in his eyes was as much to do with history as it was with fear.

The visitors drew to a halt, blowing hard. They sat down, keeping a respectful distance. Thoran let out a moderate growl. He knew it was not their purpose to challenge him, but appearances and rituals had to be observed. The fighting bear offered up a cynical snort. The Teller looked sideways, into the mist. He shuddered as the third bear floated out of it.

Thoran's weak heart pounded with relief. Astonishing. *Him*. Just as he had hoped. Only now the bear walked with magnificent grace, as if the ice was his servant and carrying his weight not merely supporting it. The limp, long ago caused by a bullet of lead lodged deep in the shoulder, was gone, healed, an incidental nuisance. Confidence shone from the once-troubled eyes. Every hair of his thick pelt glistened with power. Even the snowstorm whipping about his ears was like a child, an ice cub, begging for attention. The ice was his plaything, his to command. Here was Ingavar, Lord of the Arctic.

"You have walked a long way, nanuk," said Thoran, for on the last occasion these bears had met they had been on the other side of the world.

The fighting bear stiffened, visibly outraged by the informal greeting. But it was the Teller that Ingavar chose to glance at, as if to say, 'Remember this. Remember how this bear addressed me as a cub, for in many ways that is what I am to him, his novice.'

Ingavar swung his head forward in an arc. "This is your homeland," he said, looking west, though no trace of rock or glacier could be seen.

Thoran opened his claws, feeling the wind run between them. Cold. "Where else would an old bear come to die?" He spread his paws and pushed himself upright, wobbling slightly as he tried to stand. The curves at his sides fell inwards, not out. The Teller gulped, his empathy obvious. The fighting bear stared ahead, hard and unmoved.

Ingavar said, "I need your help."

The wind moaned and seemed to gather in Thoran's chest. "The North has changed – and I am not the bear I was."

"Nor I," said Ingavar.

The Teller shuddered again.

"This is Avrel," said his master, indicating the Teller. "Kailar to my right. They are here to witness a new beginning."

Thoran put his head back and stared at the sky. It was shifting, making shapes from the cloud: narwhal, seal, walrus, fox. His fore paws clenched and grated the ice, audibly catching in the brittle surface. "Where have you been, nanuk?" he asked.

Avrel noted what he thought was a tremor of betrayal.

"Away," said Ingavar with measured reassurance. And in every reflection of his deep brown eyes he knew that Thoran saw an image of a fire star.

"The North is dying," the old bear said. There was a drumming in his ears, a song of the Arctic. Above him, the sky made pictures of The Men.

Ingavar raised his snout to the wind. "I have come to free you from the burden of caring for it."

The sky darkened then and Avrel caught his breath. A light had appeared in the ice beneath Ingavar. It was at once both blue and colourlessly blue. He watched it spread into his master's body, turning him from flesh and bone into . . . what? He looked across at Kailar as if to say, 'Do you see this? A legend coming to life? The fire that melts no ice is upon us.'

But Kailar clearly had. He was edging back, head lowered, physically shaken. He checked around his paws. The ice there was sound.

Thoran tilted his head and stared into the radiating eyes again, looking for something that perhaps could not be seen. "When I was imprisoned in this mortal body, I heard the wind whisper that you had burned in the tears of Godith. Are you really the bear I knew?"

Ingavar padded slowly forward, creating footprints of fire in the snow. On his forehead there now appeared a telling mark, three lines the North knew as the mark of Oomara. He turned his head sideways, scissoring his jaws. White flames danced on his tongue as he spoke. One word was all he uttered. "Sometimes."

"Then I am yours to command," said Thoran.

And the icefire leapt from Ingavar's mouth, into the jaws of his old companion.

Avrel, remembering all he had journeyed and all he had seen, now added the following to his stories to Tell:

he saw how the body of the ice bear Thoran burst into flame, then broke into a blizzard of snowflakes and sparks which set themselves into the wind and were gone. And he noted, keenly, how the heart of the blaze appeared to move out of the body of Thoran into the body of his master, Ingavar, and what change took place in Ingavar because of this. He saw the morning sun rise. He heard the ice moan. And he witnessed the brightest of auroras above. A spirit-dance. A passing. A changing of Ways. And when the lights had settled and all was darkness and spinning cold again, Ingavar, standing with his back to them, said, "Do you know of an island called the Tooth of Ragnar?"

The fighting bear, Kailar, was disabled by sickness, the last contents of his stomach in a pool by his feet. So Avrel answered for the two of them, saying, "Lord, the Tooth was destroyed by . . ." He dared not go on. Some tongues said that the island had been brought down by Ingavar *himself*.

Ingavar nodded. "In that vicinity, Kailar will find a raven, a bird frozen in a block of ice. He is to free its head and feet but not its body. When he has done this, he will have it *walk* to me."

"And me, Lord?" said Avrel. "What am I to do?"

"You are the Teller of Ways," said Ingavar. "You

34

will walk with me." And he turned and a legend was instantly recorded.

He was Ingavar. Ice bear. Bringer of fire.

Ruler of the North.

And his once brown eyes were blue.

The Healing Touch

People said it was a 'blink and you miss it' kind of place. A narrow shop, barely three times the width of its doorway, sandwiched between a beauty salon and a larger shop selling computer supplies. Zanna had bought it on a sudden impulse shortly after graduating from Scrubbley College, when the royalties from David's books had amounted to a sum that demanded she make them work for her. One night she had come home later than usual, sat down in the kitchen with Alexa on her knee and said to Liz, "I want to run a shop."

"Really?" Liz had turned to her, sounding thrilled.

Unlike Lucy, who had looked up from her homework and said, "Why?" in a cursory, offhand manner.

Zanna said, "It's something that I've always wanted to do. I was passing that estate agent's, *Burroughs*, in town, saw an advert for it, went in and got the sheet. It's on the High Street. It's perfect. I'd easily have enough money to put down a deposit."

Liz patted her hand. "That's a super idea. What do you plan to sell?"

"Anything 'new age-y'. Crystals. Incense. Semi-precious stones. Gothic jewellery – I really fancy

36

making some. Books. Cards. Even some bags and clothing perhaps."

"A magic shop?" said Lucy, twisting her nose.

"I'd prefer 'place of enchantment'," said Zanna.

Lucy gave a hmph. "Well, at least it's not your hippie veggie stuff." She glared at the bag of nuts Zanna was snacking from. "How can anyone eat so many nuts?"

"Squiwels," said Alexa. She kicked her feet and smiled upwards at her mum.

"Hmm," went Zanna, giving her a cuddle. "They eat *lots* of nuts, don't they? The shop is close to the library gardens. We might have squirrels queuing up outside – if we decide to take it on, of course."

This last remark was addressed towards Liz, but it was Arthur, feeling his way into the kitchen, who asked the question, "Why wouldn't you?"

Zanna took a deep breath. She glanced at Lucy, who scowled and pretended she was focussed on her homework. "I'd need help, looking after Lexie."

"Are you a nutbeast, Mummy?" Alexa said.

Lucy paused, closed her eyes, then went on writing.

"Not a problem," said Liz.

"I don't like to put upon you. You're all so good to me as it is."

Liz cupped a hand round the back of Zanna's head.

37

"Sweetheart, it would be a joy," she said.

"Do you have a name to trade under?" asked Arthur.

"Yes," said Zanna, brightly. "*The Healing Touch*, because everything in the shop will have therapeutic potential. I'm going to take some courses as well. I'd like to offer people aromatherapy and reflexology – for a start."

"Feet?" said Lucy. "You want to touch feet?"

"Honey, don't, you'll fall over," Zanna said to Alexa as she tried to lean forward to touch her own toes. "Reflexology isn't always done on feet. It could be hands or ears." (Lexie held her ears.)

"It's still gross," Lucy muttered.

"It is not," said Liz. "You have my backing, Zanna. I think it's wonderful."

"A great adventure," Arthur added, smiling.

"Thank you," said Zanna. "I appreciate that. Erm, there is one other thing I'd like to run by you." She waited till she had Liz's gaze again. "I want to sell tinctures, made from flowers."

Liz glanced at Alexa, who was curling her hair in rings around her fingers. "You want to involve Gretel?"

They both glanced at Zanna's special dragon, who was sitting on the table, casually jabbing an orange with a cocktail stick. Gretel was regarded (mostly by herself) as the most powerful dragon in the Pennykettle household. She had the ability to make potions from flowers, anything from a sleeping draught to a hay fever cure.

"She can't," protested Lucy. "She can't use Gretel's powers."

"Hrrr!" went Alexa.

On top of the fridge, the listening dragon frowned and noted that the David child had literally said, 'hrrr'.

In a level but guarded tone Liz said, "She can – if it's done for the right reasons, of course."

"But she's a—" Lucy bit her tongue, an act which only made Zanna glower.

"Go on, Lucy, say it. You know you want to. Witch? Sibyl? Spawn of Gwilanna? Mad, bad, dangerous to know?"

"Zanna," said Arthur in a calming voice.

"All right," Liz pitched in. "Everyone cool down. I do not like being a referee in my own kitchen."

"But—?"

"Lucy, that's enough." Liz's manner was definite. "Zanna, you know I can't stop you doing this, but please remember you have a great responsibility to use Gretel wisely and to keep us out of the public eye."

"Is Gurlanna a dragon?" Alexa asked.

"And that's just one reason why," Liz said.

Zanna nodded and answered her daughter's question. "No," she said quietly, placing a protective kiss on her head. "Forget I said that. Mummy was annoyed." She looked again at Liz. "I wouldn't ever let you down."

Liz filled a glass with water and raised it in a toast. "Then we wish you well. Here's to success, and *The Healing Touch . . .*"

And that was how it started. In the months that followed, Zanna's life had been a turmoil of phone calls, deliveries and general moving in. Fortunately, there were barely any structural changes to be made. The previous owner had run the property as a small gift shop and had passed it on with all the fittings in place. Pine shelving racks occupied the two long walls and a glass display counter faced the door. Behind it, curtained off by bamboo strips, were two utility areas which served as stock room, preparation room and kitchen. The two rooms upstairs were as bare and dusty as Mother Hubbard's cupboard, but over the next three years, as her turnover increased and her reputation for producing effective 'lotions and potions' expanded, Zanna was able to decorate throughout and turn them into her consulting area, for clients requiring her unique brand of healing.

And so it came to be that one March morning, some five years after David Rain's disappearance, the door chimes tinkled and a young man with short-cropped, salon-cut hair walked in. Zanna was sitting on her stool behind the counter, resetting a tray of earrings at the time. "Hi," she said. "Feel free to browse."

"Thanks," he said, smiling, but not at her. His voice had traces of a soft Scottish accent. He looked left and right, taking in most of the shop in one sweep. He pored over the card rack and dream catchers a moment, before a large block of amethyst caught his eye. He weighed it in his hand and put it back. "Wasn't she a maiden turned to stone by the goddess Diana – something to do with protecting her from tigers?"

"Sorry?" said Zanna.

"Amethyst," he said. "In the Greek legend, Dionysius wept tears of wine and stained her purple. Something like that. She makes a beautiful crystal, don't you think? Mind you, I have to confess that whenever I see stones cut and polished like this they always remind me of the middle of strawberries. Or those kiwi fruits, sliced in half."

Zanna put the tray into the display case and locked it. "Let me guess: you're the mystery customer from the Ministry of Crystallography, come to make sure I know what I'm selling?"

He laughed at that and looked at her directly. He wore wide rectangular spectacles with frames as black as his hair and stubble. His eyes were quick and intelligent. Blue. "My name's Tam. Tam Farrell. I hope you're Suzanna?"

"Well, if I'm not, I'll be arrested for fraud," she said. "What can I do for you, Mr Farrell?"

He swung to his left, eyeing up a shelf of homoeopathic medicines. "I hear you do wonderful things with herbs?"

In the back room, working on a pot pourri mixture, Gretel pricked her ears and paused to listen.

"Flowers, actually. It's not the same thing. I am a trained herbalist, but I prefer to make up tinctures based on ancient natural remedies. Is there something I might be able to help you with?"

"Necks," he said. "How are you with them?"

"How many are we talking about?"

"Just this one, here." He tapped his shoulder. "I do a lot of computer work." He wiggled his fingers to indicate a keyboard. "Always getting stiff."

"Then it's possibly just your posture, the way you're sitting."

"Tried all that," he said, looking round. "Chair height. Rests. None of it seems to make a difference.

I get headaches, too. I work long hours. I don't believe the spin my doctor gives me. That's why I'm here – on the trail of something . . . different."

Zanna reached for a diary. "I'd have to book you in for a consultation."

"And what would that involve?"

"I take your details, do a little basic reflexology, make an assessment. If I think you need a tincture, I'll have one made up."

He hummed indecisively. "Sounds sort of deep. I was hoping for something over the counter, actually."

"Then there's a chemist just down the road," she said.

"Ouch." He reeled back, smiling, with a hand across his chest, giving Zanna a chance to take him in fully. T-shirt. Jacket. Designer jeans. Casual, but street smart. Shoulder bag. Trendy.

"That was my ego smarting, not my neck," he offered. "Didn't mean to offend. How much do you charge for a consultation?"

Zanna considered his question a moment. His humility was genuine, she was pretty sure of that. "Give me your right hand."

He offered it, palm up. "I've been told I've got a pretty long life line."

She pressed the tip of his little finger, working down

it with short intense bouts of pressure. "It might shorten if you don't let me concentrate."

"I'll shut up, then," he said. "Erm, what is it you're doing?"

"Zone therapy," she answered, leaning forward. "Each organ of your body is represented by a specific point on your hands. By feeling the points I can detect which bits of you have a blocked energy flow. If I massage the blocks, I should be able to stimulate the production of nutrients and blood to those zones."

"Well, I'm all for a decent blood flow," he said, taking the opportunity to admire her face. "Do you mind if I ask how you got into this? I mean, where does a young English maiden go to learn the science of ancient medicines?"

"Scrubbley College, two evenings a week," she muttered, looping her hair behind her ear. "We dance naked round the campus, invoking spirits."

He laughed and said, "When's the next meeting?" His eyes travelled to the leather band around her neck, following it down to where a pendant fell against her smooth white— "Ow, that hurt!"

"Hmm," she went. "That area needs attention." Her thumb was hard in the centre of his palm.

"Is that my neck zone?"

44

"No, your liver zone," she said, and let go of his hand.

He stood back, flexing and stretching his fingers. "Is this a subtle way of telling me I drink too much?"

Zanna smoothed her palms as if clearing away his scent. "I don't diagnose. I redirect energy. Strangely enough, it seems to be flowing reasonably well through the region of your neck."

He sighed and held up his hands in surrender. "OK, I give in. You're pretty impressive. First you cut me down in a couple of sentences, then you bring my scepticism into doubt: you're right, I was testing you about the neck thing, and right again, I do put too much away."

"Then maybe you need temperance, not a tincture," she said.

"Or a chaperone," he came back quickly. "How are you fixed this Friday night?"

In the kitchen, Gretel scrunched a nettle in her paw.

"Fri—? Are you asking me out?" Zanna said, her volume raised, her tone incredulous.

He glanced at her hands. "Don't see a shiny ring."

"I'm spoken for." Her tone was as flat as a wall.

He rocked on his heel. "Drat. Lucky guy. Absolutely no chance?"

"None. I have a daughter."

The blue eyes flashed. "Daughter? Really? Just a baby or—?"

"She's nearly five," said Zanna, folding her arms. "And we seem to have gone off the subject somewhat. If you're here to chat me up, you're wasting your time. If you've something you genuinely wish to consult me about then make an appointment. Otherwise, good day."

Tam pushed back his glasses. His tongue made one swift tour of his lips. "Consultation. Right. Can I think about it?"

"Naturally."

He nodded and glanced at her arm. Apart from her bangles, it was bare to the elbow. On her fair skin, three distinct weals stood out. "That's a pretty nasty scar."

Zanna lowered her sleeve. "Playground accident."

"Right," he said. "Wouldn't put a guy off."

She breathed in sharply.

"OK, fair enough." He stepped back a pace. As he did, his gaze dipped towards the glass display case. Zanna rolled her eyes as he hunkered down in front of it. "How much are the dragons?"

"Fifteen pounds each."

"Did you make them?"

"They're done by a local artist."

46

"They're cute," he said. (In the back room, Gretel winced.) "My . . . niece would like those."

"They're very popular," said Zanna, trying to retain a professional air. "I've got one myself."

Tam stood up, tapping his fingertips together. "I'll take him at the back with the green soppy eyes."

Zanna unlocked the case. She took out the dragon and let him inspect it. "That's a female, actually, from an exclusive run of twenty."

"*Gudrun*," he read from the tag on its tail. "Is that Norse?"

"No, it's from the south side of Scrubbley."

He chuckled and put the dragon down on the counter. "Fifteen quid, yeah?" He opened his wallet and counted out the cash. "I suppose you could say you'd given me a 'gud run' for my money?"

Zanna rang up the sale.

While she covered the Gudrun in two layers of bubble wrap and chose a suitable box, Tam asked, "So is that where you make your tinctures, through there?"

Zanna glanced over her shoulder at the bamboo strips. "Yes. Why?"

"You said if I needed one you'd have it made up, as if you buy them in. Or was that just a slip of the tongue?"

More questions. Zanna broke a piece of sticky tape

47

off the dispenser. "You're a very inquisitive man, Mr Farrell."

He gave a blameless shrug. "Always had a curious streak. Good job I'm not a cat. I'd be long dead, I guess."

That produced a twitch in one corner of her mouth.

"Sorry, I think I might have amused you."

Zanna allowed herself to smile properly. He was smart, she had to give him that. She sealed the box and handed it over. "I have an assistant who helps me, part time. She makes up the tinctures. Will that be all?"

"I'll think about that consultation," he said, and at last he turned away, but not for long. "Oh, poetry. Nearly forgot."

"Poetry?" she repeated, looking blank.

He flipped his satchel open and took out a flyer. "Allandale's book shop. They have regular readings in their upstairs room on a Sunday night. Nice atmosphere. Good people. Wine and nibbles. Easy on the liver." He put the flyer on the counter and pushed it towards her. "Thought you might like it." He nodded at the wall behind her head.

On a poster were the words:

> . . . *until the stars have blinked their last,*
> *wherever on this Earth you walk,*

he will arouse, excite, inspire,
my Valentine, my one dark fire . . .

"No strings," he said. "Bring your partner."

He noted her shudder. Then he turned and walked silently out of the shop.

A gift for the garden

"He asked you *out?*" gasped Lucy, almost jumping from her seat.

Liz turned the car onto a potholed car park, the entrance to *Benson's Garden Centre.* "There's no need to sound so horrified, Lucy. You don't become an old maid at the age of twenty-five."

"Six," said Zanna. "I'm twenty-six."

"And very attractive with it," Liz added. She glanced hopelessly at Lucy again. "Some boy will chance it with you one day when you finally stop acting like Switzerland."

"What?" said Lucy, screwing up her nose.

"She means when you come out of neutral," laughed Zanna.

"I don't get it," Lucy grumbled.

"You will," said her mum, opening the door above a large, grey puddle. A shower of sleet drummed ripples in its surface. More 'weather'. More false predictions from the Met Office.

The three of them stepped out of the car together. Lucy, on tip-toes, avoiding puddles, picked her way across to Zanna. "So what did you say?"

Zanna thought about her brolly, but kept it closed. "I said 'no', of course."

Lucy chewed her lip and nodded. "What else did he ask?"

"Why? What's it to you?"

"Just asking," Lucy bristled. She folded up and shivered. "It's not a crime, is it?"

"Don't start, you pair." Liz was striding on already, getting out of the rain. "We're here to buy plants, not start a small war."

"He bought a dragon," said Zanna.

"Good for him," Liz said. "The man can't be all that bad, then, can he?"

"Was he handsome?"

"Lu-cy?" Zanna stared at her, hard.

"*What?* Why don't you want to talk about it?"

"Because it's meaningless."

"Yeah, like, so why'd you bring it up in the *first* place, then?"

Liz stopped at the entrance and turned to face them, her feet rustling in the thick coir bristles of a welcome mat. "You know, the way you two squabble, no one would ever believe that you weren't bona fide, first-generation handbag-swishing sisters! I suppose I should be grateful that there's only a sliver of a family connection or we'd never see a day without bloodshed in the Crescent. I'm not going in here with the pair of you bickering like a couple of . . . gnomes!"

"Gnomes?" said Lucy. There were a group of them for sale on a pallet nearby.

"Liz, gnomes are gentle," Zanna pointed out.

Liz thought about it quickly. "Not if you steal their fishing rods," she said, causing Zanna to erupt with laughter.

"This is dumb," Lucy tutted. "You two are mental."

"Hey!" Liz scowled at her hard for that.

"OK, truce," said Zanna, knuckling Lucy's back. "I admit I found Tam interesting. He was witty and yes, quite handsome in a . . . *Guardian* reader kind of way. But my commitment is to David and always will be." She picked up her skirts and jumped for dry land.

"So why won't you try harder to find out where he is?"

"Lucy, not here," her mother said quietly.

A ring tone sounded in Lucy's pocket. She was standing in the rain like a little lost child and her eyes were filming over when she spoke again. "Maybe he needs us to make the first move?"

Zanna looked sideways and saw, of all things, a caricature sculpture of a smiling grey squirrel. "Your phone's ringing," she said quietly, and pushed the door of the garden centre open.

Despite its war zone of a car park, *Benson's* was a comfortable, easy-going store which sold a wide variety of plants and trees, plus every kind of accessory the home gardener could wish for. As well as tools and foliage, there was a well-stocked gift area selling everything from candles to spiced pears in syrup. It was here that Liz caught up with Zanna.

"You OK?" she whispered. She looped her arm and tugged.

Zanna sighed, "Why won't she let go of it, Liz?"

"Because she's sixteen. It's her job to be awkward. Every year she sees you writing a Valentine to David and she feels left out, so she has to compete for her own little part of him. She misses the man who wrote charming tales for the little girl that's still inside her. He's her hero and she loves him. End of story."

"But it's not, though." Zanna threw up a hand. "I love him dearly, you know I do. But I'm not forever trying to, you know . . ."

"Resurrect him?"

A bright tear rolled down Zanna's cheek. "I want him back as much as anyone, she must know that. But he's

53

never going to come back, is he? Is he?" She sobbed and fell against Liz's shoulder.

Liz turned her aside, guiding her away from the eyes of an over-inquisitive assistant. "Shall I drive you home?"

"No," Zanna said, recovering quickly. She sniffed and cut the air firmly with her hand. "This has to be faced. I have to deal with this and just think about Lexie. If David is anywhere he's in her, right?"

"Absolutely," said Liz, handing her a tissue, "and Lexie is a wonderful reminder of him . . . but you have to think about yourself sometimes. David would expect nothing less, I'm sure."

Zanna blew into the tissue and tucked it in her sleeve. "I don't understand. What are you saying?"

Liz picked up a gift set of bath oils and soaps. "Maybe this chap who came to the shop is what you need right now?"

"You think I should go out with him?"

"I think you need a life, Zanna, a different kind of companionship than we or Lexie or the dragons can give you."

Zanna lowered her head.

Liz took her hand and swung it. "What harm could it do? No one's saying you should have a relationship with

Tam. You're not betraying David if you go out and have a little fun with a friend."

"I don't think Lucy will see it like that."

"Oh, you leave Miss Switzerland to me. I understand fiery redheads, remember?"

Zanna's response was muted and sceptical, but she closed her arms around Liz all the same and said, "You're beautiful, Mrs Pennykettle, inside and out."

"I only want what's best for my girls," she replied. "So you'll see him?"

"I don't know. I'm slightly wary. Call it that old sibyl sixth sense, but I got the feeling he was checking me out somehow. I don't mean there was anything dodgy about him, but he knew who I was and what kind of stuff I did. I got the impression he knew a bit more than he was letting on."

"Perhaps he knows someone you've treated in the past?"

"Maybe," said Zanna, dropping her shoulders. "Whatever. Come on, let's buy plants."

"No, let's buy *this*." From a nearby shelf, Liz picked up an ornament, an arch-shaped door about a foot tall, with a mint green frame and two working copper hinges. It was painted with autumnal leaves and flowers to give it a rustic, woodland look.

"What's that for?" asked Zanna, opening and closing it.

"Fairies," Liz said, grinning like a child. "You pop it in the garden, up against a wall, and the fairies come and go as they please."

Zanna rubbed her brow in despair. "Liz, you've got to stop buying Lexie presents. She's spoiled to high heaven as it is."

"It's not for Lexie, it's for the *garden*," Liz said. "But she'll be free to play with it, if she wishes." She popped it into a wire basket. "There, done. Now we'll buy plants."

For the next forty minutes, Zanna and Liz trawled around together, chatting about nothing in particular. They managed to purchase an outdoor wind chime and a pair of thermal gloves for Arthur, but not a single plant made it into the basket. Liz was commenting on this irony when they walked into the café in search of Lucy. "Thing is, when is the right time to plant anything now? You think you'll get frosts and you wake up to butterflies. You think you're in for rain, and you end up watering. On the news last night they were warning us to expect winds at up to ninety miles per hour. We might see tornados. *Tornados*. In Kent!"

"It's Gaia," said Zanna. "The planet's kicking back."

Liz shook her head. "I don't know. It's very worrying. Ah, there she is, on the phone as usual."

Zanna dropped a shopping bag on the seat beside Lucy, who almost knocked her milkshake over in surprise.

"Whoa, what's with you?" Zanna said.

"Nothing," said Lucy, hiding her phone. "Do you mind not creeping up on me?"

"If we'd known you were having a private conversation we'd have left you in peace," Liz said.

"I was *texting*," Lucy said.

"Of course you were." Liz sighed and dropped her bag onto a seat as well, only for Zanna to say, "I don't think I want that cup of coffee after all."

"Oh, great," said Lucy. "So it'll be, like, my fault you didn't get your caffeine hit?"

"What *is* it with you?" Zanna said, squaring up.

This time Liz did not intervene, and when Lucy realised no support was forthcoming, she stormed away saying, "I'm sick of you two. I want to go home!"

As she swept past the tills, she checked her mobile connection again. The link was still live. One message, from Tam:

OK. Met her. David's partner, right? Baby by him? Good lead, thanx. Checking her out. Tam. PS What's with her scars? Real or self-harmer?

And for the umpteenth time, or however many times one can change a text message in forty minutes, Lucy tried again, this time deleting everything she'd written in favour of one word. She read it back, heart pounding, then posted it into the ether. She was doing this for David, she reminded herself. Someone, one of them, had to make a move. But even as 'sent' flashed up on the screen, she wished she could have clawed the message back. Just one word. Maybe Tam wouldn't get it? Or maybe he would.

One small word.

One legend.

Oomara.

Arctic ice cap, no specific region

For the first six or seven years of his life, the ice bear, Avrel, had led a fairly commonplace polar existence. The smaller cub of a two-litter family, he had never stood out or troubled his mother, and had easily survived his yearling stages largely by virtue of learning through obedience. Born into the seal-rich waters of Svalbard, he had rarely had to cope with lasting hunger. Even in the summer months, when only the most careless of seals could be stalked, he had always grubbed for rodents in the shoreline vegetation or settled for grinding his teeth on kelp. And because the hunting had always been plentiful and serious hostilities with other bears few, he had never strayed far from those sketches of land.

All this changed on the day he met Ingavar.

It had been one morning, during the very late spring, when the sea birds were squawking and the space between the ocean and the clear blue sky was growing ever more hazy with heat. Avrel was wandering the drifting pack ice on a pessimistic lookout for any blubber-rich seal that would care to ease his stomach through the oncoming summer, when he'd picked up the scent of an unfamiliar animal. It was weak in strength, which meant the animal was small, but as pungent in its way as the foul-smelling walrus. He tested the wind with a bob of his snout. The creature was behind him, lost in the slight miasma of haze that sometimes settled between the ice and the sky. It might even be following him.

Curious, he turned and rose up slowly. The ice field was relatively flat and sea-washed, but away to his right a small cluster of undissolved ridges offered visual protection for anything less than the size of a bear. In this direction, the scent was at its strongest. So he set down and slid himself into the water, swimming between floes until he neared the ridges. There he saw it. A small creature with greyish-blue fur and a tail half the length of its skinny body. Thinking at first it was a free-running dog, he grew wary and looked around for signs of men. But the animal did not move like a dog, it trotted along in playful steps, keeping its snout very low to the ice, obviously hunting for scraps of food.

Calculating no threat whatsoever, Avrel hauled himself onto the floe. The creature paused. Avrel must have seemed like a monster to it, dripping wet, thickset, heavy of claw. Yet the thing merely looked up as though it had been expecting him. It had an elegant face and remarkably small ears. There were barely five mouthfuls of flesh on its bones, but in the absence of seals, it would have to do.

Avrel swaggered forward in a cloud of breath, pools of water running off his flip-flopping paws.

The animal's dark eyes screwed into his. "Aren't you at least going to ask?" it said.

Avrel came to a snorting halt. Most prey, if it spoke, limited its output to squeals of alarm. To be asked a question was . . .

"Exactly," the animal said, as though it could read his puzzled mind.

And puzzled he was. The instinct to hunt had overtaken his natural inquisitiveness, but now, stopped in his tracks by this dialogue, the questions were there: What was this creature? Why was it here? Why hadn't he seen its kind before? "Are you . . . fox?" he grunted, though he did not understand where the reference had come from.

"Sometimes," it said, which puzzled him even more. Annoyed, he cut short all other queries in favour of: *What do you taste like, I wonder?*

He padded forward again. Unalarmed, the 'fox' trotted off behind a crest of snow. Avrel mooched on, in no particular hurry. The floe was detached from the rest of the field. Unless this creature could fly like a bird or outswim a seal it was only a matter of wearing it down. It was quick, no doubt. Silent, too, on its furry little feet. But how long could it hold out against a bear? It might as well offer itself up and be done with.

"Only a bear with a head full of stories would know what I was," its voice said suddenly.

Avrel swung to his left. The 'fox' was sitting on a plinth of snow, staring down at him as if it owned the whole white world.

"What *are* you?" Avrel grunted.

"What are *you?*" it said with a tilt of its head. "How did you know to call me fox when fox are never found in these waters, bear?"

Avrel blinked and thought about this. His mother must have taught him, but he couldn't recall it. A guess, perhaps? But how could he guess at what he didn't know existed? And yet when he nuzzled down deep into his thoughts, he could picture these creatures in strange locations, stealing food, running with young, their bluish fur turning white in winter. They were *there*, in his memories. Arctic fox. As clear as this one in front of him now.

"Tell me a story, Avrel," it said.

What? He looked up. The plinth was empty. Nothing

to left or right of it, either. Avrel moved forward, purpose in his step, his chest heaving in time to his heart. Was he dreaming? How did this thing know his name? He lunged forward at the crest, certain that the fox would be cowering behind it. It wasn't. It was ahead again, riding another floe.

"Tell me a story," it said across the water. "Tell me of Ragnar, Lorel and Aluna."

Avrel shook his head wildly. Suddenly, pictures were pouring through his mind. It was as if he'd been buried for years in a den and now someone had punched a bright hole in the roof. He saw bears. Great bears, in battle with men. In conflict with each other. On nine great pillars. Memories, running the aurora of time. All the way back to the dawn of the ice. Generations. History. Adventure.

Stories.

He looked up again. The fox was trotting across the ice, north. This was impossible, he told himself. How had it crossed the gap so fast when there was ten bears' length of water between them? "Wait!" he cried.

"This way," the fox replied. Its voice was lower now. Deeper. Rounded.

Avrel took to the water again. He swam for the floe, but it seemed such a long, long time in coming. When he eventually saw the white edge, the sky had darkened and he knew in his heart he was a long way from home. It occurred to him then he might have been dying, on a dream journey heading for the far side of the ice.

In truth, he was about to come alive, to awaken.

Just ahead, he could see the feet of his quarry. But they were no longer stick feet, nimble and clean. They were rugged, fur-straggled, heavy of claw. He looked up then, into the eyes of eternal wonder. The bear he would come to call *Nanukapik*, Ingavar, was gazing down at him. "Tell me a story, Avrel," he said, and he carried all the souls of the North in his voice.

Avrel knew without knowing that the real story began here. He dragged himself tiredly out of the water, shook himself down and gathered his thoughts.

"Where am I?" he asked.

"Everywhere and nowhere," Ingavar said.

Avrel tested the ice. It was sound. "My head . . . ?" he began. "These memories . . . are they mine?"

"For now," said Ingavar, looking at the sky.

"Are you a spirit bear? What do want with me?" Avrel could feel himself trembling now.

"Walk with me," said Ingavar, and the fur on his head seemed to separate into three until a mark was burning in white fire there. "You are Avrel, son of

Lorel. My chosen Teller. Walk with me, nanuk. Watch, learn, remember . . ."

. . . and now here they were, many, many months later, under a grey sky that seemed to walk with them. "Lord, look at the clouds," said Avrel.

"They are not clouds," said Ingavar, continuing.

Avrel peered at them again. Where he usually saw twisting vapour, he could now see a flock of spirit people, walking. They were dressed in the furs of the Inuit natives. Some carried harpoons, others drums. Some drove long sleds, pulled by dogs. Avrel rose up, reaching out a paw. "Who are they?" he asked. Everything his claws raked turned to fog.

"The dead," said Ingavar, "mourning their home."

"Why are they with us?"

"They are always with us," Ingavar said. "You will see them when we need them, and we need them now."

He came to a halt. A drum beat sounded, echoed by another and another and another, till the sky shook with a thunderous hum. The cloud people formed a gigantic circle. From their throats, they chanted *ai-ee-yah! ai-ee-yah!* stirring the wind into flurries and moans. They clapped and danced and sang to the ice, beckoning a great spirit into their ring.

Avrel felt a rumbling vibration in his feet. The ocean was angry. Something was surging up from below. "Lord!" he cried urgently. "Lord, we must run!"

But Ingavar threw back his head and howled, a sound no bear should be capable of making. In the sky, every sled dog joined his call. Avrel, nearly deafened, flattened his ears and saw the ice break with a rolling crack. A great spout of water gushed into the sky and came crashing back in clinging waves, over his paws. Then from the crack came the body of a woman with the tail of a fish. She crawled out, looking round, hissing threats. Her upper half was dressed in the furs of the natives. Her hair was long and matted with algae, her face crusted and twisted by shells, her eyes yellow with the rot of death. On one hand, all her fingers were missing. On the other, all that remained was a thumb.

The spirit people sighed. The drumbeats softened. The dogs ceased to howl. Ingavar also. "Do you recognise this creature?" he asked his Teller.

Avrel nodded in fear. He had seen what he had seen, and here it was to Tell: the story of the day he had walked with the souls of countless men, and seen the blue-eyed Nanukapik, Ingavar, call the sea goddess, Sedna, up from the deep.

A meeting of minds

The Pennykettle house was full of many strange and special dragons: the inspirational Gadzooks; the healer, Gollygosh; the mysterious shape-shifting time-travelling Groyne; the feisty potions dragon, Gretel. But the dragon known as Gwillan was not considered 'important'. He was special in the sense that he could fly like the others and speak in dragontongue like the others and turn his oval-shaped eyes from green to violet (stasis to life) just like the others, but he had no *magical* abilities to hurr of. His had always been a life of service and simplicity.

Until the morning he spotted Gwendolen acting strangely.

His duty was to *snuffle* – or to put it another way, to clean. He was excellent at it. Truly committed. There was barely a speck of dust in the house (including on the scales of his fellow dragons). No crumbs on carpets. No dried autumn leaves just inside the hall door. No falls of ash down the open chimney. All of them snuffled up and burnt to cinders. (Cinders, of course, were *puffled* away later, usually round the roots of the yellow rose bush which grew near to the garden rockery.)

He was hard-working, uncomplaining and incredibly efficient. As well as keeping dust motes in order, he was able to turn his paws to many other domestic chores, such as pegging out the washing, feeding Bonnington or chopping up vegetables with his tail. Any small task that might help Liz run the house more smoothly. Putting stray socks into the wash basket, for instance. Fetching the post. Tugging Lucy's wild red hairs out of the plughole. Anything. Gwillan loved his work – especially watering the plants.

He had seen a lot of things during indoor gardening, but he had never witnessed anything as frightening or bizarre as the intense beam of light that poured out of Gwendolen's eyes that day, the day she sneaked into Zanna's room. Gwillan almost dropped his watering can (a tiny replica of the big ones used by Liz). His first instinct was to hide, but he was already hidden in the overhanging leaves of a flourishing coleus. Through the greenery, he saw papers being picked up and turned. And when the light went away, he saw it disappear into Gwendolen's eyes.

Gwendolen. She was Lucy's dragon, who, like him, never had adventures or ever got *involved*. Why would she be here, on Zanna's desk?

For several days he lived with this knowledge, though

he wished that he could puffle it into smoke. He carried it around, but it rattled his scales. If he tried to ignore it, it nagged him like the grime in an awkward place to clean. People noticed he was out of sorts. A potato peeling was found on the floor of the kitchen. Arthur's slippers were arranged the wrong way about. Bonnington got a bowl of polystyrene chips for tea.

Bad. Questions began to be asked.

Eventually, Gwillan himself, realising that his standards were slipping, made up his mind to tell someone what he'd seen. That someone was Gollygosh, the healing dragon.

Golly was a kindred spirit. He and Gwillan were an unofficial team. While Gwillan ran errands, Golly fixed things – like fuses in plugs, or blown light bulbs, or the TV reception, or Bonnington's cat bell. He was making the ink flow in Liz's favourite pen (by hurring gently on the barrel) when Gwillan came up and asked for advice.

Golly thought about it and said perhaps they should mention this to Gretel?

Gwillan gulped. He didn't like to tangle with the potions dragon who was, after all, the fiercest thing in the house.

So, together, they approached G'reth. The wishing dragon had travelled the universe and boldly gone where no dragon had gone before. Surely he would be brave enough?

No.

The three of them spoke to Gadzooks, perhaps the most respected dragon in the house. He was curious, but also worried. He identified the papers as a letter. Every year he watched Zanna writing one, he said. And every year, including this, he watched Gretel burn it (under Zanna's instruction). He suggested Gwendolen might have read it in some way. But why?

They checked with Groyne, who could offer nothing more. So then the five of them called in Gruffen, who was recently returned from the shop. This was a security matter, they decided. Who better to deal with it than a guard dragon?

Gruffen did as he always did. Long ago, when he'd been made by Liz, he had been given a book of instructions, a manual of 'what to do in difficult times'. He consulted it now, under 'S' for Security. He found just six words: *If in doubt, tell the Liz.*

Every dragon sighed. They knew this instruction was wise and correct, but if Gretel was left out . . .

It was no good. She had to be told.

They approached her in Zanna's room. She was practising a form of acupuncture on Bonnington, using pine needles she'd collected from the Christmas tree six weeks before. The needles were sticking out all over his head. He looked like a tabby cat version of a conker shell.

A-hurr, went Gruffen. There was no correct way to approach a dragon of Gretel's status. One just pitched in and hoped she wouldn't scorch.

"What?" she said.

A-hurr, he coughed again.

She twiddled a pine needle and pointed it at the guard dragon's chest.

He got on with his report.

As predicted, Gretel was immediately suspicious. "Bring Gwendolen to me," she said.

Gwillan flew upstairs and brought her down.

Outnumbered and surrounded, Gwendolen told them what she knew. (It was either that or be zapped by Gretel's magicks.) She didn't think the Lucy meant harm, she said.

"What was in it?" hurred Gretel, meaning the letter.

Gwendolen hunched up and flicked her tail. "Words, to the David."

Gadzooks gulped and stared longingly at the notepad he carried. The corners of the pages were beginning to curl and the paper itself was yellowing with age. Every now and then he tore a blank page off, in the way he'd seen Liz remove dead leaves from plants. It hurt him to talk about messages to David when none came through to him any more.

"She didn't finish reading it," Gwendolen said, "but . . ."

But. The biggest word in the universe. Every single dragon lifted his or her ears.

Gretel waved a solitary flower, a warning to Gwendolen that she had better speak up or feel the effect of a truth scent in her nostrils.

"She sent a message, what she calls an email, to . . ." Gwendolen gave the address.

Every dragon held its breath. Inklings of doubt and distrust were gathering in Gretel's intelligent eyes. Tam Farrell. She remembered him clearly. At the time, when he'd walked through the door of the shop, she had paid very little attention to him. Why should she? Hundreds of people came to the shop and many of them spoke at length to her mistress. But none of them left any kind of impression. He was different. They'd been talking about Tam at home for two days. Something about this wasn't right.

"Are we going to tell your mistress?" G'reth asked quietly, hearing Zanna's voice outside in the hall.

"No," said Gretel, growling at them all, suggesting there'd be trouble if any of them did. "We—"

"She's coming in," said Golly, twizzling his ears.

"Scatter," hurred Gretel, and in a flash each dragon found a separate location as Zanna swept in, with Liz close behind, saying, "It's probably with my stuff. Yep, here you go." She lifted a *Benson's* bag from the floor.

"Mummy, Mummy! G'lant wants to see!" Alexa scooted in, bouncing with excitement. She held the cup of her hands up close to the carrier bag.

Zanna hoisted it higher. "G'lant will have to wait until we go into the garden."

"All right!" Alexa dashed outside.

"G'lant?" asked Liz.

Zanna gave a rueful nod. "I told her about him on the anniversary. Not sure it was a wise idea. She's been talking about it ever since." She glanced tight-lipped at Gadzooks. The writing dragon had turned to face the window.

"Well, I wasn't supposed to blab about the fairy door till we'd installed it, but I did," said Liz. "Maybe it was simply time that she knew. Come on." And resting a hand in the middle of Zanna's back, she guided her out of the room.

As soon as they were gone, the dragons that were not

already on the windowsill flew there to watch what was happening outside. Gretel immediately said to Gadzooks, "Tell us about G'lant." It was a dragon name. A good one, ringing with authority.

Gadzooks made a whimpering sound in his throat.

"It was the last thing he wrote on his pad," said G'reth.

"I know *that*," said Gretel, scowling at him. "The David child speaks as if she can *see* him."

G'reth shook his head, "I think she just wishes it."

A sudden jingle of wind chimes made them look out at the garden again. Liz was hanging up the set she'd bought, dangling them off a bracket she'd previously used for a flower basket. Though her voice was muffled Gretel heard her say, "There. When you hear them bongle, the fairies will be in the garden."

Fairies? someone hurred.

Gadzooks said, *Mythical creatures, I think.*

Gretel watched Alexa clap her hands, then shifted her gaze a little wider to Lucy. The girl had gone outside, but clearly under sufferance. She was hovering, arms folded, looking cold and bored. Suddenly, she looked up and saw the dragons watching. There was the usual grin of recognition, but when she saw Gwendolen among the others, her eyes narrowed slightly. She was wondering why.

74

Gretel gave Gwendolen a jab with her tail. "Are you with us?" she hissed, from the corner of her mouth.

Gwendolen nodded. It was a difficult choice, but dragon was dragon.

"Then wave," said Gretel.

Gwendolen waved a paw. All the dragons did. The flurry made Lucy smile.

"We need to know more about the Tam," said Gretel.

"An outsider?" said G'reth. "How will we do that?"

Gretel produced a big broad smile, one that brought her nostrils together in a sideways 'eight'. "He bought a dragon," she said.

The others gulped uneasily, wondering what was coming.

"Who can make themselves into a *Gudrun?*" she asked.

Sea ice, near to the last known location of the island once called The Tooth of Ragnar

As missions went, it seemed impossible. Walk to this region and find *a raven*? A useless (and generally annoying) black bird, preserved in a block of ice? It would be easier to point to a glinting star and turn it into a flake of snow. This must be a test, Kailar told himself. A demonstration of allegiance. A measure of faith. But why would Ingavar need that of him when he had already sworn to fight for him till death? Snorting heavily, he trudged on again, pace after weary paw-dragging pace, using the patterns of the stars to guide him, and the memory of the wind, and the motion of the ice. And as he walked, he let his mind drift back in time to his first encounter with the bear he called Nanukapik. It had been a night, much the same shape as this, when sickness had brought him collapsing to his knees, and he had lain down, panting in short dizzy bursts, not sure if he was dying, half-wishing that he were. That was when Avrel had appeared beside him. He winced, remembering the shame he'd felt to see a bear with a pelt like untouched snow and eyes as soft and innocent as the moon. For there was he, Kailar, a son of Ragnar, once the most powerful of fighting bears, all but glued to his place on the ice, his path across it marked by poisonous black smears.

"What . . . what happened to you?" asked Avrel, his voice expressing tenderness at first, then fear. Tenderness. Not something a fighting bear was used to.

"If you're going to kill me, strike quickly," said Kailar. Despite the toxins swelling his tongue, his voice was still able, fearsome and low.

Avrel gulped and shook his head. "Are you Kailar?" he asked. Instantly, he knew this was too quick a prompt. The fighting bear shook with confusion and rage, an act which only increased his suffering and made him cough spots of bright red blood.

"Be calm," Avrel said, shuffling back. He trod his paws anxiously, fretful that the fit would end the bear's life. And where would his mission be then?

"How do you know me?" Kailar said. The words were a gargle of air and bile. His brown eyes rolled and he saw the sky shift. He put out a paw, as if to touch it.

"I am a Teller. I was sent to find you," said Avrel.

"Teller?" said Kailar in a whisper of death.

"Listen to me! You're not going to *die*!" said Avrel. He stamped the ice hard, making Kailar snort himself back to full consciousness. Avrel stepped forward and sniffed at the awful, bitter-tasting substance that covered nearly three parts of Kailar's body. Twice he reeled back, for the stench was foul. And the texture? Like blood, half-gelling into blubber. "This is oil," he said, as a memory of it came to him. He and his mother had once swum close to a small vessel – a boat, steered by men, that leaked this dirt. She had made him taste it, not to ease his hunger but to warn him that some things were worse than hunger. On the water, the oil had seemed harmless enough. On Kailar, it looked like a coat of death.

"How did you come to be like this?"

"What does it matter?" Kailar replied. "Who sent you? How could you find what you do not know?"

But Avrel was no longer listening to him. His gaze was fastened into the distance where the dome of the sky was steadily changing. He could feel a strange wind rising off the ice and prayed for the help and relief it might bring. "Look!" he gasped suddenly. "Look ahead of you! Now!"

Kailar had already seen it and thought he must be dreaming. Far ahead was another landscape of ice, somehow in the sky but tilted towards them. It was not a reflection, for the patterns of the leads and ridges were different and the sky there was brighter, like another season. Neither was it upside down. This he could tell because walking across it was a large male bear. It was padding towards them.

"Turn around, Teller," Kailar said wearily. "This spirit is for me. Go, or he might take your ears for a prize."

"No," said Avrel, standing his ground. "His name is Ingavar. He is your Nanukapik, come to be with you."

Kailar looked up and saw the air shimmer. When it was still, there was one lot of ice but two bears over him. Nanukapik? The word bubbled through his head like water emerging out of a seal hole. He was a cub the last time he'd heard this term. It meant 'greatest bear'. Was this the nature of death, he wondered? Regression? A swift return to the den?

Ingavar looked at the stricken body. "You have done well to find him," he said, even though Avrel thought he could see a great fury raging in Ingavar's eyes. How deeply it must pain him to see such a proud bear wounded so.

"I am dying," said Kailar. "Leave me in peace."

"You were strong once, you can be strong again," said Ingavar.

Kailar snorted and closed his eyes.

"Listen to him. Trust him," Avrel said urgently. "You saw him walk out of another world."

"Then maybe he could lick this poison off me!" Kailar

79

said bitterly, trying to growl. His head thumped back against the ice once more. Nanukapiks. Tellers. Death by spoiling. Would this torture never end?

Ingavar slowly circled the body, pausing at last by Kailar's head, where a paw print of oil was clear on the surface. "What would you do for a new life, Kailar?"

"I have nothing to give," he said.

"All I ask is your devotion," Ingavar said. And he placed his paw briefly where Kailar's had stood. Avrel shuddered as a circle of flames leapt off the ice, eating up the space where the oil had been.

Kailar saw them and snarled. "Do what you want to me, spirit. I was born into the line of the ice bear, Ragnar. I will fight your fire to my dying breath."

Ingavar came forward and raised his paw. "This is the fire of life," he said. "Believe it, if you want to survive . . ." And from each of his claws came a short burst of light. When he stepped back again, Kailar was burning.

It was the most chilling sight Avrel had ever witnessed. Twice before he had seen the spectacle of fire and even once seen a careless bear singed by its heat. This was different. Kailar was immersed in a purifying blizzard. A white fire that neither made the ice around them zing nor sent smoke lines curling through the air.

It consumed his whole body from tail tip to snout. And Avrel saw – for an instant, before terror turned his head – the dry bones, the frame, the peltless Kailar. Only when Ingavar said, *It is done*, did he find the courage to look back again.

Kailar was alive. Alive and unstained. The only marks on his creamy pelt now were old battle scars. The tattoos of his life. The symbols of his lineage, importance and strength.

He got up groggily, as far as one knee. "My name is Kailar," he said – a gesture of formality. "Everything I am is yours to command."

"Rise," said Ingavar, and when Kailar was standing he addressed both bears. "You are my chosen companions: a bear from the noblest of fighting packs, and a Teller's son." (Avrel tipped his head.) "We are on a journey of life," said Ingavar. "The ice is changing. The North is under threat. Bears are starving because the seasons have altered. The spirit that is Gaia, goddess of the Earth, is restless and wanting to act upon these changes. All living things may suffer if she does."

"Can we fight this spirit?" Kailar asked boldly.

"No," said Ingavar, "we must work with her to bring about the means for change. There will be stories to Tell," he said to Avrel, "some battles to be fought," he said to Kailar, "but the greatest battle is here, inside us." He turned a paw inward, close to his chest. "Soon, the world will turn its eyes north, and the ice will be melting in the souls of men—"

"Men?" said Kailar, deep in his throat. Avrel glanced uneasily at him. Kailar looked taller now, prouder, dangerous.

"The enemy and the saviour," Ingavar said. "We must appeal to them, Kailar. We must make them understand that protecting the North protects them also."

"How do we do this?" Avrel asked. He was thinking back to the oldest stories, of the Inuk, Oomara, and the war with Ragnar.

"We make our struggle known to them," Ingavar replied. "To as many as we can, in all the ways that we can. Some of these ways you will not understand."

"And then?" Kailar remembered asking.

"Then something wonderful will come of it," said Ingavar. And he struck the ice with fire once more, sending a blaze far back across the pack until, in the distance, a light could be seen on the ocean itself.

It was a flicker of light, not as bright as fire, which brought Kailar's thoughts back into the present. He glanced at the sky where a star was winking. There was nothing unusual in that, but the more he looked at this weak yellow speck, the more he thought it resembled an eye. He let his gaze widen and thought he could make out a shape around it. A bird's head. A raven's head. *A raven.*

A sign.

He looked down. Just ahead of him, a pressure ridge had formed with a heavy collection of snow at its base. Instinct told him that was where he should dig.

He went in with powerful scoops of his paws, throwing back layers of compacted snow as if they were no heavier than the fur around his ears. Soon, he had a hole as large as his body. But still he ploughed on, convinced he was correct, until – fortune: his claws struck ice. Ice within ice that resisted his raking. He shuffled his position and dug sideways a little, uncovering a block that seemed to measure almost the width of his chest. Before long, two sides were completely revealed. He grew impatient then and threw his body weight behind it, pushing with all of a fighting bear's might. The block spilled out and tumbled to the flat. It was filled with fracture lines and opaque patches, but even in dim light the shadows at its centre were unmistakeable. Feathers. Feet. A raven in flight.

Kailar snouted it and eyed it for life. He had been

enclosed in some dens in his time, but never one quite as tight as this. The creature looked perfect, but had to be dead. Even Ingavar's fire couldn't bring it back, surely? But if the Nanukapik's words were true, this thing would walk once its legs were freed. Intrigued, he knocked the block onto its side, where he had a better overall view. The bird's frozen yellow eye unnerved him for a second. So he rose up and laid a paw over the chunk, blocking the stare from view. He tapped the ice with his stronger left paw, working out where best to make his strike. He knew he must be accurate – forceful, but restrained. One serious blow would crush the whole thing, and all that would be left would be water and smears.

He punched it. A corner broke off with ease. He punched again, harder, and heard the ice groan. Once more and it split along an internal rupture. Kailar scraped at it and thumped again. Away came the uppermost section of the chunk, freeing the raven's head in the process.

Success.

"Bird, can you hear me? Speak to me, raven." Several times he repeated these words, even tilting his ear to the animal's beak to try to detect any whispers from its lungs. But there was nothing. And he dared not touch it. The slightest pressure from his clumsy paw would snap the head right off the body. Legs, he thought, would be even more fragile. What should he do? Leave it? Wait? Eat it and be done? He chose to wait, lie down and sleep for a while.

Later, when the journey back to Ingavar was about to begin, he wished many times that he had not been so patient or so lenient. He was sleeping soundly when an awful *caark! caark!* ripped through his brain. He shook himself awake, unsettling several light ridges of snow that had collected around his eyes and ears. The raven had not been so lucky. Its head was entirely covered with snow, apart from a minor breathing hole created by the constant spitting from its beak. *Caark!* it went again, making Kailar jump. He approached, half-thinking he might kill it anyway just for having his sleep disturbed. But he relented and merely blew the snow away, as much as he could remove by snorting, anyway.

The raven shook its head. One eye swivelled forward. "Oh, perfect," it sneered. "That's all I needed. Stale seal breath from a snow-shuffling lump of pot-bellied fur. Let me go, you squinty-eyed piece of . . ." The insults went on and on, but Kailar was tired – and the blizzard was beginning to increase in strength. As the first cold spicules pinged his snout he remembered some advice his mother had given him. "When you can't sleep, imagine your ears are filling with snow. Count the flakes and sleep will take you." Kailar settled down again.

"*What?*" screeched the bird.

Tomorrow, or however long it took to wake, he would free the bird's legs and they would search for Ingavar—

"Lemming brain!" it spat.

—if he hadn't rolled over and flattened it by then.

One flake, two flakes, three flakes . . .

An evening at Allandale's

It was during the final weeks of her pregnancy, and for the first months after Alexa had been born, that Zanna had found she missed David the most. Liz was always on hand to support her. Lucy, too, had been a tower of strength then. And though Gretel had helped with restful potions, especially at night when Zanna had often tried to cry herself to sleep, no one could calm her quite like Arthur. It was during this stressful phase that he had first invited her to meditate with him. Peace, he told her, came from inner silence. In the silence she would find contentment and truth.

Arthur was no stranger to the concept of silence. He had spent many isolated, troubled years at an island monastery, trying to understand the nature of the universe and how it related to human consciousness, a journey that had shown him many wonders and dealt him many blows. The blindness he endured, caused by the agent of an alien life form in the struggle to protect a guardian of the universe, a dragon known to them all as Grockle, was both a hindrance and a blessing. In his daily life, the darkness was inconvenient. But in the Dragon's Den, locked away in deep contemplation, it was a catalyst of enlightenment, a window which opened on the quality of devotion. For these trials, ordeals and years of hardship had finally brought him here, to this house, to Elizabeth.

Everything happened for a reason.

Everything.

So when Zanna sat with him that Sunday afternoon, before she chose to go out and meet Tam Farrell, Arthur listened to her, not with the ear of a priest or its surrogate, but with the ear of a man who felt nothing but unconditional love for her. A state in which he could not pass judgement. A pool in which she could mirror her thoughts.

"I mean, I feel . . . I don't know what I feel. Help me, Arthur. I'm . . ."

"Be calm," he said. "Breathe slowly. Breathe deep."

Zanna synchronised her air flow again. The third time she'd done so since the session started. She pulled her left foot tight against her thigh. That was a measure of her tension, she thought: cramp, sitting in the lotus position. She glanced at Gwillan. *Would she like him to hurr on her toes?* he asked.

"No," she said gratefully, and set herself again. "I mean, I see Liz's point, but I feel mixed up."

"Are you frightened of letting go?" asked Arthur.

"Of David?" She sounded alarmed. "I could never give him up. He's . . ."

Arthur parted his lips again. "Are you afraid of letting go of yourself, Zanna?"

She tipped her head forward, sending her long hair cascading down her cheeks. After a few seconds lost in thought she replied, "I told Lexie about G'lant." She looked up for any sign of a reaction, but his face was a model of stillness and serenity. "Was that letting go? Or was I just passing the buck to my child because I can't cope alone with the burden of carrying that invisible flame?"

Gadzooks, sitting on a stool behind Zanna, shifted his wings uncomfortably.

Arthur opened his eyes. She preferred it like this. Although he could not see her, it seemed as though he did. It felt more personal. "When I was blinded by the Fain," he said. "I was terrified, but not for the reason you imagine. In the moment I commingled with that extraordinary creature, I was exposed to a greater part of the universe. I saw worlds I did not believe I could imagine. I sensed feelings . . ." He swallowed and closed his eyes again. "Every light is visible somewhere, Zanna. Your love for David is alive. You created it. On some level, you can be certain he knows you care for him.

And that's enough, enough for you to open your hands and let G'lant fly free."

"I know, I know, I know," she repeated, dragging the back of her hand under her eye. "But I don't want to feel I'm betraying him, Arthur."

"Let go," he counselled her, quiet and assured. "Follow your instinct. Follow your heart."

Zanna sighed and looked up. On a shelf just behind Liz's work bench was a dragon called Gauge. He was a counting dragon and the most accurate 'clock' in the house. She raised an eyebrow and Gauge in turn raised his paws for her, making the hands for 7:10pm. Fifty minutes before the poetry reading began.

Zanna uncrossed her legs and nudged her feet into her shoes. "Follow my heart?"

"Always," said Arthur.

She nodded, bent forward and gently kissed his cheek. "Thank you. I know what I have to do. We'll speak again tomorrow. Love and light."

"Love and light," he said in return. "Enjoy yourself."

Zanna knew Allandale's book shop well. When David's first book *Snigger and the Nutbeast* had been published, the shop had organised a small promotional event to celebrate the success of their most local — and mysterious – author. This was the first time the readers of Scrubbley had come to discover that the man who had made their library gardens famous was doing so posthumously. A journalist and photographer from the *Scrubbley Evening Echo* had turned up that night, hoping to talk to the 'family' of Mr Rain. Zanna, by prior agreement with Liz, had opted to stay anonymous, and it was Liz and David's editor, Dilys Whutton, who gave the paper what they needed to know: *David disappeared tragically, presumed drowned, on a scientific expedition to the Arctic. His next – and last – book,* White Fire, *would be set there. For the sake of his nearest and dearest, that was all they wished to say.*

Zanna caught her breath. It was the same room, set out in just the same way, with three arcs of soft-backed chairs and a small lectern at the front. The main ceiling lights had been turned off, and the room was illuminated by filtered blue halogens built into the two walls of bookshelves. Ten or a dozen people were already randomly seated, poring over programme leaflets, but Zanna's eye was drawn to a larger group, clustered around a table where wine and fruit juice was being served. She spotted Tam Farrell in quiet conversation with a spiky-haired woman, whom she knew to be the book shop owner, Cassandra. He was dressed almost identically to the way she'd last seen him, but without his glasses. He seemed more handsome, if less stylish, for it. Zanna gulped at the embedded disloyalty of this thought and almost turned to leave, but by then he had spotted her and was waving in acknowledgement. He finished off his drink and came hurrying to greet her, hand extended.

"Hi. Glad you could make it. Come on in. What would you like to drink?"

"Oh, white wine," she said. "Just a small glass."

"No problem." He was about to turn to get it when she caught his arm and said, "Erm, Mr Farrell, may I introduce you to someone?"

Tam glanced at the elderly man beside her.

"My neighbour and mentor, Henry Bacon. He's a librarian. He likes poetry, don't you, Henry?"

"Not this modern rubbish," he muttered, scowling his way through the pages of a pamphlet.

Tam's mouth fell open. "Well, you're full of surprises, Miss . . . ?"

"Martindale," she said, "but you can call me Zanna."

Tam nodded in the style of an old-fashioned gentleman and smiled again, as if he'd won a small but important victory. Hands in pockets, he turned to Mr Bacon. "I'm a Blake man, myself. What about you, Henry?"

"Too many angels," Mr Bacon grunted.

"There's nothing wrong with angels," Zanna chided him.

"You like Blake?" Tam turned to her again.

"Had to read him at school." Stroking her hair, she quoted one of his lines, "If the doors of perception were cleansed, every thing would appear to man as it is, infinite."

"Fair assessment," said Tam, looking impressed. "White wine, then, and . . . ?"

"Tea," said Henry. "Where are the toilets?"

Tam flapped a hand. "Oh, at the back of the shop, I think. Sit down where you like," he said quietly to Zanna. "I'll be back with . . ."

"Tea?" she said wryly.

"Tea. Right." He drifted away.

Zanna chose the back row of seats. Suspecting that Tam might elect to join them, it was her intention to use Henry as a buffer between them, but Mr Bacon's insistence on having an aisle seat (because of his gout) left the chair beside her free, and sure enough Tam chose to sit there. To his credit, he kept a respectful distance and only spoke once or twice throughout the first reading to whisper the odd comment. "Too intense," he suggested about one poem. "Probably better off the page," he said of another. Zanna said nothing in return. With her hands in her lap she struck a high-chinned pose which she hoped might make her appear to be listening, even though she was finding the poetry dull and Henry's bad-tempered shuffling difficult to cope with. She was mildly surprised that Tam had not gone to sit with friends or even tried to introduce her to them, an embarrassment she'd been steeling herself for since her arrival. And why hadn't he known where the toilets were, if this was one of his regular haunts?

The answer became clear when the second reader was announced – none other than Tam Farrell, a 'highly respected' name on the poetry circuit, with many publications in small press magazines. She clapped benignly as he stood up.

"Seems I'm not the only one with surprises," she said.

"It's not Blake, but I hope you enjoy it," he replied.

He read about Scotland. He read about his childhood. But most of all, he read about love. His voice, in turns both lyrical and commanding, hung in the air with the ethereal quality of a good radio broadcast. Despite her better wishes, Zanna found herself moved. At the end, the applause was rapturous and deserved. He nodded modestly and thanked them all for coming. She was pleased that he did not try to look at her.

The readings concluded there and Tam was drawn away to a table at the front. Cassandra announced that his first collection of poetry was available to buy and he would be happy to sign copies if anyone was interested. A small crowd soon gathered. To Zanna's surprise, Henry Bacon declared he was going to join them.

Zanna didn't know what to say. She looked over at the table where Tam was smiling broadly, already handing a book to a gushing fan. How many times had she imagined David doing that? "I'll just browse," she said to Henry. "Let me know when you're ready to go."

Half an hour later she was standing beside the section labelled New Age/Spiritual glancing through a book about the Wiccan religion when Tam's voice drifted over her shoulder. "Ah, thought I might find you here."

"In the nutters' section?" She reached up and slid the book back onto the shelf.

He clicked his tongue. Touché. Again. "You know, that really is a nasty scar," he said, daring to hold her arm a moment. "You must have encountered some brutes in your playground?"

"I fell," she said, releasing herself with just enough

force to suggest that she didn't approve of the contact. "Where's Henry?"

"Treating Cassie to a discourse on libraries."

"Then I'd better go and rescue her."

Tam swept a path clear. "He asked me to give you this." He held out a copy of his poetry pamphlet.

"*The Fire Eternal*," she mumbled, reading the title.

"It's a metaphor – for everlasting love," he said, letting his gaze wander over her face. "Not too subtle, but folks seem to like it. Read the inscription."

Zanna opened the book. On the title page were the words, *To Zanna – I hope this opens a small door to perception, Tam Farrell.*

"Henry asked me to sign it for you."

Speechless, she chewed her lip.

"Kind man," he said. "Interesting, too – once he's put you in your proper place, of course. Forgive me if I'm about to wade in with elephant-sized feet, but . . . I take it he's not your partner?"

Zanna shook her head. "No. No, he isn't."

"He couldn't make it, then – your guy?"

"I have to go," she said, loosening the flap on her knit shoulder bag and pushing the pamphlet hurriedly inside. "Thank you for a pleasant evening."

"My pleasure," he said as she swept away. With an

96

unresolved sigh, he followed her back to the signing table.

Henry was still in deep discussion and had regressed from the library system into the war years. Cassandra, who seemed grateful to see another female face, interrupted him to ask if Zanna had enjoyed the event.

"Yes, very enlightening," she said, her attention still diverted to her bag. It had felt awkward for a moment when she'd opened it, but she couldn't quite understand why.

"Impressive, isn't he?" Cassandra was nodding at Tam.

"Mmm. A revelation," Zanna mumbled, absent-mindedly buttoning up her bag.

"He gets better. You should come to these events more often. Haven't I seen you before, anyway?"

"I work in the High Street," Zanna replied quickly. "I pop in now and then."

Cassandra nodded. "Tam, about your fee."

"You pay him?" said Henry, who clearly felt that literature ought to be free to the masses.

"In kind," she said. "Choose a book, Tam. Anything you like, hard or paperback."

Tam looked around a moment then walked across to a display table and picked one up. "I'll have this." It was a copy of *White Fire*.

Zanna felt her breath moving forward in stutters.

"Fine choice," said Henry.

"You've read it?" Tam half-lifted an eyebrow.

"I've more than read it, boy, I—"

A nudge from Zanna stopped him short. "Henry, I think it's time we *went*."

Tam opened the book at the back page. "No, please, go on. I'm interested to hear what Henry has to say. There's quite a cult growing up around this. Thought I'd find out what all the fuss is about. Local chap, isn't he?" He pointed to a small photograph on the inside of the book jacket. David in the library gardens, feeding a squirrel.

Cassandra nodded. "He died – a few years ago."

Tam hummed thoughtfully. "Tragic. So young." He let the pages flutter. "Polar bears, the Arctic, Inuit legends." He looked pointedly at Zanna, then at Henry. "Doesn't strike me as your sort of thing, Henry?"

"I'm a librarian," he said. "I'm widely read."

Good answer, thought Tam. Cleverly evasive. He smiled, accepted it, and opened his satchel. "And you, Zanna? Have you . . . ?"

"Yes," she said, trying not to look away. "It's a brilliant book. Naively written in places, but refreshing for it. It sends out a clear environmental message to the world and I think everyone who cares about this planet and the welfare of its wildlife should read it. Now, I'm sorry, but we really must go."

"Yes, of course," he said, standing aside to let her go past. "Oh, about my consultation?"

She came to an imperial halt.

"Would next Wednesday at eleven be OK?"

She thought a moment. "Twelve-thirty would be better."

"OK, twelve-thirty it is. Oh, and Zanna?"

"What?" she said, turning, crunching the word.

"Thank you for coming."

He meant it, she could tell. She stared at him a second, then noticed Cassandra smiling in the background and hurriedly escaped before her cheeks lit up.

That night, Tam Farrell drove home to his Thames-side apartment in Canary Wharf, thinking endlessly about Suzanna Martindale. His mind should have been fixed on the article he planned to write for *The National Endeavour*. Instead, his thoughts danced in the rain and the headlights, lingering on her dark-haired beauty, her calf-length Indian cotton dresses, the braids in her hair, the bangles on her arms. So much passion. So many secrets. So much he still wanted to know about her . . .

The rain beat down. Tam tapped his head. *Come on, it's a job*, he told himself. *Just another feature. Stay professional. Not too close.*

He glanced at the cover of *White Fire* where it lay on the passenger seat beside him. It was the original version, a polar bear in close up at the edge of the ice cap, its head low, its brown eyes angled upward as though it was aware of something in the distance. Suddenly, the exterior street lighting changed and on the head of the bear Tam thought he saw a mark. He walloped his brakes, slewing to a stop just a bumper kiss away from the car in front. The driver remonstrated and drove off angrily. Tam gestured in surrender and pulled into the kerb. The mark on the polar bear's head had gone. Thinking at first it was a holographic projection cast in the foil effects on the jacket, he held the book up to the light from the windscreen. No amount of tilting could reproduce the mark. And yet he was certain he hadn't imagined it. He scrambled in his satchel, pulling out a sheet of A4 paper. An image, downloaded from the internet that morning. A three-pronged symbol. The mark of Oomara. The subject of several Inuit legends. The same mark that was gouged into Zanna's arm. The symbol he'd seen on the cover of the book.

A spray of rain lashed into his driver's window. For the first time since he'd begun this feature, a thread of fear wormed its way around the intrigue. "What *are* you?" he whispered, clenching his teeth. He picked up the book and stared at it again. He stroked the bear's face and thought, ironically, about the doors of perception. When they didn't open, he pushed the book and the image deep into his satchel, unaware that as he did so he was covering up something that had stowed away there. It was an artefact, patterned with Inuit etchings, fashioned long ago from the tusk of a narwhal, a creature thought to have magical properties – which might have explained, had Tam been aware of it, how he came to be carrying an invisible dragon called Groyne into the heart of London that night.

The door opens

When Zanna arrived home, the only person still up was Lucy. She was in the front room, sitting cross-legged on the sofa, watching TV. Zanna poked her head round the door and said, "Hi."

"Um," Lucy grunted, without once taking her eyes off the screen.

Just in front of her, Bonnington was sitting on the hearth rug. He was in his favoured 'panther' mode. His ferocious yellow eyes were glued to the broadcast. Zanna always found this a little unnerving. It was easy to see how a domestic cat might be fascinated, in passing, by this animated glowing box (her parents' cat, Pippa, used to like watching golf balls being putted across a green) but Bonnington, or rather the hybrid he'd become, watched it with critical intensity. No one would have been at all surprised if he'd donned a pair of spectacles or set the DVD. He was that kind of cat now.

"News 24?" she queried, reading the corner of the screen. A music programme or a soap opera, maybe; it was unlike Lucy to be watching the news.

"It's about Patagonia."

Patagonia. Right. Zanna perched on the arm of the sofa. "Homework?"

Lucy lowered the sound. (Bonnington's ears immediately pricked up.) "They have these ice fields in the Andes mountains. They're melting too fast, because of global warming. While you were out listening to poetry, the southern ice sheet probably lost an area equivalent to the size of a football pitch."

'Right,' thought Zanna. 'And I'm to blame for that, am I?' She laid her hands on her knees and pushed herself up again. "Sorry, I'll try not to be out so long in future."

"Sea levels are rising," Lucy added casually. "About a millimetre a year – on average. Doesn't sound enough to cause major flooding, does it?"

"Lucy, it's not my fault, OK? I'm just as concerned about climate change as you are."

"No, you're not."

'And there it is,' Zanna told herself. 'Damned before I can make a case.' She shook herself together with a clatter of bangles. "I'm going to bed. Goodnight."

"Aren't you going to tell me what the poetry was like?"

Zanna opened her bag and threw the pamphlet towards her. "I'm tired. Check for yourself."

"Is this *his?*" Lucy said, making no attempt at all to disguise her shock.

"He's a fine writer," Zanna said a little pompously. "His poetry's very moving. Why don't you read it? He's coming to the shop for a consultation next Wednesday. I'd appreciate it if you could pop in during your lunch hour and cover for me."

Lucy read the inscription and put the book down. "Did he ask about David?"

"No, why would he?"

Lucy gave her a questioning glare.

Sighing heavily, Zanna replied, "He seemed relieved that Henry and I weren't an item, if that's what you mean? And bizarrely, he took a copy of *White Fire* home to read."

"Are you going to tell him?"

"He's a client, Lucy. I don't discuss my personal life with clients."

"Not even if you fancy them?"

Raar, went Bonnington, and trotted out of the door.

"OK, forget it. I'll ask your mum if she's free next week—"

"Oh, talk about 'sensitive'." Lucy gurned a face. "Take a chill pill, will you? I'll cover. I always do, don't I? Might as well see if he's 'worthy', I suppose."

"Thank you," Zanna said, performing a minor curtsey. "Now, if Her Majesty approves, I'm going to retire to my bedchamber. Goodnight."

"'Night," Lucy said with an aggravated drawl. But as Zanna turned away she sparked up again, saying, "Oh, by the way, Lexie drew a picture."

Zanna jiggled her house keys, a measure of her annoyance. "Lexie's always drawing pictures. What of it?"

Lucy aimed the remote, making the television channels flash like a zoetrope. "It's an ancient dragon. Not like one of ours."

On the mantelpiece, Gwillan rattled his scales.

Zanna hunched her shoulders. "And your point is?"

"Nothing . . .'cept she's never drawn one like it before – and it's got blue eyes."

Blue eyes. Zanna turned the thought aside. She couldn't face that path. Not tonight. Not after Tam Farrell's heartbreaking poetry. "I'll see you in the morning," she said and walked away. But as she entered what used to be David's room, the words were still with her, doing their best to conjure up ghosts in the way that poems make worlds between their lines.

She slid her bag off her shoulder, sat on the bed and stared at Alexa. The child was at peace, sleeping soundly, her pretty face catching the light of the moon. One small fist was resting on the pillow. Inside it was a fan of drawing paper. Zanna leaned forward and teased it out. From the corner of her eye, she saw Gadzooks twitch.

"Have you seen this?" she whispered, using soft dragontongue.

He sent her a quiet *hrrr* of acknowledgement, but his gaze was clearly taken by something in the garden, making Zanna ask, "What is it? What's the matter?"

Beyond the glass there came the faintest tinkle of a wind chime. Gadzooks immediately peered at Alexa. Her eyelids twitched as though she was dreaming and from her lips came a gentle murmur of dragonsong.

"Oh, baby," Zanna whispered, cooing inside. She touched her hand to Alexa's cheek. "Are the fairies talking to you?"

Alexa fell back into sleep once more. Gadzooks blew a thoughtful smoke ring and frowned.

"Has she been doing that all night?"

Gadzooks *hurred* again.

"Has it woken her?"

His tail flicked sideways, but he shook his head.

Zanna nodded and opened the piece of paper. As Lucy had said, it was a drawing of a dragon. A child's effort. More of a sketch than a picture. In outline, it had the classic dragon shape: small head, umbrella wings, sinewy body. None of this came as any real surprise, for any talented child might reproduce that. But the eyes made Zanna catch her breath. In the pale light, she could not see their colour properly, but the detail around them was quite astounding. Scales. Dozens of tiny scales, small below the eye, larger above. And she had tried to draw something in the pupil as well. Something reflected in the dragon's vision. Some kind of star, perhaps?

Just then, Alexa burbled in her sleep and squeezed her empty fist against the pillow. Zanna folded up the drawing and reinserted it between the soft pink fingers. "Dream it," she whispered, using one of Liz's favourite expressions. She stroked a lock of hair off Alexa's temple and was about to turn away when a pair of yellow eyes in the darkness made her jump.

"Oh, Bonnington!" she tutted. "What are you doing there? You gave me such a fright!"

The cat was sitting on the dressing table, looking like something from a pharaoh's tomb.

"Turn back into something less spooky," Zanna said. "I can't see you in black. You're not allowed up there anyway. Come on, shoo."

She chased him to the floor and headed for the bathroom.

But no sooner had she gone than Bonnington jumped onto the table again. He briefly exchanged a look with Gadzooks, but the dragon made no attempt to criticise the move, and Bonnington settled to his pose again, this time angling towards the mirror, looking not at himself, but at the moonlit reflection of the sleeping Alexa . . .

The next morning, during the hubbub of breakfast, Zanna showed Alexa's drawing to Liz.

"Mmm," she went, through a mouthful of toast. "Gosh, she *is* coming on. That's brilliant. How did it go last night, by the way?"

Looking fragile in her Japanese nightgown, with her hair tied back and pale of make-up, Zanna said, "Fine."

Liz raised an inviting eyebrow.

"Fine," repeated Zanna, slapping Liz's arm. "Stop it, you're making me blush. He read some poetry and he was charming. Period."

"Mum, look harder at the drawing," said Lucy.

I'll tell you later, Zanna mouthed.

Liz smiled and cast a glance at the dragon again. "Yes. It's very good. Those eyes are fantastic."

"They're blue," said Lucy, scooping up cereal.

"That's not what I meant," Liz murmured in reply. "She's always liked to blob colours around, but I've never seen her add so much detail before. That's really impressive. Look at how she's used this stunning shade of green for the outlines of his body. So lifelike."

"But the eyes are *blue*," Lucy repeated.

"All right, we know where you're going," Zanna tutted, taking a yoghurt out of the fridge. She ripped off the lid as if she'd like to do the same to Lucy's head. "Blue's her favourite colour. We're not reading anything into it, OK? Anyway, she's probably just modelled it on Groyne."

On the counter top, Gretel was picking the nuts and seeds out of a piece of wholegrain bread. At the mention of Groyne, she coughed a huge smoke bubble and spilled her entire harvest onto the head of a very bemused Bonnington.

Zanna frowned at her but didn't pursue it. "What gets me is, she hasn't had that much exposure to dragon imagery, yet here she is producing realistic-looking eyes. I mean, what's made her draw that triangular-shaped socket?"

"It's called a scalene," said Lucy, and when Zanna and Liz both stared at her she added, "a triangle with no equal sides. We did it at school once. What's your problem?"

Liz glanced at the drawing again. The eye was wedge-shaped, slanted forward with a tented lid. From the back of it, Alexa had drawn three jagged extensions which helped to exaggerate the intensity of the stare. "That *is* remarkable," Liz confessed. "Is it looking at something, do you think? What's this shape she's tried to draw inside it?"

"I don't know. I wondered about that," said Zanna.

"I think it's a fire star," Lucy said.

Which made Zanna catch her breath and sigh again.

"Well, what do *you* think it is, then?" Lucy said, huffily.

"Why don't you just ask her?" said Arthur, coming in. He touched Lucy's shoulder, which mollified her feisty attitude a little. "I heard your description. Very accurate. Very apt. Grockle had characteristic scalene eyes."

Zanna waved a spoon, mid-air. The listening dragon on top of the fridge leaned back, wary of flying spots of yoghurt. "But she's never seen Grockle, or any dragon like him."

"Perhaps she doesn't need to," Arthur said, "now she's been given the opportunity to dream one." He reached for a chair. The ever-helpful Gwillan guided his hand through the extra space.

Zanna put her yoghurt aside. "You think she's drawing G'lant?"

"G'lant?" said Lucy, on it in a flash. (Gretel and the listening dragon peered intently at one another.) "How does she know about G'lant?"

"I told her," Zanna said.

"What? And she can see him?"

"Lucy, that's enough now," Liz cut in, calming a potentially explosive situation. "We all know Alexa is a bright little girl. She's stretching her imagination, like children do, that's all."

"Alexa is sending her thoughts into the universe and the universe is sending her a dragon back," said Arthur.

"An ancient dragon?" Lucy pressed. "One with proper *scalene* eyes?"

"He was her father's thought form; he's real to her," said Arthur.

But for Zanna, that was a line too much. "Please," she said, clamping her hands to her head. "Can we please stop bringing everything round to David and blue eyes and fire stars and—?"

"Yes, we can," said Liz, interrupting again, warning Lucy off with a violet-eyed flare. "If nothing else, I'm tired of this continual bickering. Where is Alexa, anyway?"

111

"Garden," said Lucy.

"Garden?" Liz repeated, sounding shocked. "But it's freezing today! Why have you let her go out there?"

"Oh, what? So I'm her nanny now, am I? Thanks!" Pushing her breakfast bowl aside in a huff, Lucy stormed out, making dents in the stairs.

"Oh, for goodness' sake," Liz said. She put the drawing on the table and bracketed her hands as if she'd like to strangle the girl. "Someone tell me I was never like that when I was her age . . . please." She stepped outside to call Alexa.

Zanna laid a hand on Arthur's shoulder. "I'm sorry. I didn't mean it to sound like I was blowing up at you."

He covered her hand and pressured it slightly. "Alexa has dragons in her soul, you know that."

"I know," Zanna said, glancing through the window. Liz and Alexa were up by the rockery, hunkering beside the fairy door. "It's just . . ."

"What is the dragon doing?" asked Arthur, letting his fingers flutter over the drawing.

Zanna studied it again. "Nothing. It's just . . . looking. There's something in its eye, like a distant reflection."

"*Is* it a fire star?"

She gave an incredulous laugh. "Arthur? Come on."

His expression didn't waver. "Every light is visible somewhere, remember?"

"She can't know about such things. Please don't do this."

"Alexa has a gift," he said with authority. "A gift all children possess: the pure, uncluttered ability to create reality in their dreams. What we don't know yet is how far Alexa can take that ability. When her father used that same talent he was able to distort time and bring probable realities into being."

"Arthur, stop it. You're scaring me now. She's just a creative little girl, OK?"

"David's little girl," he reminded her, "and yours. A seer and a sibyl. Interesting combination, don't you think?"

On the worktop, Gretel tapped her paws in thought.

Just then the door opened and Alexa ran in to collide with her mother.

"Oh, *look* at your dirty feet," Zanna scolded her. "What were you doing in the garden in your slippers?"

"There was a bongle," said Alexa, gripping Zanna's skirt and swaying on it. "The fairies nearly came. But it was too cold for them to play outside today."

"Mmm, wise fairies," Zanna said, hugging her. "Well, when it's too cold for them, it's too cold for you. Don't go running out there too often, OK?"

"OK," Alexa said in a chirpy voice. "Bonnington's going to watch for them as well."

"Bonnington?" For some reason, Zanna felt uneasy about that.

Liz hurried back in, with arms crossed, shivering. "This weather is bizarre," she said, banging the door fully to with her bottom. "The sky's clear, but there's definitely snow in the air. I can feel it in my bones."

"Where's Bonny?" asked Zanna, peering past her.

"On another planet, where else? There's something resembling a snow leopard on the rockery. I'd guess that's him."

"What's he doing?"

"I don't know. Waiting for the fairy door to open, so he can bang his head on the rock behind it and thereby return to normality, I hope. Why?"

"Nothing," Zanna said, smiling, dismissing it. She pointed to Alexa's drawing. "Who's a clever girl, then, drawing this? Shall we put it on the wall with the others?" (Alexa's drawings were a feature of the kitchen – and useful for hiding the odd missing tile.)

"Yes," said Alexa, beating her fists.

"It's very good, poppet," Liz said kindly, propping it up against a vase on the windowsill. "Better still from a distance. He's very fierce, isn't he?"

114

Alexa nodded.

"What's he looking at?" asked Zanna.

Arthur tilted his head to listen, but though Alexa opened her mouth right away all that came from it was a slight, "Don't know."

"Does he have a name?" asked Liz.

Alexa bounced on her toes. "It's Daddy's dragon."

"G'lant?"

"Yes."

And there it was. Arthur nodded sagely to himself, Liz glanced at the drawing again and took a moment to reflect upon her long-lost lodger, and Zanna applied her domestic hat. "Yes, well, look at the time. Come on, Alexa Martindale, I need to brush your hair." And she took Alexa's hands and whirled her out of the kitchen (with Gretel following on close behind).

Liz opened a cupboard and put a few boxes of cereals away. Behind her, she could hear the slow *tap tap* of Arthur's foot and knew that he was working up something to say. She turned back to him and smoothed his hair off his forehead. Since returning from the abbey he had let it grow out. Its grey streaks, peppered like a squirrel's fur, charmed her.

"This drawing," he said, making circles on the table with his fingertip. "What do you see in it?"

Liz lifted the pot and poured him his morning mug of tea. "I see a child's idea of a dragon, nothing more. Why, what am I expected to see?"

"A light in the shadows of the universe, perhaps?"

She laughed and dropped a sugar cube into the mug. "Haven't you got students to confuse instead of me?"

"Not until my seminar this afternoon."

She smiled. "Tea's hot, be careful. Gwillan's doing toast. I'm off to make the peace with Princess Lucy, then I'm popping round to Henry's for half an hour. See you later." She kissed the top of his head and was gone.

A few moments later the cat flap opened and Bonnington came flowing in. Arthur immediately lowered his hand. Bonnington padded forward, butted up and nuzzled it. To any casual observer, this would have seemed a typical act of greeting. But for a cat and a man both damaged in their different ways by the Fain, both carrying a residual trace of the aliens, the contact between them was always significant. When Arthur laid his hands on Bonnington's head, the resultant effect was more than just the physical sensation of stroking, it was the commingling sensation of *knowing*. In the quiet, secretive world they shared, the doors of perception were never closed. Arthur saw what Bonnington saw. And Bonnington reported seeing this: when the winter

116

wind had blown and the chimes had responded, the door in the rockery had opened for a second. And it *might* have been the pressure of the wind that had moved it. But that would not explain the faint crack of light behind it. Or that unmistakeable hazy ripple, characteristic of a shift in the fabric of the universe.

The legend of Sedna was almost as old as the ice itself. Like ice, it had many variations, fashioned by slips of the tongue on the wind. But the version which came to the Teller of Ways as he watched the sea goddess thrash her tail and squirm from her ocean home was this:

She had been a beautiful Inuit woman, courted by many worthy suitors, hunters of strength, agility and passion, all of whom would have crossed the ice for her, drunk the ocean, sewn the clouds together with spears. But Sedna was vain and refused them all. She preferred to sit by her father's igloo, admiring her reflection in the waters of the ocean, all the while combing her shining dark hair.

One day, her father grew tired of this. He said to her, "My daughter, we are starving. All the animals have deserted us. We do not even have a dog to slay. I am old and too weary to hunt. You must marry the next hunter who comes to our camp or we will be nothing but sacks of bones."

But Sedna ignored him, selfishly, saying, "I am Sedna. I am beautiful. What more do I need?"

Her father despaired, and thought to take a knife

to her and use her as bait to trap a passing bear. But the next day, while he sat aboard his sled, sharpening his blade and his will to live, another hunter entered the camp. He was tall and elegantly dressed in furs, but his face was hidden by the trimmings around his hood.

The man said, "I am in need of a wife." He struck the shaft of his spear into the ice, making cracks that ran like claws.

Sedna's father was afraid, but he boldly said, "I have a daughter, a beautiful daughter. She can cook and sew and chew skins to make shirts. What will you give in return for her, hunter?"

"I give fish," said the man, from the darkness of his hood.

"Ai-yah." Sedna's father waved a hand, for he thought it a poor trade: fish – for a daughter! But fish was better than a hole in his stomach. And so he said this, "Tomorrow, bring your kayak, filled with char. Row it to the headland, and I will exchange the char for my daughter."

The hunter made a crackling sound in his throat, but his face did not appear from his hood. He withdrew his spear from the glistening ice, pulling out with it a swirling storm. From the eye of the storm he cried,

"So be it." And he was gone, as if the wind had claimed him like a feather.

That night, Sedna's father made up a potion, a sleeping draught squeezed from the bloodshot eye of a walrus, that laziest of Arctic creatures. This he stirred into a warming broth, made from the boiled skin of his mukluks, his boots. "Come, daughter," he said, singing sweetly in her ear. "Come, eat with your aged father." And he gave Sedna a bowl of his broth to drink. Within moments, she had fallen asleep at his feet. Her father then wrapped her loosely in furs and in the morning carried her out to his sled. Still she slept on as he tied her to it, unaware of the trade that awaited her. But there was little remorse in her father's heart. For Sedna was idle and char were char. With a great heave, he pulled her away from their camp. She had still not woken by the time they reached the headland.

The hunter stood by his kayak, waiting. Its skins were bulging, brimful with fish. Their dead eyes watched a soulless father unload his daughter and roll her out at the hunter's feet. The hunter made a chirring sound in his throat. He told the old man to empty the kayak. The Inuk, driven by greed and stupidity, gathered too many fish in his arms, and slipped and skidded and fell upon his rump. As his head struck the ice his gluttonous gaze softened. His dizzied brain recoiled in horror as he watched the hunter pick up his only child, grow a pair of wings and fly away with her to a distant cliff. "Come back!" he cried and reached out a hand. A fish slithered out of it and lodged in his mouth. It was rotten from the tail bone through to the eye.

When Sedna awoke she found herself lying in a nest of hair and night-black feathers. She was on a high ledge, surrounded by ravens. Far below her, the sea was rushing at the rocks, dashing itself to foam and spray. "Oh, my father! Help me! Help!" she cried. Then appeared by her side the hunter who had claimed her.

"I am your husband now," he said.

And he threw off his furs, to show himself to be a raven. The king of ravens. The darkest of birds.

Sedna screamed and screamed, until her voice broke to the cark of a bird. Her fear was so great that the north wind wrestled with her terror for weeks, finally carrying it howling to her father. It beat about his ears, his soul, his heart. *How could you do this?* it whistled at him. *How could you marry your daughter to a bird? Do you want to be known as the grandfather of* ravens?

The old man was wracked with sadness and guilt. He chattered to his heart and his heart chattered back. He must go out and rescue his daughter, it said.

So, the very next morning, he loaded up his patched old kayak and paddled through the frigid Arctic waters, until he reached the cliff that was Sedna's new home. Sedna, who now had eyes as sharp as any bird, had seen him coming and was waiting at the shore. "Oh, my father," she said and hugged him tightly, smelling his furs which still reeked of fish.

"Quickly," he said, "while the mist is about us." And they climbed into his kayak and paddled away.

They had travelled for many hours and still had the calm of the ocean all about them when Sedna saw a black speck high in the sky. Fear welled up inside her, for she knew this was her husband coming to find her!

"Paddle faster!" she urged her father.

But her father's arms were slow with age and exhaustion. The raven was upon their boat as swiftly as a ray of sunlight. It swooped down and set the kayak bobbing. "Give me back my wife!" it screamed.

Sedna's father struck at the thing with his paddle. He missed and almost fell into the water. "Trickster be gone!" he shouted in vain.

The bird *caarked* in anger and swooped again. This time it came down low to the water, beating one wing against the surface. A ferocious storm began to blow and the waters became a raging torrent, tossing the kayak to and fro. Sedna screamed, but not as loudly as her father. Once more, cowardice had rooted in his heart. With a mighty shove, he pushed his daughter into the ocean. "Be gone! Leave me be! Here is your precious wife!" he cried. "Take her back and trouble me no more!"

Sedna cried out in disbelief. "Father, do not desert me!" she begged. She swam to the kayak and reached up, grasping the side of the boat. But the icy waters had made her arms numb and she could not haul herself back to safety.

Still the raven plunged and swooped. The storm grew worse. In his madness, Sedna's father saw a shoal of rotten char coming to the surface to feed, if he fell. Addled by terror, he grabbed his kayak paddle once more and pounded Sedna's fingers with it. She wailed in agony but he would not stop. "Take her! Take her!" he shouted crazily, believing that the only way to save his life was to sacrifice his daughter's life instead. Over and over again he struck, until one by one, her frozen fingers cracked. They dropped into the ocean where they turned into seals and small whales as they sank. With her hands broken, Sedna could not hold on to the boat. Her mutilated body slipped under the water and slowly faded out of sight . . .

. . . yet, she did not perish. Poisoned by the magic of

a raven's bile and further tormented by unresolved grief, she made her house at the bottom of the sea, where she became the goddess of the ocean, raging at men through violent storms . . .

All of this Avrel, the ice bear, knew as Sedna came up to speak with Ingavar. And his brave heart beat a little quicker for it. Sedna had domain over the sea mammals of the North. Every living creature which preyed upon seals relied upon her grace to give some up for hunting. If she refused, bears would starve and be no more. Avrel had no doubt that Ingavar would command the goddess's respect, but when he saw his Nanukapik walk into a mist and walk out of it again in the shape of a man he became agitated and concerned. How could this be? How could the Lord of the Ice be so changed? Avrel shook his head and looked again. The man was dressed in furs, like the Inuit. But he carried no spear or weapon of any kind.

The sea goddess dribbled water from her mouth. In a voice that caught in her throat she croaked, "Who is this who calls me from my house of bones?"

"I am the hunter Oomara," said the figure.

Oomara. The enemy of countless bears. Avrel snorted in confusion. Was this treachery or genius? He trod his paws. Have faith, he told himself. Watch and wait.

"Oo-ma-ra?" said Sedna. "Walking with a *bear*?"

"A time of change is upon us," he said.

She spat at him, covering his boots with algae. "I have no fingers and my hair is like *weed*."

"I have come with a comb for your hair, oh goddess."

Sedna slithered back. Her hideous body squelched at the join between humanity and fish.

The figure of Oomara stepped boldly forward. In his hand was a finely serrated shell. He plunged it into Sedna's hair. She quivered in relief as its spines dislodged sea maggots, sand beetles and kelp.

Avrel, looking on, saw purpose in this now. Had a bear tried to rake its claws through Sedna's hair she would have thought herself attacked by it. He swallowed hard and continued to watch, remembering all he would have need to Tell.

"Sedna is soothed," Oomara said, working the comb with skill through her tangles.

She gurgled with pleasure, swaying gently. Her crusted eyelids crunched as she closed them. Yellow bile oozed from the side of her mouth.

"Her fury is diminished," Oomara sang.

"She is beautiful," Sedna whispered to a long-lost reflection of her earthly mind.

"Very beautiful," he said. "Will she help those who

please her? Will she help Oomara, in his greatest hunt?"

"He needs seal?" she said.

"More than seal," he replied. He pulled tighter, raking out dead, black fish skins.

Sedna shuddered with joy. "Tell me, hunter, what is it you seek?"

"Something my arms cannot reach," he said. "It lies on the ocean bed, in a place once called the Tooth of Ragnar."

"A sacred place," Sedna said guardedly. She pulled away slightly. Her tail slapped the ice.

Oomara bowed. "Is Oomara not worthy? Does he not comb well?"

Sedna touched the stump of her hand to her hair. "I cannot feel it! Or see it!" she spat ungratefully.

"Your beauty is here, in my eyes," he said.

Sedna looked and saw the woman she had been long ago. A fine tear rolled down her plain brown cheek. "But I cannot stroke my hair," she withered.

"Then swim to the sea bed and bring me what I need, and I will give you fingers, goddess."

"And what do you need, oh hunter?" she hissed.

"The eye of the dragon, Gawain," he said.

Being Gudrun

On the face of it, it should have been a simple mission. Groyne's orders from Gretel were specific and clear: impersonate a Gudrun, spy on the Tam, report back via the listening dragon, stay in place until ordered home. It did seem (and Groyne could have been forgiven for thinking this) that the two most dangerous aspects were done: the risk of discovery in Zanna's bag and the invisible flight across the bookshop to the satchel. Neither step had been perfectly executed, but all the same here he was, on his way. For the dragons of Wayward Crescent, however, nothing was ever truly simple. But it wasn't until Tam unlocked his door and threw his satchel onto his white leather sofa, that Groyne met his first real problem: a cat.

It was no Bonnington (it had the vocal mews of a kitten), which in fighting terms made it relatively harmless. No match for the fire of a dragon, to be sure. Yet from the moment Tam put his satchel down it seemed to know something *other* was in the room. Even in the shape of the narwhal's tusk, Groyne seemed to be a sitting enticement for it. It came scratching at the buckles and pawing at the straps. When it tried to push its furry head under the flap, Groyne weighed up the risks of singeing its nose and flying away while the human was still confused. Luckily, Tam came back and scooped the cat up saying, "Hey, little monster, leave that be. You won't find any *Chunky Chunks* in there. Come on. Kitchen. Let's get you fed."

As soon as they were gone, Groyne was out and flying to the curtain pelmet.

Then came the other surprise: another human.

She was slim with fair hair and she breezed in calling, "Tmm, yow hum?" before disappearing into the kitchen as well.

Groyne lifted his paw and took a sniff of the flower band Gretel had tied around his wrist. It was supposed to help him to translate human-speak, particularly those with accents, but from a distance the words were still a little vague. In the kitchen now, he thought he could detect the awkward sound of that strange human activity called kissing. He ignored it and looked around. The room, though large, was sparsely furnished. There seemed to be a lot of white and black. But only two things really caught his eye: the spread of books and papers on the desk by the windows which overlooked the waterfront, and the green of Gudrun on the floor-standing speaker beside it.

Using his visual ability to zoom, he studied Gudrun hard. She was not an animated dragon, blessed with the icefire, so in a sense that made her more difficult to mimic. All her curves and points and scales were unnatural, but to anything other than a Pennykettle eye a fair approximation of her shape would surely do. Groyne focused his mind, pictured her – and stretched. With a remarkable all-over kind of *dissolve* he got her more or less right first time. She was a pretty dragon and there was something disconcerting about having to hold his tail in that she-dragon way, but for the sake of the mission he supposed it was necessary. Then there was her colour. She was green, like most of the Pennykettle dragons, and he was practically white. Thankfully, there was enough common ancestry in his lineage to flush out his scales with her deep, dark shades. It felt odd once he'd done it, but he was proud of his efforts. He was a better Gudrun than a Gudrun, he thought. All that mattered now was to be able to complete the transformation at speed.

He was still working on that when the door that led to the kitchen swung open and the girl came in again, cuddling the kitten. "Who's a lovely Jazzie?" she tooted, almost trying to dance with it. The cat struggled from her arms and went straight for the satchel. "Tch, what's with *her* tonight?" To Groyne's ears the girl sounded rather petulant.

Tam, following in behind her, said, "I had some fresh salmon sandwiches for lunch. I think she must be picking up the scent of them." He hoiked up the satchel and draped it on a coat hook.

Jazz gave a faintly disgruntled mew and pottered off round the back of an armchair.

The girl by now had changed direction and was walking her fingers over the desk. "So what's this you're working on? Eskimo mythology? Bit hokey for *The National Endeavour*, isn't it?"

Tam kicked off his shoes and relaxed onto the sofa. The cushions gave way with a breathy *whumph*. "I'm doing a piece on a local author."

"David Rain," she read aloud, picking up his notes.

"He's pretty popular. You must have heard of him?"

The girl fingered her lip. "Is this the guy who disappeared in the Arctic?"

"That's him. Cult figure. Man of mystery. The 'Elvis' of Scrubbley is our Mr Rain."

"You don't think he's dead?"

"Not sure," Tam said. He pointed a remote at a plasma TV, mounted on the wall above an old marble fireplace. It came to life showing some faraway news footage of a vast ice sheet in western Siberia. In the background, behind a parka-clad reporter, was what looked like the skull and tusk of a mammoth. He muted the sound, but continued watching. "Missing presumed dead is the official line, but there's something not quite right about it. I've been trying to gather background info on him, but he's not exactly easy to track. He was a student at Scrubbley College before it gained university status. There are records of him there, but beyond that, nothing. Everything about the guy leads to dead ends. Yet here he is with a best-selling book."

"Two words: publishing hype," she said, as though the mere act of saying it proved her correct.

"Maybe," he said, but with a hum which suggested he didn't agree. He flipped open his spectacles and put them on, staring at the TV more intently now.

The girl stretched a long leg out of a short black pleated skirt. "So how did you get on the case?"

"The book," he said, nodding at an open copy of *White Fire*.

She picked it up and studied the cover. "Polar bears?" She gave a disinterested smile.

"There's a buzz about it, a kind of underground vibe."

She let it go limp in her hand. "It's a kids' book, Tam."

"Not entirely."

"Well, the blurb says—"

"I know what it says, Jodie. Adventure story. Gripping yarn. Arctic fable. But there's something else riding between the lines. I've read it a couple of times and it does have a strange kind of after-effect. The whole book is a sort of spiritual metaphor. It seems to be a subtle but powerful plea calling for people to come together to do something to save the polar ice cap."

"Hurrah," she said and snapped the book shut.

"Fair enough, I was cynical, too, before I read it. But whatever you believe, it doesn't take away from the fact that there is a real phenomenon happening here. There are websites springing up about this guy. His star is rising in extraordinary proportions. And this is just the kind of stuff that's fuelling it." He pressed a button on the remote, in time to hear a TV reporter saying, "*This huge expanse of permafrost was formed in western Siberia over eleven thousand years ago at the end of the last great ice age. Beneath it is a frozen peat bog containing thousands of tonnes of methane, a greenhouse gas twenty times more damaging to the atmosphere than carbon dioxide. The ice is melting, slowly turning this sub-Arctic wilderness into a boggy terrain of mud flats and lakes, which are throwing up all kinds of prehistoric artefacts. Scientists have described what's happening here as a 'tipping point' — an indicator of an environmental see-saw, in which a small regional rise in the Earth's temperature could be the catalyst for a dramatic and widespread global effect . . ."*

Tam muted it and set a DVD recording.

"I don't get this greenhouse *gig,*" said the girl. "I read an article once that said the temperature of the Earth has always fluctuated. It goes through natural cycles. This is just one of them. The end. Hel-*lo?*"

"It's the rate of acceleration that matters," said Tam. "Since the early eighties, global warming has increased by—" Her sudden sideways movement made him pause.

"What is *that?*" she said.

From his high point on the pelmet, Groyne watched her put the book down and pick up Gudrun. At the same time, he felt the curtain underneath him ripple. From the corner of his eye, he saw Jazz at the bottom, climbing it.

Tam flapped a hand at Gudrun and said, "Oh, that's just something I bought for Millie."

"Millie? Millie hates dragons," said the girl. She turned the label. "The Healing Touch?"

"It's a gift shop in Scrubbley."

Her eyebrows invited further explanation.

"David Rain's partner runs the place. I'm

interviewing her there next Wednesday afternoon."

"And how many more of these do you have to buy before she admits it's all a big scam?"

"One clay dragon is enough," he said.

She smiled inconclusively and put Gudrun back. "What's she like?"

"Secretive."

"You know what I mean."

"It's a job, Jodie. She's a source, that's all."

"So how come you bought a dragon?"

"I needed to convince her I was an ordinary punter."

"She doesn't know you're a journalist?"

Tam sighed, realising where this was going.

"So, for 'interview' I should read 'chat her up'?"

"Jodie, you know how I have to work sometimes. I— heck, what was that?"

A cat's shriek turned both of them towards the far window.

"Jazz?!" Jodie gasped.

The kitten was vertical, clinging for dear life to the top of the curtain.

Tam moved a footstool over and stood on it to reach her. "She's terrified," he said, holding her steady while he unpicked her claws. "Her fur's on end and her eyes are like saucers." He handed her down and stared at the pelmet. "That's weird, the paint looks scorched." He stretched his fingers up and felt around.

Groyne, invisible by now, leaned back. It was one thing to frazzle a silly cat's whiskers, quite another to burn a human's fingers. He willed Tam away; it was Jodie who responded.

"Jazz and I are going to bed," she said, somehow weighting the sentence to suggest that Tam should hurry along too.

He frowned, took another long look at the pelmet and caved in. Moments later, the TV and lights were off and the room was empty, lit only by diffuse reflected hues from riverside apartments across the water.

Groyne hurred in relief and came back to visibility. Too long in the unseen state was a strain. At least now he had the freedom to move about – and spy.

The first thing he did was to fly down to Gudrun and attempt to pick her up. But this was no easy task. She was heavy and slightly awkward to hold. He thought again about the wisdom of substituting himself. It was an effort, but the logic was reasonably sound. He could stand, unnoticed, in his solid form for days. To flit about, hiding, might be dangerous – especially with that pesky kitten about.

He lifted Gudrun and staggered to the edge of the

speaker. It wasn't far to the shining wooden floor below, but the boards looked hard and he couldn't risk breaking her. There was a cat bed near the sofa which seemed to offer him a safer (and softer) option. Tensing his wings, he flew all out for it, but tired halfway and only just reached the nearest edge. He fell forward on landing, tipping Gudrun out of his arms, making her clink against a cat's toy bell. The sound split the darkness. It wasn't loud, but it was distinct. Any dragon would have heard it. Perhaps a cat would, too. Every scale on Groyne's spine suddenly stood proud. He glanced at the crack of light beneath the bedroom door and clearly heard the sound of kitten claws, scratching.

With some haste, he jumped right out of the basket and pushed it across the floor, turning it to face a unit made of cane. It had space underneath to hide Gudrun completely. Carefully, he rolled her out and nudged her under, wincing as her sharp points scraped the boards. Then he tugged the cat bed back into place and flew onto the speaker. Hrrr! Safe as clay could be.

But as it happened, all his urgency proved needless. As he posed there, tuning in to every little sound, he heard Jodie say, "Jazz, will you please stop that?" The scratching ceased and there was quiet again. A few minutes passed. A boat strung with lanterns drifted up the river. The hands of a clock ticked round. Groyne flicked his tail and rolled his eyes sideways. Silence.

Time to spy again.

He softened quickly and flew to Tam's desk, to study the mess of papers there. Although close-together writing, such as that found in books, was hard for most dragons to understand, pictures were not. He saw examples of the mark of Oomara in textbooks, and a photograph of David Rain he'd never seen before. His eye ridges came together in a frown and he thought about everything he'd heard that night. Tam seemed a good enough human to him, but he was clearly snooping and trying to fool Zanna. Gretel wasn't going to like that at all. It was time to report to the listening dragon.

He brought his paws together and defocused his gaze. The Pennykettle dragons were not telepaths as such, but they could communicate messages back and forth through a listener. The procedure, over such a long distance, required intense concentration. Groyne stared into the rippling waters of the Thames and opened his mind to picture the kitchen at Wayward Crescent. But just as the images began to flow in, something buzzed loudly right by his feet and a voice said, "*A message from the dark side there is . . .*" Panicked, he jumped up and sent a small object skittering off the desk. It skittered again as it hit the floor. Groyne realised to his horror it was a mobile phone; he'd watched Lucy use one many times, but had no real idea how they were operated (where was Golly when he needed him?!). He flew to it and hrrred on it, hoping his warm breath would stop its buzzing. It didn't. He tried punching it. That only made the thing flip open, introducing a square of blue light into the room.

The bedroom door creaked. In a flash Groyne was back on the speaker, being Gudrun.

Jodie walked in, wearing a long white T-shirt. She picked up the phone and pressed a few buttons. From the corner of his eye, Groyne watched her face. She didn't look happy. She turned away, clutching the phone to her chest. Groyne sniffed at his flower band, hoping to hear better the words she was mumbling. What he did pick up made his ear peaks twitch. *Hrrrpenny.*

Hrrrpenny?

She clicked the phone shut. "Jazz, come here."

Groyne glanced down. The stupid kitten was sniffing around him again! It was up on its back legs, dabbing with its paw. He had no option but to pull a scary face. Immediately, the cat ran away to hide – straight under the unit made of cane.

A startled kitty squeal brought Jodie over. "Oh, what *now?*" she said, kneeling down.

Groyne froze in terror. He heard the catch in Jodie's voice, and knew she'd found the real Gudrun.

Suddenly, both dragons were in her clutches. She held them up to the window and glared at them thoughtfully. "Two?" she muttered. "And why was one hidden? Just what are you up to, *Tam?*" She nodded, tight-lipped, and said, "Right."

Then she put one dragon back onto the speaker and the other she wrapped in a woollen cardigan. She stuffed that bundle into her bag and zipped it.

That bundle, unfortunately, wasn't Gudrun.

And Gretel had said it would all be so easy . . .

Arctic ice cap, in the presence of
the sea goddess, Sedna

Gawain. The name sent a tremor of excitement through Avrel, though he did not truly understand why. Like the word Oomara had spoken before it, *dragon*, it had no place in his memories to Tell. And yet he could sense real power in these words. Deep significance. A humbling awareness of a once-great being. The ice rang with it, rolled and swayed with it. A pulse of life, beyond the edge of creation, back before the time of the first white bears. Avrel reached, but his mind would not take him there. And if he pressed, all that returned was an image of fire.

Sedna, goddess of the animals of the ocean, likewise recoiled when she heard this request. *Bring me the eye of the dragon, Gawain.* There was terror and confusion in her gelatinous white eyes. Avrel knew she was asking herself: *What does a man-bear want with such a prize?* Even so, her fear was not as great as her obvious temptation. Fingers, for a piece of crumbling rock? She licked her lips with a worm-riddled tongue and said, "It will take time."

The figure of Oomara bowed his head, then sat upon

the ice with his mukluks crossed. "The ocean is deep. Swim carefully, goddess."

Sedna shook out her newly-combed hair. With a chattering hiss, she slithered back into the water again. The ice groaned with a mighty grinding action and closed itself up like a wound. Avrel was almost thrown off his feet. When he was free to stand solidly again he saw, to his relief, that the figure of Oomara was now the figure of Ingavar once more. The great bear looked exhausted. He was sitting flat, with his front paws crossed. His head was lowered and his eyes were closed.

Avrel approached him quietly, saying, "Lord, is it you?"

"Everything you see is me," said Ingavar. He instructed Avrel to lie down and rest.

This they did, for two more days.

On both days, however, Avrel grew impatient and wandered the ice a little, hoping for sign or scent of Kailar. He felt easier when the fighting bear was with them. There was danger here, he could feel it every time the wind pressed his fur. But that was not the entire reason he chose to walk alone. He was using these moments away from Ingavar to look into his mind and ask himself, 'What was this creature lying there as though dead? Was it a spirit? Was it real? Was it ever a bear at all – or merely the image of one?' In the archive of his memories there were legends of man-bears, which men called shamans, but they seemed to have no lasting substance. Yet, if he lay down against this Nanukapik, he could feel its body breathing in time to his own. It was alive, he was sure of it, and therefore not a spirit. But how could this – he held up a paw and watched the claws move – reshape itself into another form?

On the second day, he stood beside Ingavar, watching him. In all this time, the Nanukapik had not once changed his position. A fine crust of snow had formed on his back and small stalactites of dribble were hanging from his jaw. Avrel shuffled his feet, wondering just how long they would be resting here, when suddenly the great bear stirred. A portion of air went into his snout to emerge seconds later as a powerful snort.

"Lord, what do you see?"

Ingavar had opened his stunning blue eyes and was staring far ahead at an unknown horizon. He raked his claws and rose quickly to his feet. "The dragon Gawain is among us," he said.

The ice rocked and split with a plangent hew, and just as before when Sedna had appeared, a spume of water fired into the air. When all had settled, the sea goddess was on the surface again and Ingavar had reassumed the shape of Oomara.

"I have what you need, oh hunter," she said. Off her back she swung a bag made of strung-together kelp and deep sea weeds. "Give me fingers and I will give you the eye."

"How do we know it is real?" said Avrel. "And not just an ocean rock?"

Before Sedna could answer, a great shadow fell across the ice. Avrel saw it first as a thousand black speckles, flowing in like a rippling wave from the south. As the speckles ran by him they flittered on the surface and reduced in number, but seemed to increase in size and definition. Suddenly, he knew he was watching wing beats. He looked up and saw a great cluster of ravens.

"Lord?" he growled, unsure of what to do. It felt odd, seeking instruction from a man. But instinctively he backed up closer to Oomara, perhaps hoping that by the time he turned his head again, he would see his Nanukapik ready there to fight. These birds had points of evil in their eyes. Their grating cries were filled with taunts. They were circling slowly, preparing to attack. None knew it more than Sedna herself.

"My husband!" she wailed. "My husband has sent his flock to take me!"

A bird swooped down. But its object was the bag, not

Sedna's head. It picked and snaffled and tore out a weed. Avrel instinctively leapt at it, throwing out a deep growl, flashing both paws. The bird escaped by a feather and a squawk.

Now, for the first time, Avrel could view the contents of the bag. Through the criss-crossing weed he saw a lump of grey stone, humped in the shape of a lidded eye. All around it was a pattern of falcate scales. Dragon. He knew it instinctively. The goddess had kept her word.

"Protect me!" she cried, slithering and flapping in search of water. Somehow, the ice behind her had closed. For Sedna, there was no retreat into her ocean.

Oomara reached his hands up as if to touch the stars, calling out to the spirits of hunters past. Immediately, they came, engaging the ravens in battle with their spears. Many birds were afraid and wisely flew away. Those that did not were skewered or hacked and instantly turned into spirits themselves. A rain of feathers poured out of the clouds. Sedna shivered with grotesque delight. She danced as well as any fish-woman could and spat scorn upon the ravens for the ease of this victory.

But her mood was short-lived. For every feather that fell, a new bird began to grow out of it.

Avrel swung a paw as the first of the new flock dipped

around his head. Suddenly, ten were clinging to his back, nicking at his ears and tearing his fur. His paws flashed again, in devastating arcs, and his claws were soon clogged with the warm gel of death. But for every bird he crushed, six more came to plague him. He closed his eyes as they pecked and dug, urgently thinking of a way to defeat them. The water. It was his only escape. Certain that none of these predators could swim, he pounded the ice, hoping to break the crust. But for all his strength, the ice would not yield. He collapsed instead and quickly rolled over, terminating two more birds this way. But he was overwhelmed now and in need of a miracle. He was literally covered in ravens.

Then he felt the force of the white fire Ingavar had used upon Kailar. He heard screeches as the birds turned to windblown ash, yet felt no pain or fear himself. When he moved his head he saw to his relief the Nanukapik rearing, as strong and magnificent as the first spring glaciers. There was a halo of glaucous fire around him. Every bird retreated to a safer distance. But the battle was far from done. In what seemed to be an instant, the flock came together, gelling into one formidable creature. It landed on the ice twenty paces ahead of Ingavar. It had a body half the size again of a man, but the wings and eyes and beak of a raven.

Sedna slithered back, crying out in fear. "It is him! It is him!"

"Welcome back, wife," the birdman said. He gyred his wings and stared, with brooding eyes, at Ingavar. "Stand aside, shaman. I am married to the ocean. All its treasures are mine to own." His gaze fell greedily upon the weed bag.

Avrel, bleeding from a gouge above one eye, fearlessly went to stand by it.

"Wife," said the birdman, "I have fingers for you." From a pocket of the furs that covered his body, he brought forth eight old leathery remains.

Sedna chattered in excitement and fear, straining her upper half to see the prize.

"Take them," said the birdman, throwing them forward. They landed on the ice, squirming like maggots. "Touch them and they will be joined to your hands, as surely as you are joined to me." His gaze swivelled back to Ingavar again. "These fingers possess the strength of all the creatures Sedna's fingers became. Would you fight walrus and narwhal, shaman?"

Ingavar took a measured pace sideways, inviting the birdman to manoeuvre in turn. Avrel had seen this strategy before. When two bears wrestled, they circled like this. But why would Ingavar, with his gift of fire, want to brawl with this disgusting beast?

"Goddess, here are fingers—" the Nanukapik said. The fish-woman glided eagerly towards them. "—but if you touch them, I predict you will die."

"A-yah?" she chattered, pulling back. Beneath her stumpy hands, the fingers jumped, eager for the sinews of any kind of life. Avrel's temptation was to crush them, but he waited.

"They are not what they seem to be," Ingavar said.

"They are fingers!" she snapped.

"They are your father's," he said. "Murdered by this creature. The only strength you will inherit from them is the permanent ability to walk the sky."

"Treachery?" she said, even now as naive as the girl she had been long ago.

The birdman cackled, deep in his throat. "You irritate me, shaman."

Ingavar, still manoeuvring, said, "I am the fire that melts no ice."

The birdman sneered and extended his hands. From his fingers he raised ten fearsome claws. He flicked his wings, producing a storm of black snow all around him. "I will douse you and tear out your heart, still beating. Walk away, while you can. You cannot sustain your fire and your companion is not a fighting bear."

Avrel rolled back his lip and growled.

"He would die for me," said Ingavar, tensing himself.

"Then die together," the birdman said. And he raised his wings to fly to the attack.

But suddenly there was movement at the birdman's side, and now Avrel understood all of Ingavar's posturing. Roaring through the mist came Kailar. With perfect timing, he struck, unsighted, at the region under the birdman's wing, savaging the creature's vulnerable torso, until his paws were lost in a mulch of flesh. Feathers and innards spewed across the ice. The creature screamed and was carried down by Kailar's weight. In that instant it knew that the battle was lost, but as Kailar widened his ferocious jaws, ready to clench his prey by the throat, his head shook free and his eye was unprotected. The birdman's beak went back. But as it steadied to deliver its sickening blow, its head was fatally snapped to one side by a devastating strike from Avrel's left paw.

The Teller pounded again and again, making a stew of whatever he touched, until Kailar himself barged the younger bear aside saying, "It's done, Teller. Rest your paws. A thing can't be more dead than dead. It's done."

Panting heavily from fear and exhaustion, Avrel

flopped down several paces from the body, checking back at it now and then as if to be sure it would never rise again.

Kailar, black feathers sticking to his paws, left him and ranged up to Ingavar's flank. "You've been busy in my absence. What's this?" he asked, snorting with heavy disdain towards Sedna.

"The wife of the creature you have slain," said Ingavar. "Bow to the goddess, Sedna, Kailar."

"I bow only to you," he growled.

"Bow," said Ingavar, without any threat.

Kailar squinted at the quivering mess of algae and arrogantly tipped his snout at it.

"Is your fighting bear to kill me, too?" she wailed.

"You have delivered what I asked of you," Ingavar said. He gestured at the bag. Kailar sniffed at it suspiciously. "When the time comes, every creature in the North, on the land, on the ice or in the water, will sing your name in praise."

"I need fingers, not praise," the goddess snapped.

"You will have fingers," Ingavar told her. He said to Kailar, "Was your search successful?"

Kailar swung his head and looked over his shoulder. "Come forward," he rumbled at what appeared to be nothing but a scattering of ice blocks. But from behind it there emerged a comical sight: another raven, half-encased in a chunk of ice.

"I'm tired," it said, with a grating twang that made Avrel wince. He stood up, anxious to move away from the stench of pooling blood beside him. "Isn't it time one of you hairballs set me free?"

"Watch your tongue," Kailar growled at the bird, swiping loose ice into its face. He chewed a feather from his claws and spat it out. "You saw what became of the last of your kind."

The bird snorted out a speck of bloodied snow. "My kind? My kind? What would a thick-skulled seal-licker like you know of *my* people?"

"Shall I crush it?" Kailar asked tiredly of Ingavar. For days he had suffered this ill-tempered squawking. In his experience, death had many well-preserved patterns, and this bird was just one good stamp from being another.

"Of course not!" The bird spoke for Ingavar now. "If he'd wanted me dead he would have ordered it days ago. He needs me, idiot."

Kailar raised a paw. "Give me the command," he begged his master.

Ingavar blinked once and shook his head. "She speaks the truth."

"She?" said Avrel, recovered now and curious. He padded closer, twitching his snout at the thing.

"Get away, fish breath!" she swore at him.

Avrel reeled back, scowling warily.

"Look closely, Avrel," Ingavar said. "This is a creature that already has a place in your register of memories. What you have here is a woman who has lived for centuries, condemned and trapped in the shape of a bird."

"Woman?" clattered Sedna, drool pouring down her chin.

"And what are *you?*" the bird snorted into Ingavar's face.

His head tilted and his eye engaged with hers. "I am all things to all men . . . Gwilanna."

A piece of snow dripped from her open beak. "Bergstrom?" she said, for the first time sounding unsure of herself.

"Sometimes," said Ingavar, moving his jaw in what might have been a smile. "The shaman you knew as Dr Bergstrom and whom these bears encountered as Thoran is gone."

"You killed him?" she said with an agitated squeak.

"I took his auma."

"You—?" She gave a comical, almost puzzled twist of

her beak. And now the longer she stared at him, the wider her round eyes opened with fear. "Only those touched by the auma of a dragon could perform such magicks," she said with a hiss.

Avrel glanced at the bag with its eye of grey stone, then searched the face of the blue-eyed Nanukapik. "What does she mean?"

Ingavar put his snout to the sky as though he was engaging with an unseen force. Then he sat, column-like, lowering his head into the centre of his chest. Suddenly, the ice all around him came alive. Crystals swirled on every hump and hollow. The wind streaked and polished the contours of his body, gradually reshaping him into a man.

Kailar staggered back, blustering furiously.

"Who *are* you?" said Avrel, his curiosity beating as fiercely as his heart. For the figure before him was not Oomara. He was younger, lighter-skinned, and yet still dressed in Arctic furs. In his eyes shone a light from another world, as though he was carrying a star inside him.

"Stand me up!" spat the raven, who had been knocked over by the transformation. "Right me, you waddle-bellies! Stand me up!"

Avrel tipped her back to her feet.

"Impossible," she squealed, looking at the man that Ingavar had become. "How can *you* be here, among *bears?*"

"In truth, I never really left," he said. "But I have journeyed through the realms of dark matter, along with the spirit of the ice bear, Ingavar, to do what must be done to protect this ice." He turned to the bears and spoke to them together. "Avrel, Kailar, I am your servant as much as you are mine. You should call me Nanukapik." Then he turned to the raven again. "And you, sibyl, you may call me David."

Part Two

Breaking through

It was as if a small fish had risen to the top of a tranquil lake and pushed its nose through the surface of the water. The ripple was faint. Distant. Subtle. As slight as the delicate motes of time that mark the imperceptible movements of planets. Even so, the effect was still felt in certain parts of the house at 42 Wayward Crescent. In the kitchen, for instance, the listening dragon stirred.

Elizabeth Pennykettle put down the saucepan she'd been scouring and said, "What is it?"

The dragon sat up. *A signal*, it hurred. It tilted its head a little, letting its ears expand to their widest and panning them around like radar dishes.

"Dragon?"

The listener blinked uncertainly.

"Close or distant?"

Gone, it said and gave a noticeable shudder. It sat back, looking slightly disturbed. *Not dragon*, it said, *but it felt like it.*

Liz looked through the kitchen window and saw snowflakes beginning to pattern the lawn. She dipped her eyes for a moment in thought. "If you feel it again, try to track it," she said. Then she continued washing up.

Meanwhile, in Zanna's room, Gadzooks and G'reth simultaneously noticed what dragons called 'a guttering feeling', the strange sensation of the fire within flickering, as though a wind from another world had blown through their auma. Neither could deduce a reason for it, and when Gadzooks asked Gretel if her spark had been similarly affected, all she did was give an irritated snort and suggest he change position – or find somewhere less draughty to sit than the windowsill.

Gretel had been busy watching Alexa drawing another picture of the dragon she called G'lant. This time she had sketched him from the reverse angle, looking the opposite way. Again, the structure of the eye was prominent, but her efforts had been concentrated on the rounded speck of blue-green detail which seemed to form the dragon's point of focus. It was a planet. The Earth. Gretel was sure of it. She'd seen pictures of their so-called 'home world' before. But if that was correct, then where was G'lant positioned if he could frame the whole world in his eye? She was about to ask Alexa this very question when Gadzooks reported his fiery flutter. In the time it took Gretel to turn around and answer, Alexa had pushed aside her drawing of G'lant and started on another picture, this time with a pale yellow pencil.

What's this? hurred Gretel, disappointed at the shift.

"A nun-nooky," said Alexa, her face almost flat to the pad.

A *what?* said Gretel.

And Alexa said, "A boley pear."

All this time, Lucy was upstairs lost in music and Zanna was in the front room reading Tam's poetry. Later, she would remember a sudden shudder, as if someone had walked across her unmarked grave. But it was chilly in the lounge after tea that evening and all she did was rub her arms and call to Gwillan, who immediately flew to the curtains and closed them.

Only one human in the house truly and fully noticed the blip. That was Arthur. He was in the Dragon's Den, where he had been meditating for an indefinite period. His mind was the lake. His awareness was the fish. When the two came together, his eyes opened with a start. On the shelves to either side of him he sensed a collective hum amongst the dragons. And Bonnington was near, turning agitated circles. "Be calm," Arthur whispered and reached out a hand. Bonnington trotted forward, nuzzling furiously, keen to commingle and share any knowledge. Arthur suddenly had a vision of the frozen north and for a moment felt its coldness spreading up his spine, just as if the cushion underneath him was an ice floe. "Something has happened," he said below his breath, speaking to himself as much as to Bonnington. He uncoupled his legs from the lotus position and sat loosely, pressing his thumbs together. "Something has happened," he repeated quietly. He scooped up Bonnington and stroked the cat's head. "Come, we must visit Lucy."

It wasn't often that Arthur and Lucy spoke, not truly spoke, in a manner that might be described as conversational. Their daily exchanges were cordial enough, but each had rarely engaged the other beyond the necessary domestic grunts.

It hadn't always been like this. In the beginning, when Lucy had been a wide-eyed adventuress, excited at the prospect of meeting the man who had secretly claimed her mother's heart, the romance of living with the enigmatic, dragon-saving monk had entirely swept her away. But the crushing reality of life with him was harsh. Arthur had arrived a wrecked and troubled man. Blind, confused (often gabbling mathematical formulae), and as vulnerable and weak as a newborn puppy, he had needed almost constant care. It took months of fetching, carrying and feeding before he could be truly self-reliant again. In those months, Lucy often read to him: children's stories mostly. Anything from her bedside shelves. Eventually, a morning came when she found the courage to pick up *Snigger and the Nutbeast*. She was halfway through the opening chapter when Arthur raised a hand and said, in a bone-chilling fashion, "What became of David? Did he escape the Fain?"

She remembered shuddering, losing hold of the book. A chasm of despair opened up inside her as she began to tell him all that she knew, how she'd been abducted by the sibyl, Gwilanna, taken hostage to the Tooth of Ragnar, and what she had seen on that dreadful, final day in the Arctic. And Arthur did something she could neither handle nor predict: he wept openly.

And so did she.

That incident, far from bringing them together, had drawn a dysfunctional line between them. So she was remotely surprised when, on the evening before Zanna's intended consultation with Tam, Arthur knocked on her bedroom door and stepped inside to make himself seen.

Lucy pulled out her ear phones, filling the room with a tinny hiss of music. She thought about closing down the email she was writing. Tam's address was in the header. But Arthur couldn't see it, so what did it matter?

"Are you busy, child?"

He often called her child. A throwback to the early days. She still found it endearing. It was ridiculous to think he could ever be her father, but . . . "No." She switched off her iPod and swung her chair to face him.

His knees found the edge of the bed and he sat. "Would you do something for me?"

She shrugged – then remembered such gestures were pointless, but they all did that with Arthur now and then. "Sure. What?"

"Would you send a message to my friend, Brother Bernard?"

She found herself nodding. Roly-poly Brother Bernard. The monk who had first brought Arthur to the Crescent. She remembered him: a jolly man. A Friar Tuck. Kind. "Why me? I thought Mum normally wrote your letters?"

"A text message," he said. "I'd like it to be instant."

"A text?" She almost laughed. "Do monks have mobiles?"

"Bernard does."

Touché. Pointless arguing with the best brain in the universe. She picked up her phone, all the while glancing back at Arthur. He was weird sometimes, two slippers' worth of secrets. When he cradled Bonnington in his arms like this he reminded her of a James Bond villain. "OK. Shoot."

Arthur stroked Bonnington's head a few times, all the while commingling with the Fain-being inside him. Through hazy, almost monochrome feline vision he noted Lucy's yawn and saw the swing of her foot. She was impatient to return to the computer, of course. He saw the flicker of the screen but none of its content.

"My dear Bernard," he began.

Lucy put her thumb on hold. "Erm, you do know you've only got, like, a certain number of characters in a text? They're normally kind of snappy, Arthur."

"The message will be short. Please enter what I said, and do not truncate the words."

"I'm on predictive. Already done it. Go on."

He allowed himself a smile, then dictated slowly, "My dear Bernard, at last our ruminations may have come to fruition—"

"Ru— min— what?" she asked.

He spelt it for her. And 'fruition'. "Did you feel the eye of the universe open? If so, great wonders are upon us. Vincent."

"Vincent?" she queried. It was the name he had taken as a monk at Farlowe Abbey.

"When in Rome," he said. "Thank you. Is it done?"

"Number?"

"Of course." He spoke it clearly.

As she tapped it in she said, "Eye of the universe; what's that about?"

"It's a spiritual metaphor," he replied evenly, concealing everything, confessing nothing.

"Right," she said. Monk-speak. She didn't pursue it.

Arthur turned Bonnington to face the computer. "What are you doing? Homework?"

He immediately saw her hesitate. She was wondering how he knew the computer was on. Her expression softened as she reassured herself he could still detect areas of glowing light. Plus he could hear the cooling fan humming.

"I'm . . . updating David's website. Will Bernard reply? To your text, I mean?"

Arthur tweaked Bonnington's left ear. A signal for the Fain to adjust the cat's lenses. Bonnington blinked. His gaze zoomed in. Not a website. Email. Why was she lying? "Yes, when he is not at prayer. Tell me, was this a sudden impulse – to update the website, I mean?"

She clammed the phone shut and put it aside. "I do it once a month. It was time, that's all."

Interesting. She was showing no sign of sensing any presence. For one who had been so close to David,

Arthur found that strange. Was it real, then? His vision? That sense of connecting? In that meditative state he called the alpha phase, were desire and delusion interchangeable? The universe moved in mysterious ways. Was it possible he was being misled by his mind? "You must miss him?"

She exhaled deeply.

"My apologies. That was a ridiculous question."

But a test all the same. A gentle dig. She was prickly, edgy, hiding something. The images from Bonnington swam and pulsed, making Arthur feel slightly restless and giddy. Lucy's shoulder was covering the flat screen now, removing the temptation to delve into her secrets – though the temptation was great indeed. "How is the site coming along?"

"Cool. Loads of hits. They're zooming up. David's dead – I mean, he's *really* popular right now. Lots of people want to know about stuff."

Bonnington began to purr steadily.

"What kind of 'stuff'?"

"Just stuff," she answered guardedly, wishing he would go. "Are we, like, done here? I'm s'posed to be helping mum in the kitchen."

Suddenly, with a dizzying flash of movement, Bonnington miaowed and refocused on another part of

165

the room. Gollygosh had landed on Lucy's dressing table. Even with reduced, nictating vision, Arthur could tell that the healer was energised.

"What's with you?" Lucy said to him in dragontongue.

The dragon blinked at Arthur.

"He's embarrassed. He's late for meditation," Arthur said. "It is Gadzooks, I take it?"

"No, it's Golly," she said, twisting a finger inside the neck of her top. "I'm going now, OK?"

Arthur coughed and patted his chest. "With your permission, I'll rest here a moment."

She glanced back at the computer, burning secrets, burning energy. "Yeah, whatever." She flapped a hand and hurried out.

Gollygosh spread his turquoise wings and made as if he was going to go after her.

"Wait," said Arthur.

The healer folded down and gave a polite little *hrrr?*

"Were you coming to me or to Lucy?" Arthur's aptitude for dragontongue was not the best, but David's special dragons could interpret him with ease.

The dragon gulped. *I was flying to the Den, but heard talking,* he said.

Arthur nodded. "You feel something, don't you?"

Gollygosh tilted his head back and searched. His eyes

were bursting with violet wonder, as if he'd seen an angel parting the clouds. His toolbox clanked as he squeezed the handle. *Is it . . . the David?* he asked.

"I don't know," said Arthur, steepling his fingers – but there had to be a strong possibility of it. For years, he and his old friend Bernard Augustus had been hoping for contact, testing the boundaries of sensory attraction through the practice of coordinated visualisation. Together, they had 'dreamed it' as Elizabeth might say. A gateway into a parallel universe. A channel which they hoped David Rain might cross. A conduit of spiritual union. Hope. But this feeling, this ripple, suggested something more. A visitation. A return. A physical presence. Arthur thought about his sudden vision of the Arctic. The barren icecap. The restless wind. The souls in the sky, outnumbering the stars. Lately, he and Bernard had visualised Ingavar, the bear which David idolised in print, the Nanukapik returned to save his species from the ravages of hunting and planetary abuse. Might that have tipped the balance? Was he seeing the North through the eyes of a bear? And how did this relate to the spatial shift that Bonnington had seemingly witnessed in the garden? Oh, for clarity, for greater understanding. Oh, for the power he'd had on the island, when he'd been in possession of a dragon's claw . . .

The computer beeped. Bonnington instinctively turned his head towards it, flushing screen images back through Arthur's visual cortex. Arthur at first tried to blank them out, for in his heart he knew it would have been dishonourable to read anything that Lucy had received in private, but he could not avoid noticing the banner which popped up at the bottom corner of the screen. It was an email flag, and though it was gone too quickly to catch the sender's name, he did see the subject of the message.

re: David's parents

The banner dissolved. At the same moment, Bonnington arched and jumped to the floor, plunging his master into blindness again. "No, wait," Arthur called, but the cat was gone.

"Are you still there?" Arthur asked in dragontongue.

No reply from Gollygosh either.

Arthur stood up, deep in thought, circling his foot to activate the blood flow in an aching left thigh. Was this meaningful, he wondered? Who would ask a question concerning David's parents? And more importantly, what would Lucy reply? Did the 're:' before the subject header indicate a dialogue? If so, why did that make him nervous? For what could she say that would be of any consequence? She would have to answer 'no', and that would be an end to it. He brought his hands together in prayer, remembering a common biblical passage. *Honour thy father and thy mother, that thy days might be long upon the land* . . . But as he shuffled from the room and pulled his way along the landing, he was already rewriting the commandment in his mind. *Honour thy father and thy mother,* he repeated, *that thy days might be long – upon the ice.*

"No," Gwilanna squawked again, pounding her feet. She tottered around foolishly in her cube of ice. She even tried to peck at Avrel's black claws but only succeeded in falling over. "Crush me, furball. Stamp me out. This cannot be him! It can't be *him!*"

"Guard her," said David to the still-confused Teller and moved away towards the sea goddess, Sedna, who was thrashing her tail and reminding everyone that payment had yet to be given for her services.

David crouched down and looked at the fingers of Sedna's father, dropped by the raven king before their fight. The severed ends were glazed with cherry-black blood. The knuckle joints were cracked. The nails were blue. They were as old as a legend, but still twitching with life.

Sedna slithered forward. "Who are you, spirit? Where is Oomara?"

"He is here," said David, in guttural Inuktitut, and his face changed fleetingly to the taut, round shape of the hunter, and back. "You saw what you wanted to see. He promised you fingers and here we have eight."

Sedna stared at them doubtfully. "When you were

Ingavar, you said I would die if I touched these . . .
ghosts."

She gurgled at Avrel, who in turn glanced at Kailar.
The fighting bear was snorting and shaking his head,
not knowing what to make of all this.

"Avrel, come near to me," David said.

The Teller glanced at the raven named Gwilanna.
She was still lost in her petulant dance. He padded
forward and awaited a command.

"Search your memories. How many hands held the
kayak paddle which broke Sedna's fingers?"

Avrel pictured her father wielding it. "One,"
he replied.

David turned his blue eyes onto the fish woman.
"Then four of these fingers are from the hand of evil,
and four will serve you well. Choose carefully, Goddess."
He stood up, saying in a bear's tongue to Avrel. "We
take the eye north. Kailar will carry it."

"Wait!" Sedna squealed, running a tendril of kelp
around his ankle.

David looked over his shoulder at her.

"How do I know which to choose, shaman?"

The wind howled, tearing up a mist from the ice. As
it curled and made voiles in the air again, the figure of
David shifted with it, into the body of the ice bear,

Ingavar. "When Sedna was a girl, did she ever kiss her father's hand?"

"I . . . I cannot remember," said she, spreading pools of slime as she fidgeted and thrashed.

Ingavar shook his paw. The kelp snapped away and where it landed on the ice, the surface cracked, tipping the fingers into the ocean. "Try," he said.

"No!" screamed Sedna, scrambling to the place where the fingers had been. The water bubbled and surged as she thrust her hideous face below its surface. She withdrew a moment later with a frantic splash and skated back to her emergence hole.

Ingavar called to her, "Watch them as they sink. Four are touched with your innocence and love. They are lighter than the others and will take an eye's blink longer to reach the ocean bed. Only then will you be certain which of them to choose."

"A-yah!" wailed Sedna, and dived into the water.

As the lapping waves settled, Avrel said to his master, "I was taught by my mother that the ocean is as deep as the sky is wide. How long will it take her?"

"Forever," said the voice of Gwilanna. "Don't you see what he's doing, you pathetic lumps of blubber? He wants her out of the way so that *he* commands the ocean. He's up to something. You!" She turned and

172

almost spat on Kailar's snout. "You don't trust him, do you? I can see it in your slitty brown bear eyes. Go on. Say it. Ask him how he got here. Ask him how he came to have the power of transfigur— oof!"

With a flick of his paw, Kailar took the liberty of batting her aside. He fixed his gaze on Ingavar and said, "You gave me life when I thought I had none. Whatever you are, I swore to serve you. But I tell you this: I have little respect for men – or birds," he added with a scornful glance sideways. "This rock that you sent the goddess to claim? What use is it to us, to bears?"

"It is sacred," said Ingavar.

"What?" said Gwilanna, who had yet to see the contents of the bag.

"Will you tell us more about the dragon?" asked Avrel.

"Dragon?" squawked Gwilanna, slipping in slush. She flapped herself upright and wobbled back to stand in front of Avrel. "What's this dog brain talking about?"

Ingavar tipped his snout. "Kailar is standing by the eye of Gawain."

"*What?!*"

"What does it see?" the fighting bear asked, turning his head to avoid the bird's screech.

"Kill him!" squawked Gwilanna. "Kill him, you fools. Kill him and give the eye to me!"

Kailar let his tongue settle onto his teeth. Somewhere between his upper incisors was space for one more piece of raven meat, surely? He spread his claws and thrust them into Gwilanna's ice block, missing her head by the width of a feather.

Ingavar said, "Be wary, Kailar, this irritating creature does have a function. She will guide us away from here, to a place where ancient lines of power meet. We will place this piece of dragon at their intersect and use it to look into The Fire Eternal."

"NO!" screamed Gwilanna. "Don't listen to him! He's mad! He'll turn the planet inside out!"

Raargh! went Kailar. That was it! His patience was now so desperately thin that he pressed down instinctively and broke the ice block in two.

Gwilanna was almost but not quite flattened. Somehow, she managed to squirt her body free, only to have Avrel reach a paw forward and pin her down again by the tail. "What does she mean? What is this fire?"

Ingavar looked at each bear in turn. "Below your feet, at the centre of this world, is a fire as old and bright as the stars. At its core, it burns with a pure white light. At the centre of that light is all creation."

"All death you mean!" Gwilanna screamed again.

"Creatures known as dragons were made from it.

174

They were fashioned in the image of the Earth itself: a body of clay, a heart of fire. They were the guardians of this rock before bears existed. The last of their kind was the dragon Gawain, who still protects the northern lands even now."

"What are you talking about?" Gwilanna almost hooted. "He's in pieces of stone with a mile of water over his head!"

Kailar swung his thick neck towards the eye. "It seems to me that the bird speaks truly. How can a dead thing protect the ice?"

Ingavar trained his gaze on Gwilanna. "When a dragon dies it cries a tear. Contained within that tear is an element, a spark, of The Fire Eternal. Tell them, Gwilanna. Tell them what became of the fire of Gawain."

"How would I know?" she bickered, still struggling for her freedom. "The stupid girl took it to the ocean, and drowned!"

"Girl?" said Avrel.

"Her name was Guinevere," Ingavar said, staring deep into the Teller's eyes and opening Avrel's mind to the edge of his perception. "She brought the tear here, far into the north. Look back carefully. You will find her in your memories."

Despite his sturdiness of shape Avrel swayed a little as

he cast his mind back, suddenly giddy with newfound images. "She is distant," he said, stretching his neck as if trying to hear her voice on the howls of the wind, "but . . ."

"But what?" said Gwilanna, becoming interested now. "Come on, Teller. Tell us something useful! Let's see if you're any better than that idiot Lorel you're no doubt descended from."

"She is . . . everywhere," Avrel reported. "Her spirit flies with the wind. And the dragon . . ." He snorted suddenly and retracted his claws, enough to let Gwilanna wriggle away.

With a squawk of triumph she fluttered upwards. But her joy was as short-lived as her flight. With so few tail feathers to give her balance and wings still hampered by the extreme cold she spiralled hopelessly out of control and came crashing down to bounce off Kailar's rump. Kailar swept round in a hustle of fury and would have crushed her to juice if Avrel had not said, "The ice. The fire of the dragon is in the *ice*."

"What?" growled Kailar.

"What?" Gwilanna repeated with a squawk, poking her head from the shadows of his paw. "*What* did he say? What did he say?"

Ingavar rolled his shoulders. "Spare the bird, Kailar.

She can lead us quickest to the place we need to be."

"And where is that?" said Avrel, his young face almost grey with awe.

"The place where your history begins," said Ingavar. "The place where your common ancestor, Thoran, first put his claws into fire-frozen water. Where his brown pelt softened to a yellow shade of white. Where he became as one with the North. We are going to the place where the dragon lines are strongest: to the point where the tear of Gawain was dropped into the ocean we are floating on . . . "

Groyne returns

Gretel did not like Wednesday mornings. If business was quiet (and it usually was), Zanna insisted on running a check of everything she had in the shop. It was a job that bored the scales off Gretel, who was expected to fly around the shelves counting stock (sometimes even *dusting* stock) and reporting back while Zanna ticked numbers on an order sheet.

Hrrr.

The Wednesday that Jodie Simmons arrived was no different. Gretel was busy stabbing her tail into the boxes of herbal tea bags (counting them) when the shop bell tinkled and Tam Farrell's stylish girlfriend walked in. She was wearing a white knee-length coat, parted by a long red mohair scarf. From one shoulder, slung across to her opposite hip, she toted a mid-brown messenger bag, unbuckled.

Gretel sighed and adopted her solid form. Customers she didn't mind, but not during stock checks. That just prolonged the procedure unbearably.

"Hi," said Zanna, spinning round. "Is there anything I can help you with?"

Jodie's perfect eyelashes fluttered. A grain of mascara

fell on to her cheek. Pinching her mouth into a smile she said, "I'll browse, thanks." She was barely audible.

Zanna flashed a smile and returned to her list.

But almost immediately, Jodie spoke again. "Do you own this place?"

"Mmm," went Zanna, tapping a pencil against her lips. "Yes, I do."

"How long have you had it?"

"Oh, about three years."

"Profitable, then?"

"It has its ups and downs. I make most of my living from consultations and therapy."

"Therapy?"

"I sell tinctures." Zanna pointed to a rack of bottles by the counter.

Jodie picked up a business card. "Reflexology and Reiki as well. Quite a service."

"I also do Jin Shin and massage," Zanna said. "Are you interested?"

A cabinet filled with silver pentacles and gothic rings took Jodie's eye. "No, but I know someone who might be. Are you a pagan?"

"Pretty much. Are you?"

Jodie shook her head and turned towards the counter.

"And dragons, too." She had spotted them at last, in their display case.

"Mmm, they're very popular," Zanna advised, flicking through a basket of incense sticks. She frowned at Gretel who had curled up in a Tibetan singing bowl. "Shall I get one out?"

"My boyfriend's already got a couple, thanks."

"Of these?"

Jodie pointed at a Gudrun. "That one."

In the singing bowl, Gretel raised an eye ridge. Was she imagining it or could she hear a muffled hum of dragonsong? She dinked her tail against the rim of the bowl, which responded with a pleasing, dragon-like hum. Maybe not. She settled back again.

"Really? Did he buy them recently?"

"I'm not sure," said Jodie, lifting her chin.

Zanna stroked the ends of her hair as she said, "They're a fairly limited edition. And it's usually women who go for the Gudruns. I'm pretty sure I'd remember any guy who'd had two."

Gudruns? Gretel pricked her ears and peeked out of the bowl. Her eyes flashed towards the messenger bag. There it was again. Definitely dragonsong. She glanced towards Gruffen, who was back in the window, perched on a small stand. He had hooked his eye ridges into a frown. Yes. He'd heard the dragonsong too.

"Oh, you wouldn't forget this guy," Jodie said. "He's a real charmer. Perversely romantic. He'd buy anything just to impress a woman, he would."

Zanna gave an absent shake of her head. She put her clipboard down. "I'm sorry, but am I missing something here?"

"You're very beautiful, aren't you?" Jodie said, with all the frailty and precision of a clockwork doll.

Zanna straightened her spine. "I moisturise, day and night. What's this about?"

"Nice shop, too. Lovely display."

Gruffen quickly turned solid as Jodie's gaze fell upon the window.

"And your point is?" Zanna asked, looking away, disturbed by a sudden flurry of movement. Gretel had flown, undetected, into the back room, where she was sifting through a batch of dried flowers and dropping them into the quiver she carried around her neck.

Jodie opened the flap of her bag. "I'm going to give you this one back intact." She put a cardigan down on the counter top and began to unfold it as though it were a baby's nappy. "But in future, if you don't want a dragon-shaped hole in your window I'd stay away from– hhh! It's *gone*!"

Gretel zoomed in and touched down on the till. She reached into her quiver for a posy of flowers. "Wait!" snapped Zanna, warning her off with a heavily disguised growl of dragontongue.

Meanwhile, Jodie had snatched her bag open and was muttering to herself in disbelief. "That's impossible. It was here. I could feel its weight. When I left the flat there was definitely one of those dragons in my bag!"

Gretel twiddled her nose. Her clever eyes panned the room in an arc.

"I think you'd better go," Zanna said coldly. "Beige just isn't my colour. Sorry." She picked up the cardigan and thrust it back at Jodie.

Jodie stepped away, looking pale and disorientated. She clutched her upper arms as if the shop might be haunted. "What did you do, you witch?"

For the first time in years, the mark of Oomara itched on the surface of Zanna's skin. "The door's right behind you. Get out. Now."

"He only wants a story. After that, you're nothing."

"Get out," Zanna said again, with green-eyed menace.

The door jangled and Jodie was gone.

Zanna closed her eyes and put a hand to her forehead. She allowed herself the silence of the next three seconds. Then, without turning round, she said, "Where are you?"

Groyne materialised on a box of precious stones.

"Well?"

He turned to Gretel, who sighed and blew a smoke ring. The game was up, in spectacular style. She confessed about the mission to investigate Tam.

Zanna was not impressed. "*What?* You sent a special dragon *out?*"

Gruffen raised an apprehensive eye ridge.

We don't trust him, hurred Gretel, frowning in defence.

"Not good enough," said Zanna, dark with fury. "You could have exposed us. I've told you before you *never* act without consulting me or Liz. And what do you mean you went to *investigate* Tam? What did this grand 'mission' uncover exactly?"

Gretel nodded at Groyne, who told them now of what he'd seen in Tam's flat: pictures of David and the Inuit mark.

"Are you sure? Like this?" Zanna pushed back her sleeve.

Groyne gulped at it and nodded.

"That's impossible," she said, more to herself than the dragons. "How could he have made a connection like that?" She brought her hands together around her nose, thinking about her encounters with Tam, thinking about Jodie's parting comment. *He only wants a story. After that, you're nothing.* Story. Nothing. Two betrayals in one. She felt abruptly sick.

Gruffen spotted Lucy arriving and announced it.

"Not a word to her," Zanna snapped, "or you'll all be in a gift box before you know it."

The shop bell jangled and Lucy breezed in. Zanna gunned her down with a gothic stare.

"What?" said Lucy, pulling gum from her teeth. "Am I, like, late or something? What?"

Zanna folded her arms and looked her up and down. "What's with the skirt?"

The shoulders rose. The hip went out. The red lips pouted. "School uniform, hel-*lo*?"

"I've never seen you out of trousers before."

"They're in the wash," Lucy said, chuntering to herself. "Honestly, you're worse than Mum you are. Always criticising everything I do." She dumped her bag.

"And the hair?"

"It's just a *clip*."

"Pretty little clip."

"So? It's not a crime to look pretty, is it?"

Zanna didn't pursue it. "I'm going upstairs to get the therapy room ready. Show Mr Farrell up when he comes."

"*Mister* Farrell?"

"Like I said: we're not an item, OK?"

"Whatever," Lucy said, in mock surrender. She dropped onto a stool behind the counter, took out a nail file and started to rasp.

Zanna snapped her fingers. "Gruffen, Gretel, Groyne. With me."

"Misery guts," said Lucy, under her breath. She stuck out her tongue as Zanna clumped up the stairs. Cow. Some people really ought to get a life.

Three minutes later, Tam walked in. He was wearing a hooped green T-shirt and an open brown coat, faded blue jeans and distressed leather boots. Lucy stood up as if she'd been hydraulically lifted.

"Hello," he said, drowning her in his smile. "Are you Zanna's assistant?"

"Sort of," she muttered, aware that she probably needed to breathe, or run to the bathroom, or at the very least close her mouth.

He gave a quiet chuckle. "Is it me or is there something in the water round here?"

Her facial muscles responded at last. She almost said *hrrr?* like the dragons would have done, but at the last moment managed an enquiring look.

"Your hair, it's stunning."

"It's my mum's," she said, which made him laugh and

made her squirm. What was she *thinking*? How could she have said something so *totally, totally* DUMB?!

"Well, if your mum's half as pretty as you are," he said, "your dad's a very lucky man."

"My dad . . ." she began, and her mouth dried up. How cool and freaky would it have been to tell him she was actually descended from a dragon, born from an egg, delivered by a witch? She thought of Gwilanna briefly and shuddered.

"Is Zanna here?"

Zanna. Mistress of the dark. Lucy snapped to attention. "Err, yeah. She's upstairs. She's waiting for you." She moved aside and invited him through.

"Thanks," he said, peering into the prep room where Gretel worked. He gripped the hand rail and took a step up.

"I'm Lucy," she said, too quickly, too desperately. To avoid the possibility of shrivelling with embarrassment she nailed her gaze on a rack of horoscope books.

He leaned back, smiled and made sure she noticed it. "I'm Tam. Pleased to meet you."

"I know – I mean . . ." She shuffled her feet. "I've read your poems."

"Thank you," he said with plausible grace. He strobed her thoughtfully, then went upstairs.

* * *

Zanna had closed the blinds in the therapy room, leaving it illuminated by flickering tea lights. At its centre was a foam-cushioned treatment table laid with a strip of fresh, clean paper.

"Sit down, take off your shoes," she said, not even looking up as he walked in.

He settled on a chair. "You're going to twiddle my toes?"

"Yes," she said. She lit an orange blossom incense stick.

"How are you?"

"I've been better. Did your niece like the dragon?"

He eased off his boots. "She hasn't seen it yet."

Zanna swept across the room to a sideboard where she kept towels and a tray of essential oils. She opened one and put a few drops into a dish. "Socks as well."

"Socks?" He laughed. "Good job I showered."

"This is tea tree," she said. "It's an anti-fungal."

He nodded and removed his socks, trying as he did to gauge her tone. Was she being frosty? Or hard to get? Or natural?

"And your coat and watch – and T-shirt, please."

"On a first date?"

"You can cancel if you wish."

Definitely frosty. "No, I'm cool. Let's continue," he said. He tested the treatment table for comfort, then nodded at the dragons, who were sitting on a shelf at the head of the table. "What's with the posse?"

"Spiritual support."

He removed his things and threw them onto a chair. "Talking of which, I read *White Fire*. You were right, it is an impressive book. He's quite an inspired writer, Mr Rain." He waited, hoping she would make a comment, but all she gave out was a terse command. "Lie on your back with your hands by your sides and your palms face up."

His head settled on the pillow of a rolled-up towel. "You know, I've been thinking. You said you took a course at Scrubbley College, right? It must have been about the same time David Rain was there. Did you ever meet him?"

"Yes," she said, and turned fully to face him.

"Yes?"

She gave a well-controlled nod. "He was my boyfriend. My partner. I fell in love with him from the first moment I saw him: he was playing pinball, losing hopelessly. There was something strangely endearing about him. I was in the Arctic with him when he died. He's also the father of my little girl, Alexa. What's the matter, Mr Farrell? You look quite stunned. Isn't this what you wanted to hear?"

He gave the faintest of nods. "You're a very unusual woman, Miss Martindale."

"Oh, you're not wrong there," she said. She lifted Groyne and Gruffen and put them on his palms.

"OK, this is weird. Why am I holding *them*?"

"You're not," she said, moving around to stand behind his feet. "They're holding you. They have the ability to centre their G'ravity into a single point. It will feel as if your hands are being nailed to the table for a second. Then they'll just feel heavy. Boys."

Exchanging a glance too swift for any non-dragon eye to catch, Groyne and Gruffen simultaneously concentrated their 'G' force.

"Agh!" cried Tam. His head jerked up and his neck muscles tightened like steel hawsers. He tried moving his hands, but all he could flex were the tendons to his wrists. "What *is* this? They feel like two lead weights." He banged back, grimacing hard at the ceiling.

Zanna held his feet, rubbing tea tree lotion into his toes. "Which paper do you write for?"

"Paper? What?"

She squeezed hard at the base of his largest toe, making him cry out again. "That's the pressure point relating to your tongue," she said. "It seems to be having difficulty finding a pathway to the truth."

Through gritted teeth he said, "*The National Endeavour*."

"Oh, how appropriate. Henry's favourite mag. You'd have been a popular man next door – if I'd chosen to let you stay in my life." She squeezed his toes again. This time his cries brought Lucy running.

"Zanna, what are you doing?" she gasped.

"Lucy, get these dragon things off me," Tam panted.

She spoke to them in dragontongue. "I can't. I think they're hexed."

"What?"

"She's a sibyl. She can do spells and stuff."

"*What?*"

"Let him go. Mum'll kill you," Lucy demanded.

"He's a journalist. He's been stalking us. He wants a piece of David, don't you, Mr Farrell?"

"Look, I only want to help!" he cried.

"Let him go!" Lucy hissed, trying to wrestle Zanna's hands away from his feet.

"Get *back!*" Zanna snarled, throwing Lucy aside with a might well beyond her human frame. Lucy hit the sideboard at shoulder height. The tray of oils clattered. A tea light fell. A spill from one of the bottles ignited.

"I support the book's message!" Tam shouted at

Zanna. "The environment. The polar bears. All of that. But it's my job to uncover the facts!"

"You know *nothing* about us," Zanna snapped. "And you wouldn't understand or care if you did."

He saw her dark eyes blazing and realised it wasn't just anger he was watching. "Fire," he gasped. He threw his head sideways. "Let me go. The room's on fire."

"Gretel!" Lucy cried, getting back to her feet. "Quick, do something!"

Suddenly, Tam noticed that the dragon that had been above his head was on the sideboard. With one breath, she drew in the flames and swallowed them. "What the—? W-who *are* you people?" he stammered.

Zanna pulled back her sleeve. On her forearm, the mark of Oomara was weeping. "You know, for one foolish moment, I let myself believe that you could be something special, like David, when all you were giving me were lies and deceit."

"I can help you," he insisted, coughing out pungent, oil-sweet smoke. "If you tell the world the truth it will only raise your profile even more."

"Truth?" said Lucy. "What do you mean?"

Tam shook his head. "That he never existed. The author of the book: David Rain. He's a cipher. It's all just a front, isn't it?"

"*What?*" said Lucy. "'Course he existed."

"Then why doesn't one of you explain to me why I can't find any records of him beyond his time at Scrubbley College?"

"Shut up," said Zanna.

"What's he talking about?" asked Lucy, wild-eyed and frightened.

"This is the mark of Oomara," said Zanna, holding up her arm for Tam to see. "It's a symbol of the divide between good and evil. Once marked, you can never truly settle into one state or the other. And now you're going to know what it feels like to own it."

"No!" shouted Lucy. "No, you can't!"

But Zanna had already brought her arm down, to press the mark of Oomara over Tam Farrell's heart.

He screamed and his body gave a violent convulsion. Even so, he managed to force out a word, one that would trouble Lucy for many days to come. "Parents . . ." he spluttered. Then his head struck the pillow. 'Parents,' he mouthed again.

And then he passed out.

Tea with Henry

"There," said Mr Bacon, placing a large encyclopaedia down on the table and turning it round for Alexa to see. "Most famous case of fairies ever recorded. 1917. Cottingley Beck, Yorkshire."

Alexa let out a little gasp. On the open page was a black and white photograph of a young girl, a little older than herself, sitting beside a waterfall with fairies dancing around her head. She pointed to them, open-mouthed. Liz said, "Yes, aren't they lovely?"

"Complete fakes, of course," Mr Bacon said.

"Henry?" Liz growled at him under her breath.

He whispered back, "Is it wise, Mrs P., to let the child believe these things are real?"

"They were real enough for the creator of *Sherlock Holmes*," she said, referring to the fact that the world-famous author Sir Arthur Conan Doyle, the inventor of the greatest detective in the world, had endorsed the photographs at one time.

Henry responded with a painful grimace. "Bizarre," he muttered, "that one of the greatest minds in the universe believed in sprites and nature spirits. He must have had writers' block that day."

"Excuse me," Liz said, folding her arms (doing a scarily good impression of Lucy). "I live with one of the greatest minds in the universe, who also happens to be called Arthur. You'd be surprised what *he* believes."

"Ah, but he's a physicist," Henry reasoned. "Rational thinker. Finger on the pulse."

"He believes in dragons," Liz said teasingly.

Henry grimaced again. "Another cup of tea?"

"They're dancing, Naunty," Alexa said.

"Yes, they look very happy," said Liz.

"Mmm, well, if you like those," Henry said, "I suppose you might find some amusement in this." He disappeared into his kitchen for a moment and came back with a cereal packet. On the box was a series of classic fairy drawings, to cut out and keep.

"Oh, how wonderful!" Liz exclaimed. "You are a sweet man, sometimes, Henry." She popped a kiss on his cheek.

"Yes, well," he blustered, pointing his chin. "Don't suppose there's any harm indulging the girl's imagination a little. This is how it was done, you know. Cardboard stencils, secured to the earth with a series of hat pins—"

"Stop," said Liz, holding up a finger.

Henry bit his tongue, but he couldn't help trying another approach. "Of course, the photography should have exposed the nonsense. Fairies like to 'flit about', one imagines."

"Like Gretel," said Alexa. "She—"

"Hmm," said Liz, turning a page and interrupting her quickly. "Look, here's another picture. I think this fairy is giving the little girl a flower."

"They like flowers," said Alexa. "And playing with the bonglers."

"Bonglers?" said Henry.

"Short for 'wind chimes'," Liz explained. "In your next life, try to have some children, Henry."

He looked at her as if she'd been altered by aliens. "It was all box cameras back then," he went on. "Slow exposure, onto glass plates. The creatures should have been far more blurred. The slight movement you see in them is probably the cut-outs blowing in the wind."

Liz hummed and said, "I don't think that's the answer, my friend."

"Um?"

"Nothing. A joke. Go on."

Henry frowned and wiped the ends of his moustache. "Streaks of light would have been more convincing. Duped an expert all the same. Completely took him in. Hard to imagine how. Mind you, folks believed all sorts then. There was even a theory that the child might have somehow photographed her thoughts – held the desire to see fairies so strongly that she'd projected them onto film."

Liz raised her head.

"Ludicrous, naturally."

"Naturally," Liz said.

"Can we put the fairies by the door?" asked Alexa. She picked up the cereal box and hugged it like a teddy.

"Door?" Henry queried, looking at his.

"An ornamental one, by our rockery," said Liz. "That's where our fairies live, isn't it, Lexie?"

"Sometimes," said the child, after a moment's reflection, though she didn't offer up any further explanation.

Henry rubbed a handkerchief under his nose. "The Scots believed in fairies, you know. Ballads and poetry full of references. *Na Sithein* they called them. Not these diminutive dryads, of course. Theirs were a bunch of Iron Age savages who slaughtered cattle and made off with your wives and daughters."

"Hen-ry!" Liz bracketed Alexa's ears.

"Sorry," he said, coughing. "Erm, thought to be a race of special people, child, who lived in tiny houses made from pine cones and bark, who, erm, built underground portals to fairyland."

"That's better," said Liz.

"What's portals?" asked Alexa, looking up at her 'aunt'.

"A doorway into another world, sweetie."

"Mmm," went the girl, as if this made a great deal of sense.

"Of course, they wouldn't have lasted long," sniffed Henry. "Probably all wiped out by the last ice age."

Hearing this, Alexa swept around and peered out over Henry's frosted lawn.

Liz immediately turned her back again. "It's all right, our fairies will be fine," she said, pulling a 'will you please think about this before you speak' face at her neighbour.

"Dead souls, fallen angels or a mystery race," he whispered. "Take your mythological pick."

Before she could, Liz heard a slamming sound next door.

"Mummy's home," said Alexa, tossing back her hair.

Liz glanced at the clock. "Too early for Mummy. That must be Lucy, in a mood by the sound of it. Come on, petal, time to go. Say thank you to Mr Bacon for finding you the pictures."

"Thank yew, Mister Bacon."

"My pleasure," he said. Unsure of how to part, he took Alexa's hand and shook it.

"When our fairies come out, do you want to see them playing?"

Mr Bacon coughed.

"Of course he would," said Liz, "but not until the better weather comes, eh?" She patted Henry's shoulder. "Think of it as a treat. Thanks for everything. You'd have made a delightful grumpy granddad. We'll update you on the fairies next time. Bye."

Outside, the air was near to freezing. "Ooh, it's chilly," Liz said. "Real polar bear weather." She stamped her feet, thinking she would make Alexa laugh, but the girl was peering round, looking between the trees.

"Has he come?" she asked.

"Who, darling? Has who come?"

Alexa presented her face to the sky. The wind was shaving snow off the branches, turning the Crescent into a snow dome. "The Nooky," said the girl. "I keep dreaming him. He's . . ." She dropped her shoulders and blew a confused sigh. "I don't know."

"It's the cold," Liz said. "It's frozen your brain." She tickled the top of Alexa's head.

Alexa hummed, then skipped across the lawn. Suddenly, she turned and said, "Is Gwinnyvere a fairy?"

"Pardon?" said Liz, through chattering teeth. She dug her hands into her armpits and shivered.

"She was a *special* person, wasn't she?"

A breath of wind made a strand of Liz's red hair dance. "Yes, she was. What made you ask? Has Lucy or Mummy been talking about Guinevere?"

Alexa moved her head from side to side. "I dreamed her," she said, making footprints for fun. "She was flying – like a fairy." And even through the damp grey winter gloom, her blue eyes shone like clear bright water.

Liz crouched down and brought the girl's tiny pink hands together. "Guinevere wasn't a fairy," she whispered. "She was a girl, a young woman. She lived a long time ago, with big, big dragons."

"Like G'lant?"

"I don't know. Is G'lant a big dragon? Is that how you dream him?"

"Sometimes," said Alexa. "I saw fairies flying round him."

Liz responded with a light-hearted smile. But a chasm had opened up in her heart. Fairies. Guinevere. Why should that make a grain of sense, when it couldn't? "Come on," she said, recovering, "your hands are very sticky. We need to get those washed before they glue together."

And in they went – to find Zanna, leaning back against the kitchen worktop, drinking coffee.

"Mummy, I saw fairies at Mr Bacon's!"

"Were they eating a jam sponge?" Zanna said, frowning at the handprints on her skirt.

"You're home early," said Liz. "Is everything OK?"

Zanna took a long, slow, thoughtful drink. "Could be better."

Liz passed her keys to the ever-present Gwillan and tapped Alexa once on the shoulder. "Run upstairs and wash your hands. There's a good girl."

"All right," Alexa said, and was gone in a flash.

Zanna turned the mug in her hands. An image of A.A. Milne's grinning Tigger peeked out from between her graceful fingers. "I bought this mug for David, you know."

"Yes, I remember," Liz said quietly. She placed a thumb on Zanna's cheek and found some wetness there. "Is that what this is about?"

At the base of Zanna's chin, more tears accumulated. "Tam was a journalist, chasing a story. It was David he wanted all along, not me."

Liz stood away and let out a soft, deep sigh. "How did you find out?"

"His girlfriend came into the shop. She gave the game

away in a spat of jealousy. Don't worry, I've dealt with it. He won't get near us."

Liz spotted Gretel on the fridge top, listening. "You used magicks?"

"I had to."

"And he's . . . ?"

"Breathing, just about. He'll have a headache and some memory loss. No more than he deserves."

"Zanna—"

"There's more." She looked Liz in the eye. "I had a barney with Lucy. She was there. She saw it all. She tried to protect him. I don't think it was entirely altruistic."

Liz dragged a finger down the bridge of her nose. "What do you mean?"

"I think it might have been Lucy who put him on to me."

The air between them stood still for a moment. "Are you sure?"

Zanna shook her head. "Not entirely. But she stormed out screaming silly things about Tam and how I hadn't heard the last of it. I always thought he knew more than he was letting on, Liz. I'm worried that he might have had inside information."

Suddenly, the front door slammed and the stairs took

their usual afternoon pounding. Liz gave an unsettled nod. "All right, I'll deal with it." She put a comforting palm on Zanna's cheek. "We'll talk later, OK?" Then she slipped upstairs and found Lucy on her bed. The girl was staring at the ceiling, chewing. "Hard day?"

"She's here, isn't she?"

"If you're talking about Zanna, yes."

"Thought so. I can *smell* the witch."

"That's enough. This is your sister you're talking about."

"Part-sister, actually. Very *small* part. Has she told you what she did today, my *part-sister?*"

"Something to do with Tam Farrell, I understand." Liz stood back, folding her arms.

This was not a good sign and Lucy knew it. "What? What am I supposed to say?"

"You're looking very pretty."

Lucy touched her skirt. "Meaning?"

"You've got a crush on him, haven't you?"

"*Crush?!*" Lucy sat up, flinging daggers.

"Oh, it's all right, Lucy. I do understand. You wouldn't be the first Pennykettle female to fall in love with an older man."

"Mum, I only saw him today!"

"Long enough," Liz said. "Why are you so angry?"

202

"Because of her!" Lucy flung out a hand. "She cursed him!"

"He was deceiving her."

"He was—"

"What?" Liz said, keeping her calm. "What was he, Lucy? What was he to you – before you 'met' him today?"

"Nothing!" she screamed.

Liz glanced at the computer, booting up. "Were you emailing him?"

By the lamp stand, Gwendolen rattled her scales. Ohhh . . . why had she gone and done that then? She tightened her claws, knowing she'd been rumbled.

Liz's eyes turned to violet. "Do I have to ask Gwendolen?"

Lucy sighed and beat her pillow till the bedsprings groaned. "He was going to help us!"

"Help us do what?"

"Find David, of course!"

"Oh, Lucy . . ." Her mother's voice began to crack. "Darling, please listen to me. You've got to let go of this. David's gone and he's not coming back. I know it's hard, but you must accept it. Isn't it sufficient to have his memory intact and his books and his dragons and his daughter here around us?"

For a second time the bed springs groaned as Lucy

broke down and sobbed into her duvet. "No!" she cried. "I *won't* give up!"

Liz sighed and gradually relaxed her stance. She sat down on the edge of the bed and let her hand glide over her daughter's shoulder. "If I could take this pain away from you I would, you know I would."

"You're not trying," Lucy wailed. "Nobody's trying. And she's just . . . *evil*."

"No, she isn't."

"She *is*. She didn't have to hex Tam, did she?"

Liz stretched her fingers over her knees. "Zanna only did what I would have done."

"Put the mark of Oomara on him?"

"Pardon?"

"Oh, hasn't she *told* you that?"

"No," Liz said. "No, she hasn't." She looked away, troubled.

Gwendolen gulped.

"She's Gwilanna in bangles," Lucy said bitterly. "She should never have come to this house."

But Liz wasn't going to rise to that. After a count of three she said, "I'm going downstairs to make you something to eat. Please don't start any fights with Zanna. Just be calm until I've thought this through."

She stood up to go. But from the depths of the duvet

Lucy said suddenly, "Mum, can I just ask you something?"

"Yes, of course. What?"

"Did you ever meet David's parents?"

There was a pause. Gwendolen looked at Liz. Silly as it seemed, it occurred to the dragon that if Liz had been able to blow a smoke ring, she would have done.

"That's a strange thing to ask."

"Yeah, but did you?"

"Well, if I remember correctly he went home for a couple of weekends but, no, they never came here. Why?"

"It's just . . . " But Lucy couldn't get the words out and she ended up sobbing on her pillow again.

Liz left the room. But a minute later she returned with a sheet of cream-coloured paper. "Sit up," she said. "I want to show you something. Don't ask me why I kept it. Sentiment, I suppose. I don't know if this will make things better or worse, but if you want it, you can have it."

"What is it?" Lucy asked. She sniffed and turned over. Liz unfolded a letter.

4 Thoushall Road
Blackburn
Lancashire

Dear Mrs Pennykettle,

Help! I am desperately in need of somewhere to stay. Next week, I am due to start a Geography course at Scrubbley College and I haven't been able to find any lodgings.

I am scrupulously clean, and as tidy as anyone of my age (20) can be. My hobby is reading, which is generally pretty quiet. I get along very well with children and I love cats.

Yours sincerely,
Mr David Rain

PS. I'm afraid I haven't seen any dragons about of late. I hope this isn't a problem.

"This was his reply to our advert for a lodger."

Lucy read it under her breath. Then she pressed it to her heart, fell back onto the bed and cried as if the tears would never stop.

"I'll call you when tea's nearly ready," said Liz. She put a kiss on her fingers and touched Lucy's head. She closed the door quietly on her way out.

The remainder of the evening went by peacefully. Lucy spent all of it in voluntary isolation. She ate her tea in her room and when she was done she left the plate outside the door. (Bonnington grew a mane and sat for half an hour licking morsels off her lamb chops, as if he'd brought down an antelope on the landing.) Arthur rang to say he'd be late. Liz, although she wanted him home, was nevertheless grateful of one less complication. Arthur never interfered in disciplinary matters connected with Lucy, but he would ask about the cause and the reason and the outcome, and that, for one night, Liz could do without. So she and Zanna spent their time entertaining Alexa, making a mobile of the fairies from Henry's cereal packet. It was a great success. The fairies flew (with assistance from Gwillan) and now that Alexa had the opportunity of watching them spin and dance above her bed, she quickly changed her mind about planting them in the garden and dozed off that night singing her favourite song to them (*There was an old lady who swallowed a fly* . . .).

Night fell. The house slept. The Earth slowly turned. At precisely 7am, Gauge breathed a gentle *hrrr* into Liz's left ear. She rose, showered quickly and went downstairs. Within seconds, she knew that something was wrong. The kettle wasn't on. Where was Gwillan? And why was there no greeting from the listening dragon?

Simple. They had both been hexed. Not with any kind of serious magic, just a sleeping draught Gretel used on Arthur sometimes, when he needed to overcome one of his headaches.

Liz snapped them out of it with ancient words of dragontongue. They were still coming round when she found the note.

It was propped against the teapot. A single fold of paper.

Dear Mum, I can't stand it any more. I'm going away. Don't know how long I'll be. Sorry. Don't hate me. I love you, Lucy xx

Liz felt the world rush away from her heart. "No," she said and dashed upstairs. She threw the door of Lucy's bedroom open, hoping it might be just a cruel joke, thinking already of the words she would say. *I was SO frightened! Have you any idea?* But the room was empty. The bed was made. The curtains were open. The computer was off. There were slippers on the rug. *Slippers*, not shoes. The wardrobe door lay slightly ajar. The hairbrush had gone from the dressing table.

Liz fell to her knees. "No," she sobbed.

But the silence was deep and unforgiving. Lucy, her daughter of sixteen years, had run away from home.

Taking her dragon, Gwendolen, with her.

Finding Tam

According to Gwendolen's place-finding search engine, the offices of *The National Endeavour* were in a large glass building on Wellington High Road, half a mile's walk from the underground station of the same name. On her map, the thick green line of a major A road did not appear especially intimidating, but even though Lucy was no stranger to London, the pace of life here, in the rush hour, frightened her. Wellington High Road was a furious dual carriageway, yet there was traffic congestion on one side of the road, made worse by a fire engine and a clutch of police cars, which were throwing their blue lights into the rain. Lucy could not be sure whether something was on fire or a water main had burst or if a building had been cordoned off because of an emergency. She just pulled up her collar and hurried on past, half-wondering if a missing Pennykettle child would be reason enough to warrant an all-out runaway search. She decided not, and checked her map again. By now, if her bearings were correct, she should be right on top of the magazine's offices. A lorry powered by, rattling every pane of glass in sight. Then a horn blared making her squeal in fright, driving her towards a revolving door. She saw the word *Endeavour* and just kept on moving, glad to let it carry her out of the noise.

"Yes, can I help you?"

The voice floated across a spotlit foyer, decked on either side by artificial plants. A young blonde receptionist, wearing a set of light grey headphones, was just visible behind a curved beech desk.

"I want to see Tam Farrell," Lucy said, approaching.

The woman threw out a practised smile. The word 'bored' was practically stamped on her teeth. Before Lucy could answer, she had pressed a button on a switchboard in front of her and was speaking with sugar-coated chords into her mouthpiece. "Hello, *National Endeavour*? Thank *you*. Putting you through." She pressed another button and came up for air. "Do you have an appointment?"

Lucy shivered and shook her head. A droplet of water winged off her hair onto a notepad the receptionist was using. The woman drew herself up like a bear. She tore the page off, scrumpled it stylishly and threw it away. "If he's not expecting you I can't send you up. I'm not even sure he's in the building, actually."

"Can you check?" Lucy said, leaning over the desk. "It's important. Really important."

The revolving doors caught another visitor: a long-haired courier, in leathers. The receptionist signed for a package and took another call before speaking to Lucy again. "Is it about a story?"

Lucy said, "I'm here about David Rain."

"Who?"

"David Rain. The author. Can you please get Tam?"

The woman flexed her shoulders. She was small and a little too plump for her suit, showing more breast than Lucy's mother would have approved of. "Your name is?"

"Lucy – but he won't remember me."

"Then what's the point of calling him?"

"He might know me if he sees me."

The receptionist sat forward, twiddling a pencil. Her tongue took a layer of gloss off her lips. "Is this personal?"

"Sort of."

A half-triumphant smile broke across the woman's mouth. "Hmm, thought as much." She pointed to the door. "Out you go."

"No," Lucy said, bringing all her youthful hormones into play. "I'm not going back."

The switchboard buzzed again. The receptionist, stunned by this defiance, let it flash. "This isn't a lonely hearts club, darling. And I don't have time to argue, OK?" She clicked her fingers. From the shadow of a pillar, a security guard stepped forward.

"Stop. You don't understand," Lucy said, as he took her (gently) by the crook of her arm. "You can't throw me out. I've come all the way from Scrubbley!"

"Have a pleasant journey home," the receptionist fluted, giving Lucy a patronising wave.

"Come on, miss," said the guard, pulling her away. "The more you struggle, the worse it gets."

"Get off me!" Lucy said, wriggling free. She opened her bag and brought out Gwendolen, holding her up like a spiky green chalice. "At least give him this. Please?"

The guard tugged at the peak of his cap, then at the knot of his immaculate tie. A coat of sweat broke out on the lines of his forehead. After several indecisive attempts to go forward, he turned back to the receptionist.

"What?" she said, catching his look.

"She's brought him a dragon," he said. His accent was straight out of an East End market.

The receptionist ground her teeth. "I don't care if she's brought him Godzilla. Just do your job, Leroy. Throw her out."

"But it's important," Lucy pleaded. "Really important."

Leroy shushed her. He circled his hands. "Did you say it was about David Rain, the author bloke? The guy who wrote that awesome book about the polar bears?"

Sensing a breakthrough, Lucy stepped forward. "Yes!"

He held up his hands to warn her 'not too close'. "That was a cool read – no pun intended."

"She's still here," the receptionist intoned.

Leroy tapped his thumbs together. He raised a finger to indicate that Lucy should behave herself, then he loped back to the desk. "I reckon she's for real."

The woman sat back, infuriated. "It's not your job to decide, is it? Just throw her out, OK?"

"But what harm's it gonna do? Just call the guy."

"She might be hostile, Leroy!"

"Well, if she is, I'll take her down, won't I?" He grinned and tugged at his cuffs like a gangster. "Get him to the lobby. I'll stand guard."

The receptionist breathed in, as if she'd been hijacked. "This is on your balding head, OK?" She punched out a four-digit number. As it connected, her face changed from inclement to fair (like Mr Bacon's barometer, Lucy thought).

"Hi, yeah. It's Chantelle, in reception. There's a visitor for you. A girl, called Lucy. No, no appointment. She *says* she knows you. Just a moment." She muted the line. "He wants to know your surname?"

Lucy gulped. On the way here she'd thought about

this. Any mention of Pennykettle might leave a trail that her mother could scent. "Black," she said.

"Black?" The receptionist didn't seem convinced.

Lucy smiled. 'The colour of your heart,' she thought, but wisely kept her silence.

"Lucy Black," the woman said, in a voice charged with bittersweet cynicism. There was a pause. Lucy crossed her fingers behind her back. The receptionist played with a strand of hair. "OK. I'll tell her." Her expression changed again, back towards stormy. "Take a seat. Mr Farrell will be with you in a moment." She glared at Leroy and got on with her work.

A minute later, a pair of lift doors opened and Tam Farrell came striding into reception. He looked at Chantelle, who pointed savagely at Lucy.

Lucy jumped up.

"Miss Black?" he said, sounding charming but confused.

Amazing. Not a flicker of recognition. Lucy prayed to every star in the sky that her plan was going to work. "Listen," she implored him, coming up close. "My name's not Lucy Black, it's Lucy . . . something else. You know me, but you've been made to forget me. This is Gwendolen. She'll help you to remember – I hope."

She stepped forward again and tried to place Gwendolen on Tam's left shoulder. Tam backed away instinctively, looking alarmed.

"I told you. She's crazy. Get rid of her," said Chantelle.

From the corner of her eye, Lucy saw Leroy fingering his collar. He was having third thoughts, never mind second. She felt Gwendolen's heartbeat and tried again. "Please, she won't hurt you."

Tam said, "No. What is this? Who are you?" and stepped back so quickly that he stumbled and fell.

Leroy made a sound like a whale blowing air.

Lucy knew there was only one chance. She dropped to one knee beside the startled journalist and whispered her orders in dragontongue to Gwendolen. "Do it quickly. Then tumble to the floor if you need to." She threw the dragon at him.

"Wo! That's it," cried Leroy.

"Hurry," Lucy cried, as a suited arm looped around her neck and she was dragged along the floor for several feet.

Chantelle was on her toes now, baying like a spectator at the Coliseum. "She's out of some institution, she is. I'm calling the cops."

"Leave it. She's a kid. I can handle this," said Leroy. He pulled Lucy to her feet and lugged her towards the door.

Suddenly, Tam Farrell let out a short squeal. His hand felt for the atlas of his spine, where Gwendolen had just spiked him with the tip of her tail, twisting her isoscele deep into the core of his cranial nerves. In less than two seconds he'd located the pain; but in less than one she had interfaced with his cerebral cortex and downloaded a vast stream of data and images. She fell away, hopeful at best. Memory swapping was an untried process. Dangerous. Unpredictable. But if it worked, Tam would now have a bundle of memories, Lucy's memories, dating back to his visit to Zanna in the shop . . .

"Oh." He fell forward, with his face in his hands.

"What's she done?" Chantelle squealed. "He's gonna die – in my foyer! I'm definitely calling the police."

To her amazement, Tam raised a hand and croaked, "Wait." A string of saliva dribbled out of his mouth. He wiped it on his sleeve. Grimacing, he rolled into a sitting position.

"You OK, Mr Farrell?" Leroy said, still holding Lucy firmly in place.

"It's all right. Let her go. She's a friend," he replied.

Lucy gasped in relief.

Not so Chantelle. "What? But she tried to brain you with that dragon! I'll be a witness if you want someone?"

"Lucy, help me up," Tam stretched a hand.

Reluctantly, Leroy released his grip.

Lucy shot forward. With her help, Tam staggered to a broad leather sofa and plunged into the spacious cushions. "Sit still, let me look at your eyes," she said. She slapped his cheek lightly to make him concentrate. "You were hexed," she whispered, "by Zanna's dragon, Gretel. Do you remember? Upstairs, in the therapy room?"

"Water," he said, having difficulty swallowing. His pupils were dilating; a reasonable sign.

"Already on it," Leroy said, approaching with a plastic cup in hand. On the way, he crouched down and picked up Gwendolen. "This is cute. Where'd you buy it?"

"Erm, Scrubbley market," said Lucy. There seemed no harm in giving that away.

Leroy nodded and handed her over.

To Lucy's relief, Gwendolen hadn't suffered any damage or injury. Lucy praised her with a quiet word of dragontongue then slipped the special dragon back into her bag. She took the water and handed it to Tam.

Leroy backed off, twiddling his thumbs. "Think I'll let you guys . . . reacquaint." He touched his cap and strolled away.

"So, what are you doing here, Lucy?" Tam's eyes threw a bleary blue light into hers.

217

"You remember David, don't you?"

He spluttered a little and lifted his cup. "The mysterious author."

"I want to prove that he was real. Do you know where Blackburn is?"

"Lancashire. Why?"

"I want you to take me there."

"That's a heck of a journey from here. What for?"

Lucy reached into her bag again and drew out the letter from David to her mum. "Look," she said, and tapped the address: 4 Thoushall Road, Blackburn. "I want to trace him, like you said. Me and you, together. This is where he lived. We can start right here . . ."

Circles

Immediately after revealing his intention to visit the spiritual centre of the ice, the Nanukapik, Ingavar, used his healing powers to grant the raven, Gwilanna, a full set of feathers. "Fly ahead of us," he told her. "Seek out a path. You will be our eyes, sibyl."

"Give me one good reason why I'd want to?" she spat.

Ingavar lowered his snout towards her. "Because you're curious to know the outcome of this journey." And though she hopped from foot to foot and chuntered impatiently, the Nanukapik would reveal nothing more to her. He merely looked at Avrel, who nodded in acknowledgement. He too was curious, but any Teller understood that stories and legends are not always to be told in a single breath.

"Just *how* am I supposed to guide you?" said Gwilanna, dipping her beak at the windswept ice, as though to prove it was nothing but a huge blank canvas.

Ingavar's gaze travelled up to the sky, where, Avrel noticed, the clouds were shaping into seals again. "Your ability for magicks has been subdued, but your powers of perception are as sharp as ever, particularly where dragons are concerned. You have learned a great truth today. Now that you know Gawain's tear is in the ice, the sparks of his fire will be visible to you. Where they congregate is where we must be."

Gwilanna caarked sourly and flicked up her tail, throwing nubbins of ice into Kailar's face. "How can you know so much?" she grizzled. "You were just a mere . . . boy last time we met, meddling in things you didn't understand."

"I understand a lot more now," said Ingavar, angling his gaze in such a way that Avrel, looking on, thought that the two of them were communicating in some silent fashion, and this appeared to be confirmed when the raven said quietly, "You've crossed over somehow, haven't you, bear? I can sense them within you. The others. The Fain . . ."

Others? Fain? Avrel waited, thinking that Ingavar would comment. But the Nanukapik stayed silent and as his gaze remained steady the raven quickly realised that her petulant questions were going to be pointless. Even so, she tried one more. "If I help you, will you free me of this ridiculous body?"

"All things are possible with The Fire Eternal," said Ingavar.

"Pah!" she expostulated, ruffling her feathers. She preened several loose ones on the shoulder of her wing, then stepped forward until she could feel his humid breath on her face. "I don't trust you," she hissed. "And if you had any sense you'd think the same," she said to Avrel. Then, shrieking like a wild thing, she took to the air and soared away, chased by Kailar's roar.

Time passed – a day or two, maybe; in the bleakness of winter it was difficult to gauge. But the bird was not seen at all during that time and Avrel was growing ever more anxious. Now and then he would suddenly throw up his head, thinking he had caught a black wing-beat above. But it was always just a wisp, another ghost in the air – a phenomenon he was growing rapidly used to. For as well as seeing walrus and seal in the sky, he and Kailar were now being visited by the dead. These usually took the form of bears and other wildlife, but there were people, too. Old brown-skinned Inuit people, whose faces were always of the normal dimensions but whose bodies were often just streaks in the wind. They came to Avrel the most, singing their rasping songs into his ears, stroking his fur, tickling his snout, howling in the pit of his throat when he breathed. Sometimes, they stood up as if to challenge him and he would flash his paws in terror and disperse them into mist, until eventually Ingavar took him to one side saying, "Do not fear them,

Avrel. They know who you are. They want to celebrate your presence here and tell you their stories. Embrace them. They want to give you their lives. At the End of Days, yours will be the voice of the North."

"End of Days?" said the Teller, his heart racing. For he could speak in volumes of all things past, but the future was as foggy as the blizzards they journeyed through, and blizzards could sometimes hide great dangers.

But again Ingavar would say no more.

And so the three of them walked on for another two days, through a storm of souls and scintillating ice specks, in an arrow formation with Ingavar leading. As tradition dictated, Ingavar kept Avrel, a son of Lorel, at his left and Kailar, son of the fighting bear, Ragnar, to his right. But with every step they took, Kailar's patience began to grow as weary as his feet, and when they next paused to shelter among a jumble of ice blocks, he finally voiced his concerns to the Teller.

"We're going round in circles," he said, his words catching in the punishing wind and being snatched from his mouth on fragments of sighs. From the depths of his lungs he issued a great blow, then bit into a snow crust to slake his thirst. The eye of Gawain, still in its bag, but now secured around his neck like a clumsy pendant, thumped against a jutting point of ice. He growled at the nuisance and shook the eye aside.

"Be careful with that," Avrel said. He glanced anxiously over his shoulder for Ingavar. The Nanukapik had lain down further away, with his blue eyes closed and his head held level in the semi-hibernation state he often adopted. He was already covered by a skin of drifting snow.

"What is the point of this?" said Kailar, the eye swinging back and forth against his chest. "You know the patterns of the stars as well as I do, Teller. We are walking, but we are not heading north."

Avrel retracted his claws and counted them, something he did when he was nervous or afraid. "We are following our Nanukapik. What else matters?"

Kailar stared at him as though he were a fool. "This thing is heavy. So is your brain. Surely it must have occurred to you by now that the bird may never come back? And what if it does? What if it leads us to this place of fire? What happens then? What does our so-called Nanukapik want with us?"

Avrel winced and looked away into the distance. In the time of the nine great ruling bears, such talk would have cost a bear his place as a pack leader. He shook away the ice lines above his eyes. "My brain may be heavy but it does at least *work*. Let me tell you a story, nanuk."

"Don't belittle me," said Kailar, curling his lip, "unless you wish to end up dead or scarred."

"Listen," Avrel whispered, drawing close. "I have learned a great deal from these spirits that have come to us. What Ingavar said is true: Thoran, the first white bear, was made so by a dragon. He put his claws into the creature's fire and it turned his pelt from the colour of earth to the colour of ice."

Kailar let a rumble escape from his throat.

"This is no mere *den story*," Avrel said crossly, half-wondering if he dared give the fighting bear a cuff. "This is your history. Listen and learn. In Thoran's time, the ice was as wide as the sky. It reached out to many stretches of land. Before long, other bears walked onto it. They grew pelts to match Thoran's, to protect them from the cold. They mated and became the first true ice bears, living off seal and sometimes going back to the land in the summer. Thoran mated as well. Three times, with separate females. From these matings came three great bears: the first Nanukapik, Aluna; his Teller, Lorel; and your ancestor, Ragnar. All three of them were sons of Thoran. All three were bound to the fire. They sheltered in its auma, as you and I do now. That stone you carry around your neck should be as precious to us as Thoran is. Without the dragon, we would not be here."

Kailar grizzled and snorted again. "Yet we saw Thoran die."

"Not die," said Avrel, "become one with Ingavar."

"But he's a *man*."

Avrel's black tongue swept around his teeth. "No, he has the power to become a man – because he has the dragon's fire within him."

Kailar raised his head until their snouts were almost touching. "And when did you or I last turn into men? If we have the fire, why can't we perform such trickery, son of Lorel?"

Avrel grimaced and pulled away. The fighting bear's breath was as rank as walrus dung. "I don't know," he said, and he thought back briefly to Ingavar's puzzling conversation with Gwilanna about the still unexplained 'others' called the Fain. No inspiration came to him, however, and so he said to Kailar, "But I do know this. The ice is changing. The dragon's power is not as great as it was. Every winter, our territories grow smaller. The ice is melting, pulling further from the land. I have memories, Kailar, recent memories, of bears becoming stranded, swimming in search of land that never comes, swimming until they tire and drown."

Kailar dismissed this with a cursory snort. "Some bears are weak," he said, but he could not conceal a slight discomfort in his growl.

Avrel shook his head. "Not weak, helpless. And if you don't listen to me, one day the ocean may defeat a bear even as strong as you. Ingavar knows this. He is here to make a change and when he does, you and I will be there beside him – you and I . . . and many others, I think."

"If you mean these ghosts," said Kailar, swatting one.

"I mean bears," said Avrel, pointing his snout. "All around us. Distant, but closing in. That's why we're turning circles. I think he's drawing them to us."

Kailar looked over his shoulder, and back. "He's forming a pack?"

"I don't know. Perhaps."

Kailar stared at him hard.

"I don't *know*," Avrel repeated with a hiss.

This was too much for the fighting bear. With an incredulous grunt, he pounded up the nearest cluster of ice, sending chips flying outward as he scrabbled to the top. Once there, he took scents from three equal points. "I don't have them."

"You've been in too many fights," Avrel said, envying the scars on Kailar's snout all the same. "Your

226

senses are dull. And Lorel's line were always more sensitive, remember?"

Kailar tried again, breathing in even harder. "How far away?"

"The strength of it varies."

"How many?"

"I don't know," Avrel said, with growing impatience. "It's just a feeling, but…"

Kailar shifted his weight. The ridge he had climbed was showing signs of collapsing under his weight. He dug in like a cat, but the pressure only hastened the impending break and he crunched, rump-heavy, to the surface again. "But what?" he asked, punching a small prop of ice aside.

Avrel's words were stayed by a fluttering sound. Both bears turned and saw Gwilanna, claws splayed, coming in to land on Ingavar's back.

Kailar, showing none of his earlier doubts, immediately abandoned the conversation and ran straight to his Nanukapik's defence. Hearing the approaching thump of paws Gwilanna screeched and took off again, only missing being bitten by a radius of sweat on Kailar's snout.

"Typical!" she spat, leaving a wet, yellow dropping on the back of his neck. "I come with news and this bone-brained blubber mound tries to eat me!"

"What can you tell us?" Ingavar said, tiny glaciers of snow falling off him as he stood.

"That you're walking in circles for one thing, shaman."

So it was true. Avrel glanced respectfully at Kailar. The fighting bear had cannoned off a shoulder of ice and was nursing one paw with loose round movements, all the while training his eye on the bird.

"I've seen it," Gwilanna said, spiralling around Ingavar. "I landed on the place where the power lines meet. I felt its power. It's where she got the icefire from, isn't it?"

"She—?" began Avrel.

Ingavar stayed the question with a glance.

"It was Bergstrom who gave it to her, wasn't it?" said the bird, zooming over Avrel and making him duck. "Why? Why Elizabeth Pennykettle? I could have done anything with it. I—"

"You will lead us there under my command," said Ingavar, cutting her off with a roar that seemed to make the sky jump.

In defiance, Gwilanna soared even higher. "And what's to stop me flying away, shaman?"

"Your vanity," he said. "When would Gwilanna, sibyl of the ages, ever miss the opportunity to witness the

228

release of The Fire Eternal?"

The bird circled them one more time, then came swooping down to land again on Ingavar's back. She poked her beak into his small hooped ear. "All right, I'll help, but on three conditions. You keep that brute of Ragnar away from me, you tell me what you plan to do with the fire and, more importantly, you tell me how you came to *be* here?"

Ingavar gave a solemn nod.

"Good. In that case, you need to turn left."

Ingavar signalled to the bears to walk.

"That's better," said Gwilanna, bobbing up and down to the rhythm of his stride. "It's about time I was given some respect. *Caark!* Well, whenever you're ready, *David*. I think it's time you talked . . ."

In the days of the Premen

"Let's begin," said Ingavar, in a bear's voice, "by reviewing what happened to you, sibyl. You were incarcerated, alive, in a block of ice. Your auma was put into perpetual stasis. Why don't you tell Avrel how that came about?"

"I don't parley with *bears*," she squawked.

With a growl that made her feet vibrate, Ingavar said, "If I were you, I'd keep your insults down. Unless you want Kailar over here again?"

The fighting bear was eyeing them suspiciously.

"Animal," Gwilanna caarked (quietly) at him.

He squinted back at her with murder in his eyes and she was grateful when the wind seemed to take her side and draw its cold, icy curtain between them. Shuddering, she looked away to her left, where Avrel was padding along, nudging closer. "Your Teller is eavesdropping, anyway – as usual."

"Everything you say, you say to both of us," said Ingavar. "Tell him a story, sibyl. He's eager to learn. Tell him what you saw on the day you were imprisoned."

"I saw the Tooth of Ragnar come down," she said, and for the first time there was sorrow in her croaking voice.

"A whole island, the last resting place of Gawain, destroyed. The dragon was broken, sent to the ocean bed in lumps of stone. And I could do *nothing* but watch from that ice block."

"How were you put there?" Avrel asked.

"You wouldn't understand," Gwilanna said meanly.

"Try him," said Ingavar, glancing at his Teller with the same intensity he had used when refusing to answer the raven's questions a few days earlier. Avrel saw the blue eye shimmer like a star and felt as if his mind had widened slightly for it.

Gwilanna grizzled and cocked her wings. Then, in a voice so patronising that even Avrel was tempted to swipe off her head, she said, "Oh, very well. I was attacked by a life form called the Fain. It took away my powers and fused me with the ice. There, Teller, what do you make of that?"

Avrel narrowed his gaze.

"See!" the raven taunted him. "He hasn't got a clue. Why don't you run away and build a den, furball? This is way out of your—"

"Lorel knew them," Avrel muttered.

"What?" Gwilanna snorted, suddenly thrown.

"He encountered them, the Fain. But the memory isn't clear."

"That's impossible!" Gwilanna almost hooted. "The Fain wouldn't trouble themselves with low-vibrational ice-shovelers like you."

As if to call a truce, the wind swept down in a shallow hard-edged front from the north. Avrel bowed his head and swerved away a little. On Ingavar's back, Gwilanna flapped giddily to keep herself upright.

"You're wrong," Ingavar told her, bluntly. "Avrel's ancestor, Lorel, was the first of the Tellers, whose ability to remember was inherited from the Fain. It wasn't just humans the Fain explored, Gwilanna. They entered all organic life."

Avrel twitched his ears and felt unusually cold. He gave his supple, round shoulders a shake. "Entered? What *are* these creatures?"

Ingavar raised his snout to the wind. As he breathed in he seemed to calm the air around him. For a moment or two, time slowed down and every snowflake that fell across Avrel's snout appeared to him in its unique perfection. As the crystals turned in their spellbinding orbits, Ingavar's voice seemed to sparkle off their points. "There are many forms of life in the universe, Avrel. Some of them exist in planes of reality that are difficult to comprehend. The race of beings called the Fain function in the realm of thought and all that thought encompasses: dreams, imaginings, memories, consciousness. They have no physical body, but may inhabit any material form they choose. They can alter your mind in many skilful ways and make you perceive them in any way that you imagine. They came to this planet at the dawn of its evolution, seeking a particular geological environment and an organism that might be adapted to their needs."

"It wasn't bears," sneered Gwilanna.

"They chose men," said Ingavar. "Human bipeds, already questioning their sense of self-awareness and the nature of their thoughts. The Fain selected individuals they considered to be of interest and joined with them by a process called commingling. This was, in part, a beneficial development. The Fain quickly enhanced their hosts, making them see ways that they might progress, guiding them in the creation of tools and the willingness for invention. These commingled hybrids called themselves the Premen, to set themselves apart from uncommingled humans. The Premen ruled the planet as bears now rule the ice."

Avrel nodded gently as he took these words in. His clever brown eyes were almost on fire. "Why did they come here? What *were* their needs?"

"To breed dragons, of course," Gwilanna said

unkindly, looking back through a distant window of her mind. "This rock was the perfect place for them. Oxygen, water, clay. Fire at its core. There was nowhere in the universe anything like it."

"But why dragons?" Avrel pressed. "What is their significance to the Fain creatures?"

"Oh for pity's sake, stop asking 'why?'!" Gwilanna caarked. "He's like a child! He's making my feathers curl. Can't we spare the history lesson and just get on?" She raked a claw down Ingavar's neck. "I want to know how *you* became involved with the Fain."

"Scratch me again and I'll chew off your head and spit it far into the ocean," said Ingavar. He exchanged another glance with his Teller. "The Fain consider dragons to be their perfect hosts, Avrel. In time, you will come to learn why. For now, be content just to gather what you can from this bird and her ramblings. She's going to improve your memories of the Fain. She is a survivor of their time on this Earth, but she is hiding a truth from you."

"What are you talking about now?" she jabbered.

Ingavar looked at his Teller again. "The Fain are masters of creation, Avrel. They can use their powers in many profound ways. But for them to know themselves completely, they need to experience creation in a physical state."

"What he's trying to tell you," Gwilanna said, yawning, "is that they wanted to know what it felt like to *mate*."

"That is correct," Ingavar said gruffly. "Some Premen took each other as partners, and some chose uncommingled humans. Gwilanna is the product of the latter cross." He felt her coming to the boil and dipped his head as she screamed:

"I am not! I am NOT!"

But Ingavar set himself squarely and said, "Spare my ears, sibyl. I can read you with ease. You had a human father and a Premen mother. She was highly-attuned, on the brink of being illumined to a dragon called Ghislaine. She gave you the longevity and magicks you possess, and he—"

"Was a brute! An animal!" she screeched.

"Who cared for you when the Fain departed this planet."

"He slayed dragons! He helped hunt them down!"

"Driven by envy and fear," said Ingavar.

"My mother was a *Pri:magon*, a priestess," she snarled. "If they had allowed her to live—"

"She would have been an outcast. Just like you were in Guinevere's time. A cave dweller. A hermit, brewing herbs."

235

Avrel's ears by now had almost doubled in size. So much knowledge. So much history, in and around and between the words. As the argument paused, he considered his options. There was too much in this dialogue to comprehend now, so he posed the most pertinent question he could: "Lord, why did the Fain withdraw?" He looked around him as though to be sure that they had. He saw glimpses of the ghost world again in the greyness and wondered, briefly, if death was just another place to be.

Ingavar blew a great snort of air. "For three generations, the Fain remained commingled to their human hosts. More and more children were born to the Premen. But what the Fain did not realise, until it was too late, was that a strange kind of fusion was taking place. The offspring of the Premen could not be easily uncommingled; their minds were holding permanent traces of the Fain. What's more, they'd been ignited with a lust for power and the cleverness to attain it. Soon there was chaos. Battles for supremacy. The situation escalated out of control. The Fain masters, knowing there was no hope of reversing the aggression, abandoned their breeding programme, destroyed any Premen child they considered too advanced—"

"One of them being my mother," snapped Gwilanna.

"—and returned to their home world, a time dimension called Ki:mera. But the portal they opened, the fire star they created to make the journey, was raised to a frequency only wide enough for them to pass through and not the dragons they had bred. The dragon colonies were left behind, for fear that their auma had been corrupted. And it was them, not their masters, who were left to fight a war of confusion and suspicion with the human race."

"I have a memory," Avrel interjected suddenly, as though the sun had just breached a horizon in his head, "of a dragon involved in a battle. This is recent, just four or five winters ago. It comes from the memories of a female bear who was present when the Tooth of Ragnar was destroyed. She was sent there by Thoran to protect a human girl."

"Girl?" coughed Gwilanna, trying not to make her thoughts (or her guilt) transparent. But it was clear to her when Ingavar spoke again that he knew she had abducted Lucy Pennykettle and attempted, unsuccessfully, to use the girl to raise the sacred dragon, Gawain, from the dead, from his resting place in stone on the summit of the island.

"She's alive," he said. "Little thanks to you."

"I see it flying, like a giant bird," Avrel said, his eyes

filling up with new-found wonder. "Flames are flowing like water from its mouth. It . . ." He stopped walking, as if a wall of ice had hit him, causing Ingavar to pause as well. "It . . . burned you," he said, looking fearfully into the eyes of his Nanukapik.

"Not Ingavar," Ingavar said to him calmly. "The young dragon you remember is called Grockle. Grockle raged at the Fain that had entered this body; the invader had been sent here with orders to kill him."

"Did he survive?" asked Gwilanna.

"Yes," said Ingavar.

Avrel swiped a paw in confusion. "But . . . I don't understand. If these beings, the Fain, first came to this world to breed dragons why would they send an agent to destroy one?"

"For once, a good question," Gwilanna admitted.

"And one you must have asked yourself many times as you sat in your ice block counting stars," said Ingavar. He gave a grunt of approval for his Teller's intelligence. "Listen carefully, both of you. What I have to say next will have a bearing on the outcome of our journey. The Fain disrupted the human race. But in doing so, they also disrupted themselves. The commingling process worked both ways. When the human trait of aggression was introduced into the Premen, a new division of the

238

Fain began to evolve and ultimately break away, a darker breed who call themselves the Ix."

"*What?*" said Gwilanna, as though the idea was not only impossible but absurd.

Ingavar raised his head. "Things are not what they were, sibyl. It was an Ix:risor who came to slay Grockle. An assassin. One of the deadliest agents of the new order. Grockle was fortunate to survive, and so were you. The Ix want control of the realm of dark matter, the matrix of the universe which nurtures all creation. It's not a physical battle, but a war of wills. A conflict of moods. A push and pull of shadows. It has been in process for centuries, but only now is it coming to a climax. And this Earth, this one-time place of dragons, is being drawn into it again."

"But why was this . . . Grockle a threat?" pressed Avrel.

"The Ix are meeting resistance," said Ingavar, "not only from natural Fain, but human-Premen descendants who are beginning to understand the harmonics of the universe and the relationship between consciousness, creativity and time. If any living human had been able to achieve what the Fain call 'pure illumination' to a dragon, the Ix might have been swept aside. Grockle was a serious threat. They came for him and failed. He escaped through a fire star opened by the Fain. Grockle is a blessed gift to Ki:mera, but he is young and not yet developed enough to aid the Fain's cause – but they will prepare him for the conflict and the Ix know this. So they have adopted a different tactic. They plan to begin their own dragon culture."

"And? What's wrong with that?" said Gwilanna.

"The beings they will make are anti-dragons; their spark will be created from dark fire."

Avrel glanced at the raven, expecting her to comment. But her shape was now as rigid as ice. And though it was only flecks of snow spotting her feathers, she appeared almost pale.

"That . . . can't . . . happen," she said in gulps.

"What does it mean?" the Teller asked anxiously.

Gwilanna hurled the phrase back at him in her harshest tongue. "What does it *mean*? It means everything of meaning will be meaningless, you idiot. A dragon born of dark fire would be a monster. Imagine a world where every negative thought came true. That's what you'd get if you were illumined to it. How are they doing this?" she snapped at Ingavar.

"They're probing," he said, "but their source is hidden. They're almost certainly here on the Earth already."

"Probing?" queried Avrel,

"Sending out thought waves," Gwilanna said

impatiently, tutting as best she could at his ignorance. "To humans?"

"To their collective consciousness, mining it for negative energy."

Gwilanna squeezed her claws deep into the ice. "They'd never do it," she muttered. "Even if they killed every human on this planet and left some pathetic specimen to mourn for them, they couldn't condense enough negative energy to make one pure burst of dark fire."

"The Ix are not planning to kill anyone," said Ingavar. "Their methods are much more subtle. They intend . . ." But here he paused. The others followed his gaze and saw Kailar pounding towards them through the layers of the storm. The eye of Gawain was thumping hard against his chest.

"What is it?" said Avrel, as taut as a cat.

"A creature," panted Kailar, "unlike anything I know."

"Where?" hissed Gwilanna, peering into the mist. And then she saw it. A huge grey beast with long woollen fur and tusks that protruded from its head like hooks. "An *elephant?*" she squawked.

"Not quite," said Ingavar. He turned to his Teller. "Look closely, Avrel. This is a creature from the time of the Premen. It's called a mammoth."

The road to Blackburn

Tam Farrell's car rattled. Somewhere inside the glove compartment perhaps? Or maybe the rear view mirror wasn't fixed? Or there was a tiny screw or a random coin or an old sweet wrapper trapped inside the air vents? It was driving Lucy crazy. Making her fidget. And the motorway seemed to be never-ever-ending. And the rain seemed to be so non-stopping, the drops hammering on the car like kamikaze sparrows. She pushed a finger into a hole in her jeans. For the past ten minutes she had chewed her lip and promised herself she wasn't going to say this, because she'd done so as a girl on journeys to the coast and her mum had always teased her for it, but sometimes, well, you just needed to know. Looking straight ahead at the arrow-grey road through the hypnotic wipers beating triple time she said, "Are we nearly there yet?"

Tam touched his satellite navigation screen. "We're just passing Birmingham."

"Meaning?" Her hands flowered with four years of pure teen spirit.

"111.9 miles to go."

Lucy slumped down and sighed. She pressed her

knees together and let her feet explore either side of the foot well. "I'm bored. Can't we have some music on?"

Tam reached for the radio dial. Stations crackled in and out of the speakers. Pop. Country. Drama. Sports. He left it on News.

"This isn't music," Lucy griped.

"Aerial's bent. This is the only good station I can get. Besides, it might be useful – for weather updates."

"Erm, it's like . . . raining."

"Go to sleep," he said. "I'll wake you when we're close."

"Excuse me? I'm not a little girl," she griped. "Anyway, you're the one who's half asleep. Why are you so quiet? Someone throw a blanket over your cage or what?"

"I've been thinking."

"What about?"

"Everything," he said, giving nothing away. Then: "What's that around your neck?"

"My collar, of course."

He glared sideways at her.

"All right. It's a charm. It protects me from evil journalists!" She pulled it into view, a simple twist of hairs, one red, one cream.

"That your hair, the red?"

243

She bobbled her head. "Sort of—" No. Wait. How could she possibly explain it was really a lock of hair from her ancestor's grave on the Tooth of Ragnar? She thought briefly about the spirited adventuress, the real Gwendolen whom Lucy's dragon was lovingly named after. No. She wasn't going to tease him with any of that. But the devil in her couldn't resist saying, "The cream bit comes from a polar bear."

He seemed to find that funny.

"I mean it," she said. "There are things about me you'd *never* believe."

He nodded and adjusted his rear view mirror. "Like the dragon, you mean?" Gwendolen was riding on the parcel shelf, staring through the back window like a nodding dog. "She's real, isn't she?"

"Yeah, right," Lucy said and folded her arms.

Without warning, Tam yanked on the steering wheel, lurching the car into another lane.

"Hey!" Lucy shouted, slamming her hands against the dash. The car accelerated past a truck, through the blinding wash of its spray. As soon as they were clear Tam switched lanes again, just as jerkily as the first manoeuvre.

"What are you doing?" Lucy squealed. "You'll kill us, you nut!"

"Amazing," he said. "She must move at the speed of light. I can't see her doing it, but she readjusts her position so she doesn't fall over." He wobbled the car again. "No clunk of clay, look."

Lucy threw a backhander, which caught his upper arm. "Stop *doing* that! You're making me heave!"

He glanced sideways again, eating her up with his handsome gaze. "You don't get on with Zanna, do you? You think she's inferior to you and your mother. In fact, you're angry with her for all sorts of reasons. David: ok, that's understandable. But something about losing an isoscele . . . what's that?"

"It's none of your business."

"You made it my business. You gave me the memories – or rather your 'special' dragon did." He glanced at Gwendolen again. He could swear her ears had tipped back and stretched. "Who's Guinevere?"

Lucy groaned and banged back into her seat. "Oh, this was *so* not a good idea."

Tam switched lanes again, finding an open stretch of road to cruise. "Look, Lucy, let's cut a deal. If you want me to help you, you'll have to meet me at least halfway."

She rolled her head and stared at the waterlogged fields.

"Alternatively, I can pull off at the next junction and take us straight home?"

"Yeah, but then you won't have your *story*, will you?"

"And you won't know for sure about David."

"I lived with him!" she said, twisting upright. "How can you think he wasn't real? He was our lodger. I've got pictures of him. He ate with us. He . . . he . . . went to our toilet! He wrote me a story for my birthday – and signed it!"

"*Snigger*. I know." His eyes flicked up, searching, retrieving. "You always read a bit at bedtime before you say your prayers."

"How did you . . . ? Oh, this is so embarrassing," Lucy said. "You shouldn't be— hang on, what else do you . . . remember?"

"It doesn't matter. Let's concentrate on David, shall we?"

Lucy glared at him darkly.

"Really, you don't want to go here," he warned her, trying to catch an announcement on the radio. Something about a disaster bulletin . . . He fiddled for the volume, only to get a slap on the arm.

"Tell me," she said.

"Shush, I want to hear this. It sounds important."

She slapped him again. "Tell me, or—"

"I'm too old for you," he snapped.

A horn blared. Tam cursed and set his eyes back on the road. When he looked again at Lucy, her mouth was open. "I'm twenty-five," he said. "You're a good-looking kid but I live with a girl and . . . well, that's it. I'm with someone. Period."

Lucy's face turned the colour of a cherry. "I so do *not* fancy you!"

"Good. Well, that's cleared that one up, hasn't it? Now— oh no, what's this?"

Lucy looked up to see a string of red brake lights curling into the distance. Great. A hold-up. That was all she needed. Her enthusiasm for this quest was slowing down as quickly as the engine's revs.

"Obstruction," muttered Tam, reading an announcement on an overhead gantry. He joined the stream of traffic snaking into two lanes. The car rolled to a virtual halt.

"How long will we have to wait?" asked Lucy. Suddenly, everything seemed so grim, stuck in this fish tank drenched in rain, hemmed in by fumes and creeping metal. Her bedroom at home was like a five star hotel by comparison.

"Let's put it this way," Tam muttered anxiously. "Now is not a good time to say you want the bathroom."

"Oh, you're sooo funny. I can't imagine why any girl wouldn't fancy you."

"Let it drop," he said, setting the screen vents to blow warm air and effectively drowning out the radio again, "or I'll remind you – in graphic detail – of what you were thinking when I walked into the shop. Do you want to phone your mother?"

"No," she said pointedly, hiding her face.

"If we're held up too long we'll have to stay over."

"What?" she said, colour draining from her cheeks. "I'm not staying anywhere with you!"

"My aunt lives near Blackburn. She's got four rooms."

Lucy was speechless.

"We're not turning back."

"Excuse me? I think that would be kidnapping, actually."

"I'll take my chances," he said. "I haven't come all this way not to get some background on your mystery lodger."

"You said you weren't bothered!"

"I've changed my mind."

"So you admit he existed? Fine, take me home."

The car shunted forwards another few yards. "I want to find his parents, Luce, and so do you."

"It's Lucy," she snarled, putting her feet against the dash.

"Lucy," he repeated, in a softer tone. "Look, I'm not saying you didn't know the guy. It's just a little strange that I can't trace any details of him back beyond the college. It's almost as if he popped up out of nowhere, did a quick geography course, saved your squirrel, then disappeared again. For the sake of my professional integrity I need to nail this down. And if I don't," he added before she jumped up again, "someone else will. The longer you go on wrapping David up, the more people are going to come snooping. So why don't you just ease off and trust me? Is it true, for instance, that he died in the Arctic?"

Lucy chewed an imaginary piece of gum.

"I can't find the details in these memories you gave me but I can feel your sorrow. You cried for weeks and planted a yellow rose bush in the garden for him, didn't you? You had a ceremony and you held hands with Zanna. She was still pregnant at the time. Come on, what really happened up there, Lucy?"

"He *drowned*, trying to save me. I don't want to talk about it."

"Save you? Save you from what? How come you were there at all? You must have only been about eleven at the time. What was a kid from the middle of suburbia doing in a killer wasteland like the Arctic?"

"I can't tell you," she said, making claws of her fingers, "and you wouldn't understand if I did. Anyway, my mum would go totally mad – and you'll get properly zapped if Mum's on the case."

"Then why did you ever bother to 'unzap' me? Why hitch a lift to Blackburn? Why mail me in the first place? What is it you want, Lucy?"

"I want people to know about David," she said, tears springing from her flashing green eyes. "Polar bears are dying and the ice is melting and people like you don't even care."

Tam took a hand off the wheel to gesticulate. "All right, if you're going to generalise, let's at least set the record straight. It's people like me who try to present a balanced picture. You say polar bear numbers are dwindling? Yes, they are – in certain parts of the Arctic, like Hudson Bay. But in some territories, their numbers are actually *increasing*. That doesn't mean we should ignore the problem areas, but likewise, they shouldn't be used as the only barometer of what's happening up there. The same is true for the whole global warming debate. I admire people like David who stick their necks out and try to bring the issues to people's awareness, but that doesn't mean I close myself off to the scientists who argue the other side of the story. You know what the biggest trouble is from all this?"

"Erm, boredom?" Lucy suggested, who hated being lectured.

"Disinformation."

She wriggled her nose. "What?"

"While the jury's out, the politicians will have a field day. They can spin the debate whichever way they choose. That's what's known as power, Lucy. When the populace is confused, our leaders are well and truly in command."

Lucy rolled her eyes. Politics as well, now. This guy was fast in need of a tedium bypass. "I don't care about *politicians*."

"Well you ought to," he said, as if she'd just had her wrist slapped. "If you want to make David a hero you'll have to aim for the heart and find something that will strike a planet-wide chord. And that has to be done in a political sphere."

Lucy yawned.

"Want to hear what I think?"

"Do I have a choice?"

"No. But I could always leave you by the roadside with a sign around your neck saying 'annoying, arrogant, naive little girl. Please give me a home.'"

"Very funny," she said, squirming uncomfortably.

He was quiet for a moment, driving, so she said, "Well? What, then? What would you do?"

He braked again. "Remember that news story a few months back about the polar bear cub born in a zoo in Europe?"

"'Course I do. They were going to kill it."

"Yes. You know what stopped them? Public sympathy. I read an article about that bear. The most telling line in it was a quote from its keeper. 'The thing that's caught people's imagination,' he said, 'is that he – the cub – nearly died.' *Nearly died.* Transfer that feeling en masse to the Arctic and you have your quick-fix solution to global warming: you lobby the UN Environmental Agency to persuade the big industrial nations to get polar bears listed as an endangered species, using cute cub as the perfect icon. Once that motion goes through, the powers that be will be forced to protect the polar bear's habitat. That means they will have to examine what's causing the reduction of the Arctic ice cap and come clean about what they know. In other words, either they have to admit that there is a direct correlation between the amount of carbon dioxide in the atmosphere and the degree of Arctic meltdown so that they're forced to introduce strict laws to cut CO_2 emissions or they establish once and for all that it's a natural phenomenon and they pour more resources into helping the bears that are threatened. It wouldn't be perfect or painless, but it would be a start. David knew this when he wrote *White Fire*. But his book, by itself, won't motivate people to act soon enough. It's too subtle. What you need is a media crusade. That's how I can help."

"So . . . will you?" Lucy's tone now was meek. "Even after what Zanna did?"

Tam pushed a hand inside his shirt. The skin on his left side was tingling again, as it had been on and off for most of the day. His mind flashed back to Zanna's arm, coming down like a branding iron across his heart. *This is the mark of Oomara.* The first three fingers of his hand gave a twitch and he felt something stirring, as if he had connected with a distant force. Some kind of whispered chant in his head. Some kind of darkness flowing through his synapses. He shook it away and planted both hands on the steering wheel. "I can make a champion of David for you, but he's not exactly 'A' list material. I'd need an angle. Something that will take the world by storm and make people really sit up and listen."

"Like . . . ?"

"Like what's his connection to dragons, for instance?"

Lucy buried her face in her hands.

"Come on," Tam pressed. "Anything bizarre makes a real difference. Dragons are wired into the human consciousness. If people thought David could bring clay to life he'd be—"

"He couldn't," she cut in. "He's not like us!"

"Then let's talk about 'us'. You and your mum. Or . . ." He felt the stirring again. "Gawain, is it?"

"No!" Lucy shouted. "No! No! N—!"

"Wo-a!" Tam cried and suddenly pumped the brakes.

Despite the low speed the car slewed a little and Lucy gave out a little yelp. "Is that a tree?" she gasped, rubbing at the windscreen.

Just ahead, behind a cordon of revolving yellow lights, lay the severed trunk of a very large tree. At its broken end the splintered spikes of wood stood out like clean white flames, as though it were a rocket frozen on blast off. It was spread across the bottom third of the embankment reaching out into the first two lanes of the motorway. Men in orange waterproofs were waving cars past, guiding them through a coned-off region, fresh with the dust of cracked and flattened wood. A small van was on the shoulder with two police vehicles. It had been half-crushed.

Tam glanced across to the opposite carriageway.

The traffic there was flowing but had been slowed down by accident-watchers and debris spilled far across the road. In the distance, on the crest of a long stretched hill he could see a radio mast. It was swaying. Not much, but enough to suggest that the wind strength was greater than he'd first imagined.

He switched off the vents. The radio bulletin filled the space. Among the first words it spoke were '. . . *tsunami, in the Pacific* . . .'

"A tsunami?" said Lucy, vaguely concerned. She felt the rainstorm crashing in around her and shuddered.

Tam turned up the volume a little, which only seemed to increase the disaster quotient. In what a reporter was calling 'The Day The Weather Went Mad', there were stories of tornados on the east coast of England, hailstones the size of golf balls in France, and volcanic disturbances in Guatemala and the Aleutian Islands.

Perhaps the most bizarre thing of all, the broadcaster continued, *are the reports we're receiving of polar bears moving north in great numbers. They seem to be migrating, en masse, towards the ice cap. Some even throwing themselves into the ocean and swimming – to what must surely be a certain death. Scientists here in Stavanger are baffled, though they say the phenomenon is not completely* new. A year ago when the population of bears on certain areas of the Svalbard archipelago diminished in number it was discovered, from data collected on animals already collared with radio tracking devices, that they were relocating further north. But that was a Sunday constitutional in comparison to this. Scientists have commented that in human terms, this is nothing short of a pilgrimage. Our guide here joked, "Perhaps they were on their way to the conference and got lost?" One senses that a small element of these scientists wishes it were true. For it's clear that these great icons of the Arctic have been attracted by something – the question is, what?

"Bears again," said Lucy, like a frightened little girl.

"Hmm, I rest my case," said Tam, hiding his concern in his softly-spoken accent. "Have a sleep. This could be quite a drive." He put his foot down and the car sped away, rocking now and then as a gust of wind caught it.

And all the while the radio whistled and the news poured out in broken patter. Eventually, Lucy could take no more and silenced it with a petulant prod. She laid her head on her shoulder and closed her eyes. In her pocket, she felt her phone vibrate. The sixth time it had happened since she'd left the house. She glanced at it quickly. A message from Zanna. She must be one guilt-ridden witch by now. Tough. No way was Lucy going to read it. She switched the phone off but kept her hand tight around it. Home in her fist, just a button press away. But Tam was right, there was no turning back.

When she woke, a couple of hours or so later, the wind had subsided and the rain had filled out into a moderate snowfall. She rubbed the misted passenger window. They were in a suburban housing area, not unlike Wayward Crescent, though the houses here were smaller and the trees were few. Each dwelling was like a little boxed clone of the next.

"Perfect timing," said Tam. He tapped the sat nav. "According to this, Thoushall Road should be first on the left."

"I need the bathroom," said Lucy.

"Well, maybe you can go at David's house," he said, chewing a little cynicism off his lip.

David's house. The sign for Thoushall Road was looming closer, screwed to a fence just twenty yards ahead. Lucy held herself, nervously, as Tam took the corner. What would they be like, David's mum and dad? Would they be here at all? Maybe he hadn't even lived with his parents, but had lodged with someone else before coming to the Crescent? Some other Lucy, with her own injured squirrel running circles in the garden?

257

She shuddered and let the window glide open, checking the house numbers as they rolled past. They were in the high thirties.

"Far end," said Tam. "It's number 4 we want, yes?"

Lucy nodded. "You will come up to the door with me, won't you?"

He took a breath and said, "Get ready with the letter."

Lucy unzipped her bag, still counting the houses. 10. Golden Labrador chewing on a bone, caravan taking up too much space. 8. Neat and tidy, nothing special, crazy paving and a pretty box hedge. 6. An England soccer flag in an upstairs window. 2. A broken gate and a wallpapered dustbin, motorcycle covered over on the drive.

10, 8, 6 . . . 2

"But . . . where is it?" she gasped.

Tam glanced across the road to be doubly certain that the numbers there were definitely odd, then reversed the car and parked between the houses numbered 6 and 2. "I don't believe this," he said.

But it was plain to see – or not to see – like a gap in a row of teeth.

There was no number 4, Thoushall Road, Blackburn.

Dandelion alley

Instead, there was a muddy strip of earth, no more than three metres wide. It was bedded with deep-trodden cobbled bricks, and where seeds hadn't fallen on the stony ground, clusters of wild dandelions grew.

Lucy stepped out of the car in a daze. And then, as if one shock wasn't enough, across the road another car door opened and a voice said, "Forget it. You're wasting your time."

Lucy jumped back as if she'd seen a ghost. "Hhh! What are *you* doing here?"

Zanna came flowing towards her, dressed in a calf-length black velvet coat. "You forgot to take your toothbrush. So being the good and caring person that I am, I drove at breakneck speed up the motorway to make sure you'd always be popular in Blackburn."

"B-but . . . ?"

"Save the lip-flapping, Lucy. You weren't too smart, were you? It didn't take us long to work it out. First you ask your mum about David's parents, then you disappear the next day with his letter. I must admit we weren't expecting an accomplice." She glared at Tam, who was

259

watching this over the roof of his car. "How did you revive him?"

"She used her dragon," he said, noticing the flash of fear in Zanna's dark eyes. He pointed at Gwendolen, who was still acting solid. "Memory implants. Very impressive."

The spotlight fell again on Lucy.

"He knows stuff," she gulped. "Things he shouldn't."

"Your daughter's very pretty," Tam complimented Zanna.

"*You*—"

"And now here we are," he added quickly, falling back against his car and speaking up into the cloud-heavy sky, "on the trail of your enigmatic boyfriend, who sends letters from an address that doesn't exist."

"He must have written it down wrong," Lucy said frantically. "It must have been 14 or 49 or—"

"I've checked," said Zanna, cutting her dead. "I've been up and down the road. No one's heard of David. And the families either side of the gap have lived there for ages. As far as they know there's never been a number 4."

"So he's fooled us," said Tam. "Or covered his tracks. Now, why would Saint David do a thing like that?"

"Shut up," said Lucy. "David was good! There must be

a house here. It must be round the back." She slammed the car door and stormed off to investigate.

"Lucy, I've looked," Zanna shouted after her. "It's just allotments and waste ground. Get into my car, please, I'm taking you home. Lucy? Lu-cy?! Oh!" She gave up and flipped her mobile open. As she leaned her head into it, she glared at Tam.

"Allotments," he said, jiggling coins in his pocket. "Maybe he was born under a mulberry bush? Or perhaps he went AWOL on a boy scout mission, erected a tent in the corner of a cabbage patch and painted a great big '4' on the flap?"

"Why don't you crawl back into your hole, Farrell?"

"Face it," he said to her, not unkindly. "There's something wrong here. We should—"

But she had spun away by then to speak into her phone. "Hi, Liz, it's me. I've got her. Yeah. No, quite safe. She arrived a few minutes ago. No, with Tam. Not exactly. It's all a bit . . . well, it's one for Arthur's scrapbook. I'll tell you when we're home. What? Can't hear you. It's snowing a bit up here, I'm losing my signal . . ."

All the while she was speaking, Zanna was walking towards the gap, her conversation fading into the distance. She disappeared shouting Lucy's name. Tam at last saw his chance. Climbing into the rear of his car he took Gwendolen off the rear shelf. He turned her, shook her, clinked her with a fingernail, tried unsuccessfully to wiggle her tail, had an embarrassed go at tickling her feet, even blew (very warily) into her nostrils. Nothing. Nothing would make her move. Then for some reason he opened his shirt and put his hand on the invisible scars of Oomara. *Throw her*, said his thoughts. *Throw her onto the road. If she's real, she'll save herself. That's the test.*

A devil on his shoulder, or an Inuit ghost? The idea was wicked and wrong – but it excited him. Animated clay. Hold the front page. The physics of the universe entirely rewritten. The complete paranormal, here in his hand. Base elements turning to literary gold.

Throw her.

But something stopped him. A jingle of music – more like a chime. The weirdest ring tone he had ever heard. The sound was somewhere in the ether of the car. He could almost scent the notes as well as hear them. His chest itched again. This time he ignored it. Confused, he laid Gwendolen down and slipped his hand along the side of the passenger seat. Double gold! Lucy's mobile phone, which must have fallen from her pocket while she was sleeping. He flipped it open. Standard issue phone but . . . no caller's name on the display. Stranger still, no number. Instead, a single dot of light was strobing back and forth, leaving a fading grille across the screen. Tam flexed his toes. He could make no sense of what he was seeing, yet he did not feel that the phone was malfunctioning, just receiving in a different kind of way. He touched the 'yes' button. The screen lit up in a pulse of violet. At the same time, he heard Zanna's voice again and saw she was returning with a recalcitrant Lucy. In a flurry of panic he hammered the keys, trying to shut the signal off. But by now the screen was bulging with light, an ectoplasmic stream, weaving its way like a ribbon through the window. Too stunned to move, he watched it wrap around the falling snowflakes and draw hundreds of them down, compacting them into . . . He gasped and let the phone fall from his hand. There was a grey squirrel on the pavement. A grey squirrel, *conjured from snow*. In a flash, it turned and hopped towards Lucy. It paused briefly by her feet then hurried on past. She squealed in delight and began to give chase. Tam heard Zanna shout, "Lucy, come back here!" A sudden rush of air brushed the shell of his ear. When he looked again, Gwendolen was not on the seat.

Even though she had not plugged into the phone, Gwendolen could sense it was operating at a frequency well outside the range of any cellular network. It wasn't sending words or any other form of binary. It was sending *thoughts*.

She shot past Zanna and landed on a fence post right beside Lucy just as the squirrel turned and chirruped. It was sitting among the dandelions, halfway down the path.

Gwendolen let out an urgent *hrrr*, a warning to Lucy that she ought to turn back.

"But it's a squirrel," Lucy whispered and took a step forward.

And in a blinding flash of light she completely disappeared.

She came round on the floor of a darkened room. A room chilled by age and constant neglect. The rounded stone walls were mossy with damp. The only source of light was from a partially-eclipsed and rust-coloured moon, leaking in through a high slit window. Flakes of snow were puffing in under the lintel.

Lucy sat up rubbing her arms. "Hello?" she called. Her voice rang with the sharpness of a winter frost.

"Welcome," said a voice.

She squealed and scrabbled round.

In a chair behind her was a hooded figure. His

calves were bare. There were sandals on his feet. He appeared to have a mobile phone in his hand. His thumb moved across it. A small square of violet faded into the darkness.

"Who are you?" she said. "What am I doing here? W-where's Zanna? Where's Tam?"

"We *have* met," said the figure. "In . . . a previous existence."

Previous existence?

"Help!" Lucy shouted and jumped to her feet. "Help me, someone! Anyone? Help!"

"You are in no danger," the figure said, as if he was both fascinated and amused by her behaviour. "Look at me. You know me." He pushed back his hood.

"Brother Bernard!" she gasped, she fell flat against the wall. "How . . . ?"

"You are in a folly on Farlowe Island," he said, with a slight uncertain stutter in his voice, as though the words were correct but he couldn't quite justify the movement of his lips.

"But how did I get here? I was chasing a squirrel and—"

"You were probing, child. Reaching out in your mind . . . and heart. You were looking for David."

"Is he here?" She ran forward and dropped to her knees.

Brother Bernard clamped her hands in his. "Everyone is seeking David, child. Now, stand. You must come with me."

Lucy shook her head. There was something unnatural about the monk's face. And his palms felt cold and scaly, like a lizard's. "No, send me back."

"That won't be possible."

"Send me back!" Lucy shouted, and opened her lungs to their deafening maximum, but with a movement of his finger the monk put her back to sleep. And the last thing that came to her before she slumped was the reason for the strangeness in his face. He possessed all the features of the man she remembered, right down to the threaded veins in his cheeks and the bushy eyebrows and the small round mouth. He was Brother Bernard, but for one difference. There was no colour in his eyes.

The irises were black.

A *gift from home*

"How do we fight it?" Kailar said, the afterburn of running still dripping from his mouth. He looked back over his shoulder. The mammoth stood before them, as calmly as a cloud.

Gwilanna stretched her wings and took to the sky. "With any luck it will stamp you to pulp. The real question is, what's it doing here, shaman?"

"I don't know," said Ingavar, who seemed more fascinated by it than afraid.

The mammoth lifted its trunk and released a sharp bellow from the flap of its mouth.

"We should split up," panted Kailar, "attack from three sides."

"It doesn't look harmful," Avrel said, watching ghosts that had once come freely to him layer themselves all around the mammoth's body. They were gliding over its shaggy contours as though to welcome it into their midst. He saw foxes weaving round the pillars of its legs, sea birds in a spectral halo above it, seals in a mirage of pack ice below.

"What's it doing?" caarked Gwilanna, sweeping in figures of eight overhead. "Has it come for the eye or not?"

Ingavar looked at the spirits in the sky. Their mood was good. He took a slow pace forward.

"Here, guard this," Kailar whispered to Avrel. He bent his head and let the eye of Gawain slip off his neck. It landed with a ringing thud. Several lines of blue-white fire radiated out from the site of impact, all of them petering out within a few seconds and drawing back, tidally, into the eye.

"But—?"

"Don't argue," Kailar hissed. "You saw what happened with those ravens. Why should this be any different?" He nudged the eye between Avrel's paws then swaggered away on an arcing path designed to irritate the mammoth and draw its attention away from Ingavar.

"Kailar, wait for my command," said Ingavar.

The mammoth turned towards the fighting bear and shook itself playfully, as though trying to throw a million fleas off its fur. In that moment, Avrel saw a gathering of lights above it, as though half a dozen stars had just dropped from the sky and were eager to join in with the posturing. As he watched, they formed a glinting frame of tendrils spreading over the heads of the mammoth and the bears. The sky spirits reacted with an agitated horror. Their voices wailed and their drums began to beat. They became a storm cloud, turning, turning. Ingavar raised his head in alarm. Avrel saw the disquiet in the Nanukapik's face and was still considering what to do when the frame of light reduced to a single point and flashed towards Kailar, striking him directly between the eyes.

Kailar gave out a fighting growl and immediately drew parallel to the mammoth's flank. Ignoring Ingavar's previous instruction, he began pacing back and forth in a threatening manner, his head held low, his black tongue issuing from the side of his mouth. It was a gibe to the creature to come and challenge him.

Avrel tightened his claws. There was going to be trouble.

The mammoth flexed its trunk, making a deep concertina of the thick folds of pachydermal skin that bridged its forehead. It had eyes like a fish. Small, staring, expressionless orbs. It gave another high-pitched trumpeting call, which resonated right through Avrel's chest. Yet the creature did not seem hostile to him. He was hearing confusion and hurt in its roars. It was a giant of gentleness, clearly unhappy to be intimidated so. If anything, the lights were the real danger. Avrel felt it in every hollow fibre of his pelt. Giving counsel as his forebear Lorel would have done, he called out to his Nanukapik to draw back. But

Ingavar did not hear him. He was, by then, in the shadow of the mammoth, sending out a parcel of whuffing noises, trying to establish a common language. But the mammoth had turned to face Kailar instead, throwing its head about in all directions as though scooping a hole in the air with its tusks.

Kailar rose up showing his claws.

The mammoth blew a great swatch of air from its lungs.

"Kailar, no!" barked Ingavar. But the fighting bear was already loping forwards. Avrel saw the ghost clouds jar towards him as though to form a barrier or mouthpiece of contempt.

The bear swept through them like a great white arrow.

Avrel felt his chest muscles tighten. This was ill-matched. The mammoth might have peaceful intentions but it was *enormous*. If the creature were to raise even half of Kailar's inbred aggression it might skewer him before he struck a single blow. But Kailar seemed, to the Teller, possessed. There was a redness in his eye. An unexplained fury. He was roaring forward as though the risk of a gory death was of little or no concern to him.

There was a thump and a clash of bodies. Kailar's head went back and his shoulders went upwards. The ice juddered as he crashed down onto his back, held there briefly with his four paws kicking and his head thrashing wildly from side to side. But to Avrel's astonishment, his companion had not been crushed by the mammoth. He was in the grip of Ingavar. The bears struggled and separated and came together once more in a frightening knot of muscle and fur, this time on hind legs locked at the shoulder.

"What do you *see?*" Ingavar was growling, his eyes held to Kailar's in a haze of sweat.

Kailar wrestled and pushed, snarling with a savagery that Avrel had only ever witnessed in animals caught in hunting traps.

"What do you see?!" Ingavar roared again.

"Black bear," Kailar panted, saliva frothing up between his teeth.

Avrel looked again at the mammoth. It was standing there bemused, shimmering slightly, as though it was about to disappear into the mist. But it was still a mammoth, the creature from the time of the Premen race. How could Kailar have mistaken it for anything else?

"Look at me," said Ingavar, shaking Kailar violently, cuffing him until their heads came level. Then from the blue eyes there shone a white light, directly into the fighting bear's eyes. Kailar cried out and fell away heavily. His head slapped the ice and bounced back once. His left paw, his fighting paw, twitched for several seconds, but his eyes remained open, staring at everything and nothing, at ice.

Avrel ran to him, even though it meant abandoning the eye of Gawain. "Is he dead?" he panted. He put his head down and listened for tell-tale wisps of air. To his relief, a faint gurgle left Kailar's nostrils.

Suddenly, Ingavar turned his head and roared with the force of nine blizzards at Gwilanna. She had fluttered down and settled on the stone dragon eye and would have been blown away like tumbleweed if she had not stretched her wings and taken flight.

"I was protecting it!" she squawked. "What's the matter with you? There are demons at work here. Can't you feel it, shaman?"

"What does she mean?" asked Avrel, still standing over Kailar. There was a ripple in the fighting bear's shoulder. He was waking.

"Haven't you worked it out yet?" Gwilanna snorted. She banked steeply upwards then allowed herself to drop hard and fast towards the mammoth. Avrel gasped as he realised she wasn't going to stop. He gasped again as she passed right through the creature's body and emerged on the other side with a triumphant cark. "It's a projection," she said. "A cleverly made thought-form. That can only mean that the Fain are among us."

"I saw lights," Avrel said, turning to Ingavar. "They struck Kailar just before . . ."

"I know," said Ingavar. "He was attacked by the Ix. They can sense any ripple in the fabric of the universe and probe it in an instant. Kailar's mind was in the easiest state to accept them. They were testing him. They made him see what he most feared. A black bear. A nightmare from the den. I've closed the ripple, all the way to its source. But the Ix will be curious. They will try to trace it."

Gwilanna fluttered down again, this time to land on Avrel's back. "Are you saying you know where this apparition came from?"

Ingavar nodded. He sat down and lowered his head into his chest. As he closed his blue eyes, the sky spirits joined in a circle above him. Then, with one enormous breath, he drew the wind down and around him like a blanket. His pelt flattened and his shape transfigured. When the atmosphere had settled and the ice had ceased to thrum, David Rain was in furs before them again. "The mammoth is a gift from my daughter," he said.

Gwilanna clicked her beak. "You? You've got a child?" Her squawk of incredulity made Avrel shudder.

David crouched down and stroked Kailar's ear. "Her name is Alexa. You should be proud of her, Gwilanna. She's from the line of Gwendolen."

The raven tore a loose feather off her wing. "Not by that hot-headed dark-haired girl?"

"Zanna is an excellent mother," said David. He stood up and patted Avrel's neck. The Teller, still uncomfortable with the man-bear transformation, snorted once and stood his ground like a faithful dog. "And Alexa is a remarkable child. The kind you've been looking for all your life. She has dragons in her auma and the skills of a Pri:magon priestess at her fingertips. But she's young and she doesn't know what she's doing."

"Then when we are done here I will train her for you."

Gwilanna spoke these words with the cunning of a witch, but David responded with the smile of a seer. "She needs you now. She may be in danger. That's why I have to send you back."

Gwilanna looked greedily at the eye of Gawain. "But I'm needed here, as a guide. As—"

"The spell will be broken. You'll be Premen again," said

David, with unswerving authority in his voice. "Prepare yourself. The move will be sudden and nauseous."

"No!" Gwilanna flapped. "I'm not going back. I was with Gawain when he flew these skies. I have a right to the dragon. He's mine to protect. I'm staying here to see you open the eye. Someone has to monitor what you do. This pair of tubby low-lives are far too trusting."

"You'll guard Alexa with your life," threatened David, glancing sideways at Kailar as the bear began the groggy climb back to his feet. "If anything happens to her, I'll put you in front of this 'low-life' son of Ragnar one last time." He raised his hand as if to cast a spell.

"Wait! Why me? Why can't you go back?"

David looked at the mammoth, which was now no more than fading grey patches in the criss-crossing wind. "Alexa is aware of my presence in the North, but only in the way that a dragon child dreams it. If I returned to the Crescent she would do everything in her power to keep me there. I can't risk the heartache that would bring. My destiny is here, with these bears, with this ice."

"We had a deal," Gwilanna reminded him, sharply. "You promised to explain to me how you came to be here."

"I told you, I never really left," said David. "I was at

275

the Tooth of Ragnar when the island came down. It was me who destroyed the Ix:risor. But in the process, the man you knew as David Rain was speared through the heart by a shard of ice."

"And?" she said, half-guessing, half-fearing what was coming next.

"The fire of the dragon flowed into him," muttered Avrel, remembering what he had witnessed at Thoran's side.

"No!" said Gwilanna, with such severity that Avrel gave a gruff, spontaneous bark of warning. "You can't be one with the auma of Gawain. It's not possible. It's . . . How?"

David took a step nearer to her, saying, "When my spirit was released it looked for the light. Where else would it go but to the fire star, Gwilanna? In the extreme G'ravity field, my auma commingled with the auma of Ingavar and we were *both* joined to the dragon Gawain. We passed into Ki:mera, the Fain dimension, together. And as you know, many wonders are possible there."

Gwilanna moved her head from side to side like a metronome, as if trying to shake a small pea out of her ear. "But, you'd be . . . *revered*," she said, as though she'd like to spit a feather. "The Fain would look upon you

276

as . . . " But here her frustration reeled out of control and she beat her wings in a frenzied dance. "*Caark!* Why you? What's so special about you? A useless boy and a waddling lump of fur?"

"Time to go," David said. "Guard my daughter well."

"No!" she squawked. And she flew with great speed to the eye of Gawain, trying to speak an incantation into the stone. Suddenly, a light began to circle around it. For a moment she scraped her claws in triumph, thinking she'd restored her ability for magicks. But when she looked back at David, the spell was there to read upon his lips. She felt the suck of time and screamed a long and exasperated *Noooooooooo* which was partly to do with her dismissal from the ice and partly to do with the last thing she had witnessed. For in that instant of removal she, like Kailar, had seen her worst fears – in David's face. There was man and there was polar bear in his features. But there was something else, too. Something she had desired for herself for centuries.

The look of the dragon.

He had scalene eyes.

"OK, what the heck just happened?" said Tam. He stepped warily onto the first row of cobbles, his astonished gaze switching between Gwendolen (who was still on the fence post), a stunned-looking Zanna and a single green dandelion leaf which was falling to the ground like a alien snowflake.

"It was a shift," Zanna muttered, her coat tails flaring as she spun around looking for reference points. "This has got to be some sort of time corridor."

"Oh, right, so as well as keeping dragons you time travel as well?"

Hrrr, went Gwendolen, raising her wings in distress.

Zanna sent her a calming call. "Lucy's dragon thinks it might have been a trap."

Tam's grin fell apart. "She was *abducted*? Who by?"

"I don't know," Zanna said, fury burning through the dampness in her eyes. "And I don't have time to discuss it with *you*. Why don't you just leave us alone, Tam? Go back to your flash apartment and write your exposé of David if you must. One of the people I'm closest to has just disappeared, and I don't think I really care about you or your magazine any more."

"I want to help," he said. His eye line softened. A wisp of snowflakes patterned his shoulders. "Seriously."

Zanna flipped her phone open and quickly keyed in a speed dial number. "You've done enough damage."

"I brought her here, Zanna."

"Exactly. Just *go*."

He sighed, ran a hand through his unwashed hair and looked at length down the alleyway again. Gwendolen was hovering at ground level now, on the exact spot where the rift had opened. She seemed to be trying to take some kind of readings, but her movements were impossible for the human eye to follow. She just kept popping up here and there like random pixels on a computer screen. After a few seconds Tam gave up watching her and said, "Tell me what you're going to do?"

Zanna's eyes met his in a gesture of impatience. "Take advice – from an expert. Hi Liz, it's— Oh, Lexie, this is Mummy. No sweetie. No. I'll be . . . very late tonight. Did you? Oh, that's nice. Well, I'm sure if Daddy could have seen your picture of Bronson he'd have liked it. Yes. Give the phone to Naunty Liz now, will you . . . ? She's where? Mr Bacon's? Oh. All right, is Nunky Arthur at home? Good. Take the phone upstairs to him, please. Yes, then you can have an icepop if you like.

They're in the bottom drawer of the freezer. Be careful, it's cold. Ask Gwillan to help you. What? No, Lucy's not here. She's gone to visit a friend. She might be away for a little while. Just go to Arthur now, darling, OK?" She clamped her hand across the phone.

Tam said, "Who's Bronson?"

"Her toy mammoth," Zanna said. "This is a private call – *if* you don't mind."

"She draws stuff for David?"

"No, Tam, she just draws. Now— Arthur? Hi, it's me. Yeah, I'm still in Blackburn. No, there's been an incident – Lucy's disappeared."

She proceeded to tell him what she'd seen.

Arthur asked at length about the squirrel.

"It was just a squirrel," she said, sounding mildly irritated. "She chased it and *poof*. You know what she's like about Ringtails and Birchwoods."

"That rodent wasn't right," said Tam.

Zanna twisted on her heel. "Arthur, wait a second." She put the phone on mute. "Are you still here?"

"Some kind of light came out of her mobile. It made a squirrel from the falling snow. If it was a trap, that squirrel was the bait." He added as she frowned, "It's the truth, Zanna." He nodded at the phone. "See what your 'expert' makes of that."

Her fingers tightened into her palm. She relayed the information back to Arthur.

After a short pause Arthur said, "Does Lucy have images of squirrels on her phone?"

"Dozens," said Zanna. "She's always taking snaps of them – in the library gardens mostly."

She heard him take a long breath through his nose. Usually a pronouncement of wisdom would follow. This time it was fear. "Zanna, you must leave there. You are in great danger."

"But Lucy's gone," she repeated. "I can't pretend it didn't *happen*. I can't leave her, Arthur. She's a pain in the backside, but she's still . . . Lucy."

"There is nothing to be done," he said. "Come back to the Crescent."

Her fingers, china blue with cold, squeezed tightly round the phone. "No. What is this place? Why did David use it as his home address? There is no home here. It doesn't exist."

"I've told you before, existence is merely . . ."

"Don't get cryptic with me," Zanna cut in, biting down on a wave of anger. "You wrote about this. Did you bring it into being?"

"When I wrote about David at the folly," he said, "I was guided by the auma of Gawain, through his claw.

There are forces at work here that are almost impossible to comprehend. I believe we're caught up in something far greater than our own domestic troubles. Come back to the Crescent. We need to talk this through."

"There's no time," she said, pulling a braid from her hair. "Lucy's been taken and I intend to go after her."

"*What?*" exclaimed Tam.

Shut up, she mouthed at him. "Arthur, tell me how to open this rift."

"I can't do that."

"I think you can. Gwilanna always knew how to move through time. I'm a sibyl; you're a physicist. There are forces in the universe that work for us as well. While we're wasting time chatting Lucy's life could be at stake. Now, tell me what to do."

There was another short pause. Then in a voice close to freezing, Arthur said, "What became of the isoscele, Zanna?"

In the shadows of her mind, a well of fear sprang up. The isoscele? Why would he ask about that? "I've told you before. It was lost in the Arctic. What's this got to do with rescuing Lucy?"

"What you're planning is ill-advised," he said. "Even if the rift could be opened from this side there is no guarantee of a linear transfer. You might end up in a dimension of the universe you can't get back from—"

"Ask him which dimension David came from," whispered Tam, leaning in close enough to overhear and be elbowed firmly in the ribs for his trouble.

"If we had that piece of Gawain," said Arthur, "it might be possible to draw Lucy back merely by committing the dragon's blood to paper . . ."

A snowflake landed on Zanna's cheek. The dash of cold was the catalyst to make her shudder. She looked briefly at Tam. His eyes were still raising the question that was falling off her lips in silent words, *Which dimension did David come from?* Was he nothing more than . . . an entity, then? A being, a life force drawn through time?

She felt faint. Tam put out a hand and steadied her. He heard Arthur say, "Where is the isoscele hidden?"

She pushed Tam away and snapped back at Arthur, "Tell me how to open this rift or I swear I'll take Alexa out of the Crescent and none of you will ever see her again."

"Alexa may be the key," he said. "I've meditated on this at great length, Zanna – about how Gawain's claw came to be in the folly. I don't think it was mere serendipity that I found it. I think your daughter was involved."

"I'm not *interested*," she snapped. "Five seconds or I close this call. I'm not joking, Arthur. I want that information." She glanced at Tam again, who nodded supportively.

"Very well," Arthur said, straining at the edges of despair and reluctance. "Did Gwendolen go through the time slip with Lucy?"

"No. She's here. Fretting, like me."

"Then give her Lucy's phone. Ask her to try to commingle with it."

Zanna's blood ran cold. "Are you saying that Lucy was taken by the *Fain*?"

"What you've described has all the elements of their methods, though why they have targeted Lucy's phone is a mystery."

"Why are they even back?" Zanna said. "I thought David . . ." But her throat swelled and she couldn't go on with that. She gathered herself again and said, "What then, if Gwendolen makes the link?"

"She will need to trace the precise coordinates of the rift. The points will be etheric, not numerical. Gwendolen will have to feel them in her mind, then dream them consistently and purely to project them. If she succeeds, you will see a shimmer at the place where Lucy disappeared. But to open the rift for long enough to allow you through, you will need to find a power source which Gwendolen can use to magnify her thoughts. A car battery might be enough."

"I'm onto it," said Zanna.

"Wait," Arthur said. "Please think about this. If you go, you might never see Alexa again."

A tear ran freely down Zanna's cheek. "Bye," she said, and ended the call. She clicked her fingers. In an instant, Gwendolen was on her shoulder. "You got jump leads?" she asked a startled Tam.

"Erm, yeah. In the boot."

"Fetch them, and Lucy's phone. Oh, and flip your bonnet."

"What? Why?"

"Just do it," Zanna snapped. "Unhook the terminals on your battery."

Knowing better than to argue, Tam did as instructed. In the meantime, Zanna told Gwendolen what she needed to do. Gwendolen tested the battery terminals, flicking them with her tail until showers of sparks were leaping off them under the bonnet. Then she plugged herself into the phone. Closing her eyes, she concentrated hard. A few seconds passed, then she reached for the crocodile clips that were attached to each of the battery terminals and gripped them hard to complete the loop. Every scale on her body immediately stood on end. A pulse of violet light came out of the phone and went shooting down the ringlets of wire to the battery. There was a low humming noise and a slight smell of burning. A smoke ring emerged from Gwendolen's nose. And in the gap between the houses on Thoushall Road, a shimmering vertical line appeared.

"Well, here's a story," Zanna said to Tam, moving down the alleyway towards it. "The last two women who thought anything of you both threw themselves through a hole in time. Maybe you need to improve your technique. You write a nice poem, though. I'll give you that. Don't wait up for me. So long, Tam."

"Zanna, wait," he called. She was now just yards away from the rift, which was deepening and folding as it detected her presence.

She paused, ready for her final steps, when, of all things, her mobile rang. Irritated, yet glad of the excuse to hesitate, she answered it.

It was Elizabeth Pennykettle. "Zanna?" She was breathless, practically frantic.

"Liz, I'm kind of busy."

"I talked to Arthur. Don't you dare go near that rift!"

"Sorry. Nearly there. Doing this for Lucy."

"No, Zanna! No! Think about Alexa."

Zanna's lower lip tremored. "Take care of her for me."

"Wait a second. Listen."

There was a fumbling noise, then Alexa said, "Mummy?"

"Baby?" Zanna's voice was like a cracking egg.

"Mummy, where are you going?"

"I don't know," Zanna said. Tears streamed down her cheeks.

"I saw Daddy," said Alexa.

"Daddy? What?"

"Through Bronson's eye. I saw him, very small."

Zanna reached out her hand. The time rift rippled. "That can't happen, baby. Daddy's . . ."

"He was being a polar bear."

"What?" Zanna said in a small hurt voice.

The next voice was Liz's. "Sweetheart, come home. Something odd is going on here. I can't afford to lose you. Step away from that rift. It's not— Zanna!" she shouted, as a squeal came down the line. "Zanna, can you hear me? Are you OK?"

There was a rustling sound and then Zanna said, "Yes." She sounded furious.

"Where are you?"

"Sitting on my backside in a clump of wet dandelions."

"It didn't work? The rift rejected you?"

"Oh, it worked all right," Zanna said, breathing fast. "I'm gonna kill that—"

"Zanna? Slow down. Tell me what happened."

"He pushed me aside! He's gone in my place. The stupid arrogant son-of-a—"

"Who pushed you aside? Tam, you mean?"

"Yes!" Zanna railed, sounding as though she was doing a war dance. "Tam's gone after Lucy."

No place like home

The snow began to fall in flakes as big as plums. But it could do little to soften Zanna's anger or accumulated pain. For another ten minutes she spoke freely to Liz, pouring out feelings that went way beyond what had just happened with Tam. She was bordering on hysterical as she revisited her fears about David, her life with him and who he really was. Question after question. All of them rhetorical. All underscored with bewildered despair.

For Liz, it was like gathering in a sheet on a windy day – first just a question of catching on and holding, then the careful process of drawing in safely. Using all her skills of motherhood she listened patiently, answered sympathetically, and finally brought stability, simplicity and calm. "The truth is here, standing beside me, Zanna, getting messy on an icepop. Come home, where you belong. Alexa needs you. So do I."

It was enough. Zanna said, "OK, but the sky here is filling up with snow again. The last thing I need right now is to be wrapped in a blanket on some freezing motorway. I passed a small hotel just down the road. Think I'll stay there overnight. What will you tell Lexie?"

"Exactly that," Liz said. "Mummy's stuck in a storm." She heard the breathy shudders coming down the line again. "We'll sort it out, Zanna. One way or another. Drive safely tomorrow. Take your time."

Zanna said goodbye, then clammed her phone shut and went to Gwendolen. The dragon, exhausted from her recent exertions, was asleep on Tam Farrell's engine, curled up like a shiny green kitten. Her paws were slightly blackened and she'd dropped a scale or two, but otherwise she seemed unscathed. Zanna picked her up, took the keys from the ignition of Tam's car and locked it. Then she went back to her own and drove to the hotel.

In the meantime, in the Crescent, Liz was struggling to keep her composure. Despite Arthur's advice to Gollygosh, the *hrrr* had quickly gone around the dragons that David's special 'threesome' had felt some kind of 'auma wave'. This, combined with Gretel's report that Alexa had apparently 'seen' her daddy, had set up a minor earthquake of whispers. No dragon dared to act on these rumours, of course, for Liz was running off red hot sparks and had enough to think about with Lucy going missing. Alexa *seemed* unaffected, though. She was going about her usual routines, playing with her toys, drawing her pictures, and talking to the fairies spinning around her mobile as though nothing on this Earth could ever really faze her. Gretel, in particular, found this infuriating. Many a smoke ring had been blown by her that day.

The general buzz wasn't lost on Arthur. In the kitchen the following morning, while Alexa was out in the garden (planting apple pips in yoghurt pots, in spectacularly unpredictable sunshine), he reiterated his feelings about the girl to a disenchanted Liz (and a very alert listening dragon). "Ever since she learned about the dragon G'lant, significant things have been happening," he said. "The life-like drawings. Her awareness of David. The reanimation of the dragons—"

"They're barely active," Liz cut in, almost ticking him off. "G'reth was asleep when I looked at him this morning and Gadzooks had dropped his pencil down behind Zanna's desk. Golly hasn't fixed a thing for weeks. They're hardly making mischief, are they? It will take a bit more than a few guttering *hrrrs* to prove to me that David is reconnecting with them, Arthur."

Bonnington came in, then, mewing for food. Arthur reached out for his tail but missed. At the same time, the kitchen door opened and Alexa popped her head just inside and said, "Naunty, can I put the apple pots by

291

the rockery, so that the fairies can water the seeds?"

"Yes," said Liz. "But don't plant the apple seeds in the rockery, will you? We don't want any big trees growing there."

"No," said the girl. The door closed again.

Fairies. The rockery. Arthur thought about the light that Bonnington had witnessed from the fairy door. Could that be connected with Alexa, he wondered? It was too much to expect that the rockery might lie on another time rift, but was it possible Alexa had somehow created one? That her desire to see fairies was so intense that she had fleetingly opened something more spectacular than an ornamental doorway made of wood? "We should talk to her about G'lant," he said.

"No," said Liz. "I absolutely forbid it. She's a child, Arthur. I won't have her interrogated. The name is nothing more than a trigger for her imagination."

"I agree," he said, crossing his thighs in what Lucy always called his 'academic' way.

Lucy. Liz turned the agony aside.

"It's a wonderful name: noble, creatively potent and highly suggestive of dragon lore. It makes sense to me now why David sent it. I don't think it was entirely romantic."

He recognised a tight-lipped breath. "I wouldn't tell that to Zanna," said Liz.

"Zanna has closed herself off," he came back. "Even in her meditative state she has given up believing in David's survival to protect herself from the pain of having lost him – or rather, the man he *used* to be."

He heard her run the tap. Fast, splashing water. A clink of cups. Dropped items of cutlery. She was becoming flustered. "Arthur, we've been over this time and time again."

He smacked his lips slightly before replying, a sign that he was leading up to some kind of premeditated diagnostic response. "I want to share something with you," he said. "Something that may help you accept that David could come back."

On the fridge top, the listener widened its ears.

"When I was attacked by the Fain," Arthur said, "my memory was torn apart and left in scraps. As it returned, certain pieces did not fit. They seemed inappropriate to my life as I knew it. After a while I began to realise that those pieces were fragments of the history of the Fain, in particular their spiritual creed."

"Why haven't you mentioned this before?"

"There was never any need to – before," he replied. "In the past few months these extraneous memories have crystallised into a meaningful 'record'. I now understand the relationship between the Fain and dragons."

He felt the pressure of air as she turned.

"When I was at the abbey, I had a dream. I saw the universe created from the outgoing breath of a dragon called Godith. Everything was born from the fire of that dragon. A white fire. Auma in its purest sense. You and I, this physical world we inhabit, came into being when the fire cooled down to a low enough vibration to produce ingenious combinations of atoms and molecules. But in certain parts of the universe the fire remained at a higher vibration and filled the spaces between the atoms. From this aspect of the fire the Fain evolved."

"And what's this got to do with David?"

Arthur nodded slightly and pointed his toe. "There is an element of spiritual tension that binds the universe together. Humans, in their quietest moments, reach out to the etheric world of the Fain, seeking what they call enlightenment. But it is not a one way process. The Fain, likewise, have a mystical aspiration to make a cyclical journey back to Godith, back to dragonkind. They can only become truly enlightened when they commingle, unconditionally, with a living dragon's fire. They call it *illumination*."

Liz turned to the washing-up again. "This is heady stuff for a Wednesday morning, Arthur. An alien RE lesson? I still don't understand how David fits in."

"What I'm about to tell you now came to me in a meditation a few days ago. A single moment of clarity. A revelation, perhaps. We always talk about David dying, but the nature of his passing, the ice through the heart, has always seemed significant to me. You use icefire to animate your dragons. What if the ice that took his mortal body had that same capability?"

"Arthur . . ." Her hands splashed into the water.

"Please, just consider it," he said. "Ever since my mind was scrambled by the Fain, I've been reaching out for a truth like this. And now it has come. I think David has been transformed. I think he's on the pathway to illumination and his chosen name is G'lant."

Liz stood away, shaking her head. "I'm sorry, no. I just can't deal with this. David will always be a boy to me, Arthur. A lovable young man who got carried away saving animals and the Arctic ice cap. And I'm responsible for that, *and* for what happened to him. I was the one who introduced him to dragons. If I'd kept my mouth shut, if I hadn't let him get into conflict with Gwilanna he might still be . . . oh, I don't know."

"You do," Arthur said evenly. "You know that David came here for a purpose. Alexa, too."

"She—"

"There is movement," Arthur continued to press. "A great atmosphere of change. For a while it was confined to hopeful speculation and tiresome reminiscence. Our hearts were in the Artic, but not our eyes. Now we have ruptures in the world's weather patterns, the inexplicable migration of polar bears north, the seizure of your daughter through a known time rift and what I believe to be an accurate report of David's reappearance. The universe is turning and this planet is its focus. Something *major* is about to occur. David is at its core and I'm sure Alexa senses it. The truth is shown to us every day through her, but we're re-labelling it as childish babble."

"Then why isn't he here, being more of a father?" A rare burst of anger powered through Liz's voice. "Why doesn't he come back and show himself properly, instead of torturing his partner with signs and speculation?"

"Perhaps he can't," Arthur said. "Or is not allowed to. Or he is trying to divert attention away from this house. From what Zanna told me of Lucy's disappearance, it's clear she was taken by the Fain. Why they want her is impossible to say. But they may not stop at a daughter of Guinevere. We must be prepared to act – while we can."

Liz glanced through the window. Alexa was carrying a watering can to the rockery. "And do what, exactly?"

"Find the isoscele of Gawain. I don't believe Zanna lost it. Something as precious as that doesn't slip idly through the fingers. I believe she put it away to dissociate herself from the pain of losing David. We should retrieve it and test Alexa."

"She's not a lab rat, Arthur."

His marble eyes rolled. Even now, their fixed expression still unnerved Liz a little. "She saw David through the medium of her drawings. If she was aided by the auma of Gawain she could be capable of boundless creation. Dark matter might be to her what clay is to you."

That brought forth an agitated laugh. "Whatever happened to good old string theory and . . ."

"Quantum mechanics?" He raised an eyebrow, just as Bonnington leapt onto his lap. Vision, at last. He saw that Liz had her hands to her face. Crying? Exasperated? It was difficult to tell. "It might be a means of bringing Lucy back – and Tam Farrell, of course." More pain. He could see the film of moisture in her troubled eyes now. But this was crucial. He needed to push. "I tried to explain to Zanna that when I wrote about David years ago at the Abbey, my hand was guided to that time corridor in Blackburn. It was no accident. Neither was my finding one of Gawain's claws on the floor of the folly. Some force intended it should happen."

Liz gestured at the ceiling with rubber-gloved hands.

"I believe Alexa made the claw materialise."

"What? What are you talking about? Alexa wasn't born when—"

Now it was Arthur's turn to cut in. "I believe Alexa came to this planet, in this fashion, for a reason. I believe she chose her own parents. One from this dimension, one from—"

"No," Liz interrupted him, spreading her hands. "That's enough. I don't want to hear any more about this. I love you, Arthur. You're a genius and a good, kind man. But sometimes I think you spend so long in your own head that you forget there's a very real and stressful world outside of it."

"You are a descendant of a dragon princess," he reminded her. "You have the power to animate clay and speak in a language few humans could master. Don't forget *that* world, Elizabeth. It's what you really are."

He watched her knot her fingers, saw the ripple of movement in her neck when the dragon, Gwillan, leaned forward to speak to her. He knew then that she had not given up believing in what she was, but was merely frustrated by her inability to take action.

The cordless telephone rang. It was close enough at

hand for Arthur to pretend to fumble for it. He pressed 'receive'. But as he began to raise it to his ear, Bonnington let out a furious hiss, morphed into a tiger and struck the phone out of Arthur's hand.

Liz gave a yelp of fright. On the fridge top, the listening dragon took a pace back.

The phone crashed to the floor and the shell broke open. Bonnington was over it in a moment, arching, spitting, baring his fangs. The handset clicked and gave a pregnant burr. The green light on the arch of its shoulder faded.

Bonnington relaxed and morphed back into a tabby.

"What was all that about?" Liz said fearfully.

Arthur brought his hands together under his nose. "They have found us," he said.

That was all Liz needed. She yanked the door open and shouted up the garden, "Lexie, come in now. Come and have a drink of juice . . ."

On the rockery, Alexa stood up as if she'd magically grown out of a space between the stones. She smiled underneath her sun hat, wiped some loose soil off her hands and jumped down onto the path.

She was running down the lawn when she stopped abruptly and turned to stare at the fence which separated number 42 from Mr Bacon's garden.

There was a large black raven hunched on a post.

"You're *her*, aren't you?" Alexa said.

The raven cast her a crabby-eyed glare.

So Alexa repeated the question – in dragontongue.

"Oh, very impressive," the raven caarked sourly.

Alexa jumped up, clapping her hands in glee. "Are you a fairy?"

"Don't be ridiculous, child. There are no such things as fairies. They're intervital forces, sentimentally misrepresented as idealistic corporeal entities."

Alexa hooked her lip. "I've got a door for them," she said, pointing proudly at the rockery. "They'll come when the bonglers play the right tune."

The wind chimes gave a slight tinkle.

"Ridiculous," the raven chuntered. Unwisely, a fly landed by its feet. In an instant the raven's beak daggered down and the fly was devoured in a single gulp.

Alexa gasped. "Does it wiggle and wriggle and tickle inside you?"

"What?" squawked the bird.

"You're the old lady who swallowed the fly! I don't know why. Perhaps you'll—"

"Because I'm hungry, that's why," the 'old lady' cut in. "And tired of this pathetic hollow-boned form." She

300

ruffled her wind-beaten feathers in annoyance, making Alexa giggle.

"I suppose you think this is funny, don't you, child? I was meant to be Premen again. That was the deal. Your father cheated and left me coated in feathers."

"Daddy? You saw Daddy?!" Alexa lifted on her toes.

"He's a crook."

Alexa reached out a hand and cupped a flower of her father's rose. "Did he do a spell on you?"

"A very bad one, yes."

Alexa thought about this a moment. She opened her mouth, then closed it smartly (there were, after all, other flies about). "Do you want an icepop?"

"*What?*"

"You said you were hungry. We've got icepops in our freezer. I don't think we've got any fly-flavoured ones. The strawberry ones are the best. They're Bonnington's favourites, too."

The raven sighed like an out-of-shape football. She tapped a wrinkled foot. The nostrils in her black beak twitched a little and she looked as though she might fall off the fence in boredom. But then she suddenly rose up again, as if her feathers had been plumped with hope. "Did you say 'freezer'?"

Alexa nodded, setting her sun hat flapping.

The raven's eyes stood out like two black peas. It stepped half a centimetre to its left. "Is there still a plastic box in there? A grey one with a pale blue lid?"

"It's near the fosh," Alexa answered.

"Fosh? What is 'fosh'? What are you blabbering about now, you stupid girl?"

"Fish," Alexa laughed. She liked to call it 'fosh' because Lucy always did. It came from a story Lucy had read as a girl.

The raven wasn't in the mood for humour. "Bring it to me, child."

Alexa tilted her head. She put her hands behind her back and shook her dark curls. "That's Naunty's snowball. That's for the dragons."

The raven's eyes shone. "I was sent here to protect you. That . . . snowball will help me. Now stop this insubordinate behaviour and—"

But before the raven could get its words out, a jet of water from Mr Bacon's side struck it firmly under the tail and sent it flapping skywards, wet and angry.

At the same time, Liz appeared beside Alexa and gripped her hand. "I said to come in, Lexie, what are you doing?"

"Talking," said the girl. "The birdie's funny."

Liz looked up. The raven was spiralling above them.

Mr Bacon's face appeared at the fence. "Can't be doing with those things," he said. "Keep the sparrows off the porch. Bullies. Nothing more."

"She'll be mad that you wet her," Alexa said. "She might come back and make a spell on you. *Hrrr!*"

Henry Bacon could not translate that, of course.

But Elizabeth Pennykettle could. "She's a witch?" she muttered, drawing Alexa back towards the house.

"Mmm," went Alexa. "And she's very, *very* old."

Liz swallowed slowly. "Does she have a name, this witch?"

"Yes," said the girl. "I dreamed her once. She's my Naunty Gwyneth."

Testing Lucy

Grass. Long, thick, uncut grass. Glistening with water. Every blade soaked. Lucy could feel it under her palms. Damp, nerve-chilling, odourless grass.

She sat up, gasping with shock.

She was outdoors, under a thunder-filled sky. Grassland all around her. A rogue wind thieving all the warmth from her blood. A sense of the sea (as though the land was heaving to its far-away swell). Salt in the air. Turbulent, bloated cloud formations. No buildings, save a squat stone tower, which she thought might be a lighthouse but she guessed must be the folly on Farlowe Island. Farlowe Island. Yes. Surely that was where she was? Marooned in acres of ragged grassland – and sitting at the centre of a ring of standing stones.

The first shiver hit her and she clamped her arms. Her top was drenched. So too her red hair, flattened against her face by excessive rain. How long had she been here? And who had left her – alone, without any shoes or socks? Her bare feet were almost as blue as her jeans. When she stood up, the ground felt like a sponge against her heels.

It was ludicrous, she knew it, but she had to cry out.

It was a shallow form of comfort. *Help! Where am I?* The sky rumbled. A lightning bolt cracked the gloom. Lucy squealed and ran to the nearest stone for cover. The moment she touched it, it turned into a monk.

She screamed and staggered backwards, then ran for the gap between the monk and the next stone in the circle. But how could she know that escape was impossible? Or that her trajectory was always curving?

The next stone she collided with became Brother Bernard.

"You are ours, child," he said.

Then the lightning came again and struck the centre of the ring where Lucy had been lying, scorching a dark pattern in the earth. From the pattern rose a creature, half as tall as herself. In general shape it resembled a dragon. Serpentine body. Powerful wings. But it was thicker set and ugly. Cabbage ears. A gargoyle. Its feet and paws were stout and immensely strong, the claws inside them conical, tapering to points. It had no ordered rows of scales. Instead, the surface of its body was pocked and ridged as if the skin had been sheared from brittle rock. And apart from its pulsing, bile-coloured eyes, hooked green tongue and grey-tipped claws, it was completely black. Yet Lucy could see lightning spidering inside it, as though she had opened a box of mirrors. She shook her head in fear as the creature turned towards her. With a granite-like click it unlatched its jaw. From its throat came a bolt of pure black fire.

She screamed and was suddenly sitting upright again, surprised to find herself on a narrow cot in a stone-walled room. She was covered in a blanket that smelled of hay. Logs were crackling in a fire nearby. Orange light was radiating from the same source.

In a chair put together from sanded planks, a round-bodied man shook himself awake and unfurled his plumpish limbs like a cat. "Thank goodness," he said. It was Brother Bernard. He rang a small hand bell and stepped into the light.

"Get away from me!" screamed Lucy, looking for a weapon. Finding nothing but a pillow, she pulled it in front of her to use as a shield.

Brother Bernard strayed no nearer. He brought his hands together in a gesture of concern. "Be at peace, child. I have no wish to harm you."

"Where's that thing?" she yelled. Her frightened gaze probed all the darkest corners.

Bernard's thick brown eyebrows came together in a frown. "This will be difficult to comprehend," he said. "Your mind has been tampered with. You are being tested. You have been made to see what you most fear."

"I saw *you*," Lucy said, venom spitting from her mouth. "In the fields. In that tower! Your eyes were black."

"We found you in the folly, passed out," he said.

Another monk walked in, carrying a tray. On it was a bowl, a plain cotton napkin and a wedge of bread.

Lucy gave a start and drew her knees into her chest. "I'm not your prisoner. Let me go!"

"Brother Cedric has brought you broth," said Bernard. "It is made from wild rabbits we trap on the island. It will nourish you. Please eat. You must be exhausted."

The second monk, a slack-jawed man with hollow eyes and very little strength in his upper body, leaned forward and placed the tray on the cot. As he backed away, Lucy kicked it to the floor. The earthenware bowl turned over by his feet, spilling broth around the contours of his fraying sandals. In the puddle, Lucy saw a piece of cut meat. A rabbit's foot, twitching. She gagged and clapped a hand across her mouth.

Brother Bernard nodded silently at his companion. Cedric picked up the napkin and quickly cleared the mess before exiting the room.

"He will return with more," said Bernard.

"It was alive," said Lucy, shaking, looking sick. "The

soup was . . ." She vomited slightly into her hand.

Bernard sat down and placed a handkerchief beside her. "Do you hear a humming noise in your left ear?"

A tear, triggered more by shock than despair, trickled down the left side of Lucy's cheek. Humming noise. Yes, she'd noticed it. She nodded.

"That is them," said Bernard, touching the outline of a crucifix under the neck of his habit.

"The Fain?" she snapped.

He seemed a little surprised by that and took a moment to re-consider his thoughts. "Yes, of course, my old friend, Brother Vincent – your mother's . . . companion, Arthur – would have talked at length about them, but he may not have mentioned a higher order of the Fain who call themselves the Ix."

Lucy had a stinging taste of acid in her throat. "Higher order?" she said, grimacing as she gulped.

"More advanced," he said. "It is they, the Ix, who have come to the island. You will know, I think, that the Fain can possess your body and meld to your mind through a process called commingling."

"They're in my cat," said Lucy. "One of them got fused into his brain and now he can turn into any kind of . . . well, it doesn't matter." She bit her tongue, wishing she hadn't given so much away. What she wouldn't do to have Bonnington with her now, baring the fangs of a sabre-toothed tiger.

Brother Bernard smiled. "We do not know how long the Ix have been among us. They confuse our linear perception of time. They invade us periodically, then leave us at will, but we cannot entirely escape their presence."

Lucy snatched up the handkerchief. "This is an island. You must have boats?"

He steered a hand towards the window. Lightning flashed, as if by his command. The open fire flared, making Lucy jump. "To cross the water in a launch would not be advisable."

"You've got phones."

"All disabled. We are trapped," he said, very matter-of-factly.

Too much so for Lucy. She balled her fists. "Why did they dump me outside?"

"They did not. You were dreaming. Did you see yourself among the standing stones?"

Lucy glanced at him sideways. The humming noise, she noticed, had suddenly gone.

"That circle is the centre of the island," he said. "In a geological and a spiritual sense. Millions of years ago, during the formation of the landmasses here, this was an area of high volcanic activity. Eons later, when the Fain first visited this world, it became the perfect location for a dragon eyrie. Do you understand what I mean by that?"

Lucy frowned and shook her head.

"It was a breeding ground for dragons, the nest of a female called Ghislaine. On this site, the Fain created a multi-dimensional time rift. A place where a portal called a fire star could be opened and dragons, once prepared, could be sent to Ki:mera, the home world of the Fain."

"How do you know about *dragons?*" hissed Lucy. Her mouth curled into a snarl.

"We've been learning," Bernard said, turning slightly sideways. "The Ix have no secrets. They are confident enough of their own superiority to shield nothing from us."

"Then what do they want? Why did they steal me?! One minute I was in Blackburn and now . . . I'm here!"

Brother Bernard unlaced his fingers. He made a circling motion by his left ear.

"Gone," Lucy whispered, guessing he meant the hum.

His finger moved to his lips. "If it comes back, point to your ear but do not speak."

Lucy squeezed her pillow even tighter and nodded.

"The Ix are planning to return to this world in far greater numbers – to breed a new kind of dragon."

Lucy's mouth made a *what?* shape.

Bernard raised his hand to be sure of her silence. "Suffice it to say, not a dragon of your liking. The Earth was once the perfect environment for dragons and in its ecological profile it still is. But in the old times things were very different. Life was more natural. The people were fewer and better attuned to their surroundings. Some of them, like you, had great . . . harmony with dragons."

Lucy gulped. "What are they going to do with me?"

Bernard tilted his head. "You will be among the survivors," he said.

Lucy's eyes dilated suddenly. "What do you mean? What's going to happen?"

Bernard shushed her and pressed his hands together. For a moment, he could have been sculpted from wood. "What I'm about to tell you will be of deep concern, but do not cry out for that will attract them." He paused until she signalled that she understood. Then he said, "This planet is facing ecological disaster. The melting of its ice caps will cause untold damage and widespread despair. The Ix will do all they can to accelerate this process, to clear away as much unnecessary human disturbance as possible from their breeding programme."

"How?" said Lucy.

"They will prey upon your fears of destruction, child."

For a second, Lucy thought she heard the hum coming back. She began to raise her finger, but the whine was gone again as Bernard continued, "They will exploit your lethargy, make you believe that nothing can be done to reverse the decline, then encourage you to submit to the earth spirit Gaia who will wreak devastation through volcanoes and storms. There will be nothing left but the Earth, its breeding grounds and some chosen Prem:Ix."

"Prem:Ix?" Lucy jumped on it quickly.

"Their name," he said, "for people like yourself, who will be permanently, fully commingled to the Ix."

Lucy shook her head violently. "That will never happen."

His face grew rounder (and she thought a little smug), inviting her to say how it could possibly be avoided. So she gave in to her heart and began to blurt out, "David won't—" but then stopped herself quickly, for the name had caused an obvious flicker of interest in his eyes. All around her now, she thought she felt their presence. Creepy, like ghosts. Like nightmares. The Ix.

"Unfortunately, Lucy, David will be their greatest ally."

"Never!" she shouted.

This time he didn't bother raising a hand. "David's spirit has survived, and they fear him," he said.

Lucy sat forward. "Really? He's alive?"

Bernard turned to the window. "He is in the Arctic, about to make a grave mistake. He is going to use the eye of the dragon Gawain to open the heart of Gaia herself, to draw upon the well of The Fire Eternal. With it, he will crystallise human consciousness and attempt to raise awareness of the problems faced by this unstable planet. He will use human thoughts to shape dark matter and manifest . . ."

"What?" said Lucy, so tense she could break.

She saw his gaze narrow. "A solution," he muttered. "It is futile. He will fail. The Ix will intervene and quickly overpower him, poisoning human consciousness at the same time. David Rain will be helpless against them."

Lucy threw her pillow aside. "Then we've got to help him. We need to tell him somehow. There must be a way?"

At the door, the monk arrived again with soup. He had his cowl up this time, as if to protect himself from any more outbursts. Lucy tutted and shut herself up. The monk stepped towards the cot. He picked up the soup bowl and knelt as though to place it on the floor. But then, in a thick Scottish accent, he mumbled, "Brother Bernard?"

Bernard turned towards him, looking down. "What is it?"

Suddenly, the bowl came up and hot broth splashed in Brother Bernard's face. He cried out in great pain and covered his eyes. He did not see the other monk swing the tray and was unconscious by the time the second blow had struck him.

Lucy squealed in terror as he slumped.

"Shush!" hissed the monk, and pushed back his cowl. "Wow, that's one heck of a story," he said.

It was Tam Farrell.

In the chapel

"How did you get here?" Lucy gasped.

"Never mind," Tam said, already lifting Brother Bernard by the shoulders and dragging him manfully towards the cot. "Grab his feet. Help me get him onto the bed."

"Is he dead?" Lucy asked, feeling just as queasy as she had before. There were several spots of blood on Brother Bernard's habit and his normally rosy face had turned as grey as fish skin.

"No, but *we* will be if they find us," hissed Tam. "Now, pick him up. Quickly. We need to get out of here."

"Why'd you hit him?"

"Why do you think? I was outside the door, listening in. That wasn't him talking, that was the Ix."

"But—?"

"You heard what it said. They're so 'superior' they have no need to keep secrets. It was bluffing you, Lucy. Bragging, through this monk. It was telling you exactly what they plan to do. Come on, get his feet."

Lucy bent down and grasped the thick-set ankles. "Ugh, he's got varicose veins."

"Just lift," sighed Tam.

She screwed her nose and tugged. With a clumsy heave they slid the body onto the cot. Tam rolled Bernard to face the wall and covered him up to his neck with the blanket.

"Here, put this on." Tam grabbed a shabby monk's habit off a chair.

Lucy gave him her grossed out look.

"You kind of stand out at the moment," he said. "We're not trying to make a fashion statement."

She snatched the habit from his hands and slipped it on. He pulled up her cowl until her red hair was covered and her face was lost in shadow. "OK, listen. I managed to do a quick tour before I found you. There's a jetty and a boat house half a mile away. I know this island. It's not far to the mainland, even if I had to row—"

"Row?" she snapped, sounding like a small dog underneath her hood.

"University coxless fours. I can do it."

"But they'll see us."

"They're like zombies. If we act the part, we're out and gone in a matter of minutes. Follow me. Keep your head down. Shuffle. Speak to no one."

"Wait!" she hissed, and tugged him back. "What about David?"

"David? What about him?"

"We have to warn him."

"We'll do that when we get off the island."

"But I've been trying for years to reach him and I don't know how. The Ix must have a way – or how would they know so much about him?"

Tam chewed his lip slightly and looked at Brother Bernard. It was a mistake. Lucy read his face in a flash.

"You know something, don't you?"

He shook his head. "Come on."

"Stop!" She held his arm again. "I thought you wanted to find him?"

"If this is right," he said, talking low through his teeth, "all this stuff about . . . The Fire Eternal, I think David can take care of himself."

A crack of thunder almost shook the glass from the window. The rain slewed against the pane as if it had been fired from a Gatling gun. The sheer intensity of it was beating visibility down to mere yards.

"Hardly owl and pussycat weather," said Lucy. "You're not gonna row your boat safely to the shore in this."

Tam's mouth closed into a thin pink line.

"We've got to help him," she said. "He'd do the same for us."

Footsteps. Tam raised a finger to his lips. He pulled Lucy flat to the wall and stole a glance down the corridor outside the cell. Two brothers were approaching, at zombie pace. "All right," he whispered. "There's some kind of black stone on the chapel altar. I don't know what it is, but I saw it drain the colour from a stained glass window when one of them put his hand on it. The brothers near me at the time all jerked in response. We take it and go, agreed?"

She nodded eagerly.

"OK. When I signal, drop in behind me." Quickly, he gathered up the tray and bowl and stepped up to the doorway as the monks were passing. Lucy saw him give a brotherly nod to them. He paused a moment and reset the tray, then his finger tapped the side and he was moving again. She bent her head and followed him out of the door.

In the distance, a bell was tolling. It grew louder as they walked, the sharpness of the clangs almost grouting the mortar from the old stone walls. A smell of cedar wood hung in the air, making Lucy think of Arthur and his muzzy aftershave. That led her thoughts home and she found herself taking on the mantle of her clothing and praying that she would escape this place and see her mother and her dragons again, and even her annoying part-sister, Zanna. She thought of David, also, and cast her mind north. In that instant, she heard the hum

318

inside her ear and the folded brown canvas of Tam Farrell's habit briefly became an Arctic wasteland.

"This is it," Tam whispered, breaking the spell. They had stopped by a pair of oak-panelled doors. He pushed one open and drew her inside a dark, empty chapel.

"Something's wrong," she said, rubbing her arms, frightened. "I heard the hum. I think they know we're here."

But he was down the aisle already, looking around, muttering. "This is changed," he said. "It's all been stripped of colour." He pointed to the chalices, the cloth over the altar, the lights, the pew cushions. They were all just shades of grey.

"I don't like this," said Lucy, clapping a hand to her ear. The hum had suddenly faded. Or was it waiting by her shoulder?

"Sit there," said Tam. "Look as though you're praying." He guided her into the nearest pew.

She dropped to her knees and opened a hymn book. Instantly, the hum was back. The words of the hymns came together as a block and reorganised themselves into a heading that read:

The Death of Dragons is Nigh

Lucy dropped the book and gave a shuddering gasp. Monks were beginning to appear in the pews,

319

materialising as though a cloak had been lifted. She saw Tam Farrell kneel before the altar. On the altar lay a body, made from ice.

It was David.

Tam's habit fell away and from within it rose one of the awful black creatures Lucy had seen at the centre of the island. Paralysed with fear, she watched it spread its wings and hop off the altar step to land on David's body. It extended three conical claws, making the shape of the mark of Oomara. It dug them into David's chest.

Lucy screamed. A visceral howl that seemed to tear the lining clean out of her lungs.

The monks responded with reedy cries. Several began to shake and have fits. The glass in the east window fell apart, leaving a framework of hollow angels. In the sky beyond, Lucy witnessed a terrifying vision: the Arctic ice cap, cracking into islands.

On the altar, David's body imploded to water and flowed away, drenching the steps below.

Lucy was aware that she wanted to be sick. But the feeling stuttered as a wiry-bearded monk in round-lensed glasses came to stand in front of her. A hand gripped her arm and she was pulled from her seat.

The monk took off his glasses and polished them. "She is perfect," he said. "Take her to the room of obsidian."

Liz learns a truth

Among the many residents of Wayward Crescent, Elizabeth Pennykettle was one of the most well-liked. Henry Bacon had long been beguiled by her, though, of course, he was far too 'proper' to admit it. Other neighbours found her cheerful, if a little eccentric, mainly due to the fact that Liz had a tendency to make clay dragons for anyone in need, a course of action that commonly raised bemused (and sometimes sceptical) eyebrows, but had a wonderful way of resolving 'inconveniences' all the same (though no one could ever quite determine how). She was regarded as an excellent parent, actively supporting Lucy at school, and a reliable member of the local community, always willing to lend a hand at fêtes or Scrubbley town events. As a mother, she was efficient, fair and kind. She ran a good home. True, she had no shortage of help from her dragons, but *she* was the hub, the perfect mum. She cooked. She scrubbed. She mended. She loved. She was artistic, cared for animals, had magnetic letters on her fridge (an essential requirement of good parenting) and read wonderful bedtime stories. She could do anything.

Even speak to birds.

Less than ten minutes after taking Alexa in from the garden she was out there herself, pegging out a line of washing. She had her back to the fence when she heard the raven land. "Well, is it you?"

The irritated scrabble of claws confirmed it, well before Gwilanna croaked, "Guinevere's blood treats you well. You haven't changed a jot in five years, Elizabeth."

"You have," Liz said.

The raven produced the best hrrmph! it could. "It's not like you to be uncivil, my dear?"

Liz snapped a peg shut, ending the resistance of a pair of socks. "The last time you came to this Crescent you took my daughter hostage in the Arctic. Why should I express any kindness towards you?"

The raven arched its wings. "As usual, you put your tiresome humanity before your true lineage. The child was witness to a unique opportunity to raise Gawain. If I had asked for permission to take her, it would have been refused and the chance long lost."

"Lost?" Liz repeated bitterly, almost spitting the word over her shoulder. "I know what happened at that island, Gwilanna. My daughter was nearly killed and my lodger gave up his life protecting her. This household has never recovered. How can you talk to me about missed opportunities? If I could swap your life for his I'd do it a thousand times over. Why are you back?"

"He sent me," said the bird.

Liz closed her eyes. She felt a weakness in her shoulders, a slight chasm in her heart. "That's a lie," she said, before her breathing could stall.

Gwilanna dipped her beak in irritation. She looked back towards the house where Gadzooks and G'reth were sitting close together on the windowsill. "His dragons are watching. How very poignant." She snorted and turned her eyes on Liz again. "Have you lost all your dragon senses, girl? How could *they* have survived without him? I've seen him, Elizabeth. I've seen what he's become. Your lodger has found a new home in the Arctic, inside a polar bear's skin."

Liz shuddered and gripped at a shirt for support, squeezing its waist to almost nothing. She remembered Alexa on the phone to Zanna, *I saw Daddy, being a polar bear.*

"The child senses him," Gwilanna added casually. "While I was with him she materialised a thought gift: a woolly mammoth. A powerful talent for one so young. She is extremely promising. Unruly, naturally, but astonishingly forward. She should be given to me for training."

Liz whipped around so fast that her heels churned holes in the water-softened lawn. "You touch one hair of her head and I'll put you in a pie, you evil old crone."

"She's in danger."

"With you around that wouldn't surprise me. From what?"

"Her father wasn't specific. He's become arrogant, like the rest of those slanty-eyed dumplings he's bonded with."

"All words, Gwilanna. How do I know this isn't a trick?"

"If it is, it's not of my making," she said. She stretched her neck and added sharply, "The boy is alive and meddling with forces he doesn't understand. Do you remember my teachings on The Fire Eternal?"

Liz turned in a fluster to her washing line again. "Page one of the sibyl 'Book of Wisdom'. It's the breath of Godith, the source of all creation and unconditional love. The fire of life. The auma of the universe. Of course I remember it. Why?"

"Right now, I would say he's standing above it."

"Don't play games, Gwilanna. We're all above the fire. It's at the centre of the Earth."

"Ah, but according to your raised-again lodger there's a direct conduit to it, a very deep and dangerous well, located at the point where Guinevere dropped Gawain's tear into the ocean – and the polar ice cap formed as a result."

Liz stopped with a peg between her teeth. "He created the ice cap? Gawain's fire is *in the ice?*"

Gwilanna hopped sideways along the fence so that Liz could see her from the corner of her eye. "Incongruous, but true. Your little 'secret' in the freezer comes blessed with it, of course."

"Then he's in my dragons – and in David, too."

There was silence on the fence.

Liz turned round, saying, "Zanna told me he was killed by an ice spear through the heart."

"Outrageous providence," Gwilanna said bitterly.

The yellow rose bush bristled sweetly in the breeze. Liz covered her mouth. She thought back to her kitchen conversation with Arthur and his inspired 'revelation' about David's death. "So he does have Gawain within him," she said. Tears began to well in her bright green eyes.

"When you've done with this sentimental twaddle," said Gwilanna, "perhaps you'd like to get me out of these feathers?"

Liz shook her head. Gathering herself together, she pegged up the last piece of clothing and said, "So his tear wasn't lost. It was transformed into the ice, and Guinevere was responsible for that."

"What do you want, a glow of pride?" Gwilanna tutted.

"You told me she'd drowned."

"She was far out on the ocean."

"But you didn't see it. It was just an assumption. It was always an *assumption*."

"What does it matter? The girl is long gone."

"Not from here," said Liz, pointing to her heart. "She's in every breath I take. And suddenly, she's very alive to me, Gwilanna." She tossed her red hair. "So are her descendants. Lucy's disappeared. What do you know about that?"

"Nothing. How did we get onto—?"

"She went through a time-slip. She was taken by the Fain. Why would that happen?"

"I told you there was danger."

"Why do they want her? What's going on? If David is back it must be to a purpose. Are the two things connected? Tell me."

The raven did a version of the Texas two-step. "He talked about a conflict. An unseen war. Something to do with a division of the Fain who call themselves the Ix. They want to make dark fire."

"You always told me that was impossible."

"I've been wrong before," the raven said, doing its best to sniff. "The Ix plan to tap into human consciousness; your 'boy' plans to stop them. That's all I know. Now do the spell. Get me out of these feathers."

Liz shook her head again. "I can't. I'm not a sibyl. You'll have to wait for Zanna."

"And that may take some time," said a voice. The clothing parted and Arthur came through with Bonnington in his arms. Spying the bird, the cat gave a vicious hiss. "No," said Arthur, holding him back. "I believe this might be an old acquaintance."

"I'm glad you didn't say 'friend'," said Liz.

"So you took up with *him* after all?" hissed Gwilanna.

"I don't need your advice on who to love," said Liz.

She touched Arthur's arm and he said to her quietly, "Henry just came round with a message. Our telephones are down. Zanna's stuck in traffic a few miles outside of Scrubbley. There are jams all round the town."

"How come?" said Liz.

"I don't know," said Arthur. "Alexa thinks they might have come to see the fairies."

On the face of it, this was a ridiculous statement. The kind of innocent remark Alexa made every day. But it caused Liz to shudder deep inside.

"We must talk to her," said Arthur.

"I agree," caarked Gwilanna. "Set me free."

"No. You fly away. Now," said Liz. "Find Zanna and bring her home as quickly as you can. Use magicks if you must."

"I have no magicks!" the raven squawked. "My powers were removed when I was locked inside this body."

"Then teach Zanna what to do."

"The girl is headstrong. What if she refuses to trust me?"

Liz walked up the garden and broke a petal off the yellow rose. She kissed it and put it in the raven's beak. "Lucy's dragon, Gwendolen, is with her. She'll be able to verify my auma on this. Go, sibyl. Now's the time to make amends for thousands of years of deception. Go."

With a muffled *caark*, Gwilanna beat an upward path, finding a thermal that took her soaring backwards over the pepper spray of houses. As she levelled out, she tilted her head and looked down. To her surprise she saw people in the streets all around. Dozens were getting out of their cars and wandering like ants in a radial pattern. A pattern with its centre over Wayward Crescent. People, for all the world migrating.

Heading for the house at number 42.

Avrel tells a story

There was a tension in the air, a kind of resistance. The further north they journeyed, the more Avrel felt it. Even the ice seemed to drag beneath his paws. It was solid here. No creaking suggestion of water. It made him nervous.

It made him think.

For several days now his mind had been questing, collecting memory fragments on his ancestor, Thoran, in an effort to place in context the way the ice had formed. It was a critical moment in the history of the ice bears, and yet it was almost impossible to reach. The searches were tiring and mostly fruitless. Often, when he thought he was about to grasp a truth, it would fade with the slightest lapse of concentration. It didn't help that his interest kept drifting towards the woman. The woman who had been with Thoran at the start. The woman who had held the tear of the dragon. Guinevere, that's what Ingavar had called her. If he centred on that name he could picture her – just. She was tall, like the blue-eyed man Ingavar sometimes became. She had flowing red hair, bright green eyes, skin as pale as a seal pup's pelt. Charms and amulets were cast around her neck. She carried no weapons. Her strengths were her kindness and fearlessness of heart. What of *her*, this woman whom the bear had befriended? The raven had claimed she had drowned in these waters. But Avrel's instincts favoured the reverse. Guinevere had lived. He felt certain of that. But what had become of her? Where had she gone?

One morning, or night, it was impossible to tell, for there were very few breaks of genuine light, Ingavar came to join him at rest. Avrel was watching the sky spirits playing. They were sliding down a ribbon of green 'nightfire', which was the term his mother had sometimes used for the colours that formed in the arc of the sky.

The Nanukapik sat down beside his Teller. "Tell me a story, Avrel."

The sky spirits instantly rushed towards them, settling in the air like a living cloud.

Avrel, who was lying in the mouth of the wind, with one paw stretched and one tucked under his young chest said, "Lord, what would you like me to Tell?"

"Whatever is in your mind," said Ingavar.

Avrel middled his gaze. There was more than legends in his mind just then. He glanced across at Kailar. The fighting bear was battling with the early throes of sleep.

Lately, his rests had been scrappy and erratic. In sleep, the dragon's eye spoke to him, he said. It made him see things, made him *fly*, high above the ice like a ghost in the wind. Now he had fallen into slumber again, covering his snout with an involuntary paw and snoring with an irritated, broken rumble. He looked vulnerable. And he had lost condition. It was worrying, Avrel thought, but somehow touching.

"Our journey is nearly at an end," said Ingavar.

"We have reached the place?"

"We are very close."

Avrel looked about him. "There are no marks." Had the raven not reported lines of fire? A definite intersection where the tear had fallen?

"They will show themselves," said Ingavar, "when you need to see them." He folded a leg and laid himself down. The ice barely echoed to his weight as he dropped.

A spirit danced before them, a woman in skins. Avrel looked up, wondering for a moment if it might be Guinevere, for her name was playing in the shell of his ear. His chin sagged when he realised it wasn't her at all. His gaze turned inward and Ingavar followed it.

"Take away the wind and the night from your memories. Take away time. Tell me what you see."

A vision. Avrel was almost left breathless by its

swiftness. He saw the ice forming like a morning sunrise, breaking on the crust of the ocean so quickly that it might have just surged to the surface from below. At its centre was a great white fire. From the body of the fire stepped a perfect bear.

"I see Thoran," said Avrel, his head clustered with images. "He is wandering, distressed. He is looking for something . . . for the woman, Guinevere."

"I hear you," said Ingavar, tipping his snout. It was the tradition to acknowledge a Teller's story so.

"He has been walking for days," the son of Lorel went on. "He was separated from her when the dragon's tear was dropped." He flinched as he saw it happening again, another flashback, another ice cap moment. So much beauty. So much light. "The sea was in torment. The spreading ice lifted her and carried her away. His heart is in despair, for he knows she could be anywhere. He is lost and he cannot detect her scent. This landscape is strange to him, the open sky, the cold. He feels blinded by the brightness and has nothing to guide him barring courage and hope. But he will not give up. He will not rest until he knows her fate. She was kind to him once. She . . . oh."

Avrel jerked back suddenly. A twist of snowflakes gathered on his head, making the mark of Oomara in his fur. "He sees her." His slim jaws parted in wonder. "She is lying on a ridge, no higher than his chest. She is frozen to it." He paused. "She is dead."

Not dead, said a wind from another world.

Avrel's eyes snapped open. "What was that?"

Ingavar calmly raised his snout. He squinted at a snowflake on the tip of his nose.

"I heard a whisper," said Avrel. "It said she wasn't dead."

"Then pay heed and continue with your Telling," said Ingavar, his voice low and rasping but his coaxing gentle.

Avrel gave the sky a distrustful sweep before warily closing his eyes again. When he did, the story opened clearly in his mind as if Thoran and Guinevere were right there in front of him. "Thoran has settled beside her," he said. "He is anguished. He does not know what to do. Time is passing in blizzards, in storms. The days layer up in drifts against his fur. His eyes are frosted, but he cannot sleep.

"One morning, there comes a steadiness, a calm. In the quiet, he tells himself he must move on. For what good would it do to laze here and die? He must explore this new white world. Claim it, for her. There must be meaning in this miracle she helped to create?

"Suddenly, he hears the beat of a wing. In the sky, far above, too distant to identify, he notices a travelling speck, a bird. It means no harm but it makes him think of predators. What creatures, he wonders, might be roaming this place? He growls inwardly, desiring to protect her. Nothing must take her body. Nothing.

"He stands, stiff and weary, considering his choices. Perhaps he could cover her? The soft ice blown into drifts by the wind is easy to scoop and pack into mounds. But how long would it last? How quickly could it be broken into? He snorts impatiently and thinks again. He could eat her, leaving nothing but her cloth skins behind. But that alternative is just too repellent. So, in his mind, he looks to the ocean, gauging its swell as every ice bear that ever comes after him will. If he sends her there she will be lost to its secrets, but her auma will live with him forever.

"So he rises up and pounds his paws against the surface. Pounds till the shudders almost loosen his teeth. But the ice is thick. It will not break. Committing her to water will not be possible. Yet his efforts have brought about a physical change. Her arm has been dislodged from the side of her body. Her frozen serenity has been disturbed. Thoran looks at the stiff, blue fingers. Are they reaching out to touch him one last time? He drops his nose to their tips and leaves it there a moment, making a thin warm wall of vapour. Then he licks the hand respectfully and tries to nudge it back against her side with his snout. It will not go. He tries again and hears a frightening crack.

"He steps back, snuffling with hurt and confusion. What has he done? What has he done? All over her body more cracks are appearing, running up her arms, spreading across her chest, crawling round her neck like the roots of a tree. He barks at the sky as if the spirits are to blame, then calls for their help, to *anything* that can help. But nothing comes. Nothing can stop the erosion. Guinevere is falling apart before his eyes. Her skin, her hair, her clothing, her boots, disintegrate to pieces, there on the ridge. But then . . ."

"Then?" said Ingavar.

Avrel tilted his head. He kept his eyes closed, but it was clear from the twitching muscles in his face that his mind was astonished at what he was reporting. He continued in an awestruck whisper. "From the dust comes a flake. A single white flake. Followed by another. And another. And another. A small blizzard is rising up from the remains. He is seeing her auma, turning to snow . . ."

Not snow, said the voice on the wind. The sound

whooshed through the tunnels of his ears. As it came to a peak his mind opened like a shell and he saw . . . not snow, but small creatures with wings.

Avrel jumped and opened his eyes. The present-day North came rushing back. But the setting had changed. Ingavar was no longer at his side, but sitting column-like, just ahead. Kailar, now awake, was staring wild-eyed into the distance. Before Avrel could determine why, the ice around his feet began to glow a shade of green. And now, in whichever way he moved his head, he saw a line of coruscating green in the distance, like blood trails lit with fire. And he knew what he was, and why he was. And he felt all history coming to a point. He was sitting on the place where dragon lines meet, over the channel to The Fire Eternal.

And when, at last, he did raise his head, this is what the Teller of Ways recorded: bears, young and old, approaching in their thousands.

Now he could understand Kailar's anxiety.

The three of them were surrounded.

The Power of Obsidian

The walls were circular and constructed of coarse grey stone. There were no windows and the air was dry with smoke. It was a tower room, lit by rippling torches, set at angles, in iron frames, at equal heights. The monks had left her on a splintered wooden floor which creaked in several places as she rose. In the centre of the floor was a polished brown boulder. It was huge, like an outrageous cancer. How it had been carried there, Lucy could not guess. The top had been levelled off to make a table. On the table were a cluster of jagged black stones. They had a lustre in the torchlight and looked like pieces of petrified liquorice.

Sitting up, she called out, "Where am I? What do you want?"

The flame nearest to her danced hypnotically. There was no reply.

She stood up and tried the only door. It was locked, but she'd expected that. There was a keyhole, but nothing really visible through it. Shadows. Maybe a winding stair.

"Please?" she called out. "Please, I'm cold." She clamped her arms but the chill was in her mind. She remembered the chapel. The monster. David. "Please," she said again, and hunkered down.

Suddenly a voice said, "The creature you saw is called a Darkling."

Lucy squealed and jumped back to her feet. Brother Bernard, or what was left of the man, was standing on the far side of the table. Blood had crusted against his temple. His habit was torn. His eyes were black and largely inert.

"How did you get here?" Lucy hissed. Her gaze darted frantically all around. Had she missed an entrance? High up, perhaps? All she could see were aged rafters.

The monk slid back his sleeves. "What do you know about obsidian, child?" He played his hands above the rocks on the table.

Nearest to Lucy was a spear-headed piece. She snatched it up, wielding it like a dagger. "I'll use this stone, I will, if you don't set me free."

"Stone is a weak description," he said. "Obsidian is a volcanic glass, made from fast-cooling molten magma. During the Fain's early breeding programme, it was thought that dragons might be fashioned from it. The prototype bodies were aerodynamic but never flexible enough to sustain the desired range of movement. They fractured too easily, because of impurities in the chemical structure. And when it was discovered that the glass was incompatible with The Fire Eternal, it was put aside in favour of clay. This island is a mine of the purest obsidian. From it you will make the Darkling you saw."

"In your dreams," said Lucy, and lunged at him.

But he was gone, like vapour, to reappear in an instant at the opposite side of the table.

"Your bravado is very ill-placed," he said. "If you were human, I would kill you in an instant."

"I *am* human."

"You are not. You are a hybrid. An offspring of the dragon Gawain and the woman Guinevere who partially commingled with him through his fire. You were birthed by an ancient means of parthenogenesis. Your kind self-replicate. You will introduce this quality into the Darkling. You may begin."

Lucy hurled the stone at him. It struck his shoulder, making him wince. Worried that she'd made a physical contact, she took a pace back. "Why would I make anything for you? You're not Bernard. You're *them* inside his body."

The figure of Bernard turned towards the door. It opened and two more monks came in. They threw Tam Farrell into the room. His body, still clothed in its stolen sacking, fell heavily and he rolled awkwardly onto his back. Blood was spilling out of one nostril. Lucy ran to him and put her ear to his mouth. There was a faint warm breath.

Very faint.

"What have you done to him?"

"He is nothing," said the Ix. "Probing his mind reveals no uses. But you, you have a history of dragons. With it comes a powerful ability to visualise. What you saw in the chapel was a projection of your fears. A waking nightmare. You will use this ability to construct the Darkling."

"And if I don't?"

"It would be a simple task for an Ix:risor to enter your mind, make you see the worst means imaginable for this human's death, and convert it into reality. If you want him to survive, you will make the creature."

"No," said Lucy, shaking with anger. "He'd rather die than see that evil thing flying."

At that moment, Tam stirred and his eyes flickered open. He whispered Lucy's name and accepted her hand as she slid it into his. He felt cold, almost frozen, and very weak. "I'm sorry," he said. "We should have run when we could."

Lucy forced her gaze away. That was her fault, the

chapel. They could have escaped. Guilt and indecision spiralled freely in her mind, followed by a flash of another nightmare: Tam's body falling from the roof of the tower. That was them, playing with her mind again, she knew. She cut the image off and said to the Ix, "How do I know he isn't a projection?"

The monk's head nodded, as if this was a sensible question. "By a simple exchange of energies."

"Yeah, right. Can I have that in semi-human-speak, *please?*"

She felt the hum in her ear. Bernard's eyes seemed to blacken again. His mouth moved to the commands of the Ix inside him. "The girl-dragon knows which energies are required, but the human element is conditioned and unwilling. Exchange love with this human and you will know that he is real."

Lucy looked down at Tam's dark, stubbled face. She'd read his poetry. She understood.

To that which beauty must forever bow
Love is the fire, the eternal now

She put her mouth over Tam's and kissed him.

Real. Very real. Her relief flowed into him.

They parted slightly and she caught his breath in hers.

She let her fingers brush his ear.

For a second time his bloodshot eyes flickered open.

Human.

Real.

She was about to pull away when he grasped her hand and pressed it flatly against his heart. Their eyes met. *What?* she mouthed. He was trying to communicate something to her, without saying or thinking the words. He parted her fingers awkwardly with his, hearing her gasp as they tingled slightly. He nodded once then passed out again. She thought she saw a flicker of relief in his face before his head came to rest on the boards once more.

"All right, I'll make your creature," she said, "but only if you set Tam free. He's human. No threat to you. Send him back through the rift."

The lifeless black eyes rolled towards Tam. "He is not strong. The atomic dissociation will kill him. Is this what you desire?"

"No. Of course not!"

"Then he must be held." The Ix picked up the rock that had bounced off his shoulder and placed it back on the table again. "Choose two pieces. Concentrate, as you would with clay. The pieces will meld as you bring them together. Make the Darkling exactly as you saw it."

Lucy stood up and studied the rocks. Obsidian. She did know something about the stone. Zanna sold bracelets and necklaces from it, along with what she called some loose 'conchoidal' fractures – broken pieces with highly-polished curves. She wiped the sweat off her palms and said, "I don't get this. Obsidian brings out the warrior spirit." (Wow. Zanna would have praised her for that.) "It's a grounding stone that helps you find the truth inside yourself. It's s'posed to drive away negative energy. So how does that work with your dark *thing?*"

"Create," said the Ix, refusing to answer. "Bring the stones together. Dream it."

That was a dreadful moment for Lucy. "How do you know about *that?*"

"Build," it said.

This time it was an order. She felt the hum rising and shied away. "All right. Don't. No more nightmares." One imagined Darkling was quite enough.

She selected two pieces. They clacked sweetly as she knocked them together. It seemed incongruous to think that they could ever be joined, but as she closed her eyes and conjured up the Darkling, the stones softened into a flexible jelly and flowed around her hands like cold lava. It was difficult to work with, hard to contain, but in time she grew used to its unique malleability and

343

discovered, to her amazement, that shapes formed best when she drew her hands away a few millimetres from the surface and used her *thoughts* to make the mould. When she opened her eyes, she had constructed a foot.

"Excellent. Proceed with the rest," said the Ix.

It took as long as it took. When it was done, the creature sat squat on the boulder like an old church gargoyle, hideously perfect, about twice the size of a Pennykettle dragon.

Lucy stood back, clammy and cold. She was terrified of the beast, yet fascinated by its savage beauty. Every surface of it shone, even down to its studded tongue and the twisted horn that made the tip of its tail. Torchlight glinted off its blueberry eyes. It was exactly what she'd seen, but it wasn't moving. It had no auma. No light inside.

"What now?" she asked.

The door opened again and in walked the bearded monk she'd seen in the chapel.

The Bernard figure said to him, "It is done."

The bearded one stepped forward to inspect the Darkling. It rested a finger on one of the upright wings that sat out like a pair of unnatural shoulder blades. Lucy held her breath, thinking the Darkling would spring to life. It remained unchanged. "What's it for?" she snapped at them. "What are you going to do with it?"

"It is a weapon against dragons."

"There *are* no dragons! We don't have them any more."

"The Fain you call 'David' will soon create a channel."

David. Fain? Lucy felt as though her heart was a maypole, strings tearing it apart in all directions.

"Dragons will come to him," the bearded Ix said.

"He'll destroy you," said Lucy.

She felt the hum in her ear and wished she'd kept her mouth shut.

"What is this?" said the bearded one. He pointed to a single piece of obsidian.

"I didn't need it," Lucy said. "It was just . . . left over."

The monk rolled it between his hands. It was roughly the shape of a small root vegetable, slightly swollen at one end and tapering to a sharp twisted spike at the other. It could have easily passed for a knife. He put the tip of it onto his tongue. For a moment, Lucy thought he was about to make a cut, but he pulled it away again and said to her, "Take it."

Lucy shook her head indignantly. "Why?"

"In this form, it is poisonous to humans."

She saw death in his eyes and took a pace back. "I did

what you asked. Let me go. Let me *go*." But, suddenly, the hum was overpowering her again and she passed out with a stifled cry, falling in a half twist over Tam's body.

The bearded Ix turned to Brother Bernard. "The dark energy in this sector of the universe is peaking. The Fain David is about to open the core. Modify the rift coordinates and send an Ix:risor back within the girl to your old brother, *Vincent*. The risor will ensure there are no interruptions." He placed his hand on the Darkling and stroked it. "We are ready," he said.

Supernova

They agreed to wait until Zanna was home. No conversations with Alexa till then. In the meantime, Liz was growing ever more concerned about the people gathering in the Crescent. They'd been coming by in dribs and drabs all day long. But now they were staying. Now they were a throng. She and Arthur (and a very studious Gretel) had installed themselves in Lucy's bedroom window, from where Liz could see the huddle growing. There was no gate at the end of her drive and so far no one had trespassed down it. But on the pavement they were swelling like a football crowd, pressing against the hedge and even climbing on the cars. Trying to get a glimpse of something.

But what?

"Arthur, I'm frightened. Tell me what's happening?" Liz hooked his arm and put her face against his shoulder.

Arthur allowed Bonnington to step onto the windowsill, still near enough to have his tiger's tail stroked. "Do you recognise any of them? Or are they all strangers?"

Bonnington and Gretel panned the crowd intently.

"Most of them are strangers," Liz replied. "But some

are people I've known for years. I mean, what are *they* doing? Why aren't they complaining?"

Arthur put his head against his interlaced fingers, something he did when he was wrangling with a crossword or the workings of the soul or the mysteries of the universe. "Do you feel anything? A sense of inner bliss?"

Liz frowned and shook her head. "Is this Arthur or Brother Vincent talking?"

He pursed his lips and nodded. "Perhaps you're too close to it. Lucy was the same. But the dragons . . . they are waking up. So are these pilgrims."

"Pilgrims? Arthur, what are you talking about?" She gave him what she called a 'practicality prod', a literal jab in the ribs to remind him she was his partner, not his student.

He took her hand briefly and stroked it. "Remember the news reports about the bears migrating? This is its human polarity. To use a cosmological analogy, these people are on the edge of a collapsing star. They are being drawn here because they cannot help themselves. They have come to witness a supernova. Something . . . extraordinary is about to happen."

"That was my hedgerow cracking," said Liz, as the weight of the crowd finally pushed the hedge over.

Arthur turned his gaze to the Crescent. "I think these people are David's readers. Come to fulfil their connection with him."

Liz shook her head and hurred to Gwillan, who flew to Lucy's TV and switched it on. A special news report flickered straight up, from the Conference for Climate Change at Stavanger. *There are thousands of people here, the reporter was saying, filling the streets around this magnificent building. The fjords are ringing to their chants . . .*

"Do you hear it?" Arthur muttered, swaying almost drunkenly. He brought his hands together in a gesture of peace.

Liz jinked the voiles aside. The crowd in the Crescent had begun to chant, in eerie synchronicity with the TV. She whipped around and stared at the wall to the Den. "The dragons are humming it."

Bonnington leapt off the windowsill and went haring from the room as if he'd been stung.

Liz glanced at the sky. A feisty wind was spiking the tops of the trees and stirring the clouds in a circular motion, blending them into a uniform grey.

"A mantra," Arthur muttered. "They are chanting a mantra."

No, not a mantra, Liz decided. For she could hear a

sequence of notes now, too. Hollow, tonal harmonies. That was a *chime*. Suddenly, alarm bells sounded in her head. "Lexie?!" she yelled. She sprinted to the landing and leaned over the banister. "Lexie, where are you?!"

"Here, Naunty!" The child's voice floated out of Zanna's room.

Liz hammered downstairs and burst right in. "Are you all—?" Her words failed when she saw what Alexa was doing. On the bed lay the plastic box from the freezer. The girl was holding what was left of the snowball. David's four dragons, Gadzooks, G'reth, Groyne and Gollygosh were sitting on the windowsill facing her. Alexa gathered up a piece of ice and put it on the healing dragon's snout. It melted through his nostrils, turning his eyes an intense shade of violet, the same colour, Liz noticed, as the other three dragons.

"Alexa, what have you done?" she gasped.

"They have to go now," said the girl.

"Go where?" said Liz, half-sinking to her knees in confusion.

Gretel, who had followed Liz in, hurred and pointed to the cardboard mobile. The fairies were jinking madly as they turned, though there wasn't a breath of wind in the room.

From the garden came an urgent yowl.

350

Liz stood up with a start.

"Come on," Alexa said and put out her hands. The dragons came to her like pigeons to a grain-covered bird table.

"No, stay there," Liz said, backing out. "Gretel, don't let her out of your sight." And clutching her sleeves into the middle of her palms, Liz ran outside to go and find Bonnington.

Alexa looked at Gretel, Gretel at Alexa. Alexa pointed to her drawing pad. On it was a sketch of the dragon she called G'lant. Around his head were several flying creatures, like the fairies in the mobile but not the same.

Gretel asked for an explanation.

"They're *nearly-fairies*," Alexa announced. The wind-chimes *tonged*. Alexa picked up the note and in dragonsong hummed the rest of the melody. Gretel jolted in surprise. The picture had suddenly come to life. The scales around the dragon's eye compressed as he blinked. The Earth at its centre began to turn. The planet tilted north towards the polar ice cap and the 'nearly-fairies' began to shimmer.

"Naunty Guinevere's helping Daddy," said Alexa, hurrying out and leaving Gretel quite mesmerised.

By now, Liz had caught up with Bonnington. She had

found him by the rockery, facing the fairy door, stretching and yowling in the way he sometimes did if he was going to vomit. She hunkered down, not sure whether to touch him or not. He did not appear to be in any sort of pain, but his coat was going through rapid changes, as if he was moulting in time-lapsed photography, or speed-dialling a number – or flashing out a code.

Suddenly, he halted on plain brown tabby.

There was a click. Violet light strobed the bottom of the rockery.

The fairy door opened and a being fluttered out. Liz gasped and now she did grip Bonnington, though he was showing no signs of fear. The creature hovered in mid-air, beating wings as barely visible as drifting dust motes. It was the size of a large rose petal and just as fragile, the main part of its body taking the form of a semi-translucent, flexible membrane. When it moved (in the way that certain marine animals swam) light flowed through it in pastel-coloured waves. As more beings appeared Liz noticed that they had a humanoid appearance, though their faces were characterless and impossible to tell apart. One of them settled on Bonnington's nose. It put out what appeared to be a probe of some kind and touched the space between the cat's eyes. A gradient of light from lilac to violet pulsed simultaneously through the creatures.

Bonnington gave a contented purr.

Alexa knocked her fists together in delight. "They just said hello to the fairy in Bonnington."

Liz turned her head. The girl was right behind her, with David's dragons. "Lexie, stay away. They're not fairies. I think their proper name is *fainies* – and they're not very nice."

Do not be afraid, said a voice.

Liz squealed in fright and fell back with a hand clamped across her left ear.

Alexa knelt down and let the dragons fly free. Immediately, each dragon was surrounded by fairies, guiding them like tall ships onto the rockery.

"No!" cried Liz, trying to reach out and stop it. "The Fain attacked Arthur! They attacked me. Lexie, don't—"

Not us, they said, and several came to settle on her arm.

Liz rocked back again. Her head felt light, like a room that had just been cleared and aired. As she struggled to find a focal point, the garden seemed to fold itself away and for a moment a whole new world appeared. A place of high mountains and lush vegetation. A stream bed.

A village. A place of dragons. And that voice . . . ?

We are like you, Elizabeth.

When she looked again, the fairies had red hair.

We must commingle with the image of Godith, they said.

And as she watched them fly away, one fairy went to G'reth and literally flew right into him, dissolving through the hard scales on his chest. The same thing happened with Gollygosh and Groyne. When it came to Gadzooks' turn, Liz saw him tremble and shake his wings. He lost his footing briefly, sending loose stones tumbling down between the rocks. He had the airy look of a newborn bird. When he coughed, a jet of white flame erupted from his throat.

The fairy door opened a little further.

"Wait," said Liz, as the fairies guided the dragons towards it. "I made these dragons. I can't let them go without knowing what will happen to them."

Alexa picked at her red gingham dress. "Say bye bye to G'reth," she said.

The wishing dragon was on the threshold, looking deep into a matrix of swirling colour. He stroked Bonnington, who had padded forward to sit beside the door like a great furry bouncer, then disappeared through it with a quick snap of light. Groyne and Gollygosh quickly followed. Gadzooks was the only one to cast a glance back, first at Liz, then at his beloved suburban garden. *Hrrr*, he said.

Liz laced her fingers and hunkered like a pixie. "*Hrrr*. I love you, too," she whispered.

There was another snap of light and the door creaked shut. Alexa went to it and tugged at the handle. She peeked in, but all that could be seen behind the doorway now was rock.

Just then, a thin crash of metal from somewhere near the house made Alexa catch her breath and whirl around.

"Hi, did you miss me?" said a girl's voice.

And there was Lucy, feet outstretched, clanking back and forth on her rusty garden swing.

In her lap was a knife of poisoned obsidian. And on the patio next to her, lay a broken wind chime.

Part Three

For only the second or third time in his life, Kailar felt truly afraid. In fourteen or so winters roaming the ice (the precise number blurred like the hairs thinning yearly on his prominent snout) he had fought many bears, survived the harshest blizzards, dug his way out of an avalanche (as a cub), escaped men and their dogs, nearly had his eye taken out by a walrus, been imprisoned near a dump town, laughed at starvation, tasted poison and very nearly died from it, run with spirits, watched a blue-eyed bear turn into a man, come to know every pore of his body through the power of a purifying white fire, carried the eye of a creature called a dragon and endured the prattling words of a Teller. But he had never seen anything like this before, every ice bear (or near so, surely) drawn together into one huge pack. He shuddered to speculate how it was possible. It worried him even more to know by what enchantment they were being kept calm. It terrified him to wonder at their fate.

"What is this?" he demanded, with the growl of a brave, indignant champion.

"This is a new beginning," said Ingavar. He looked

outward and nodded his head. To Avrel's astonishment, the first row of bears began to lie down. Like trees falling, the rest followed suit.

"I like what I have. What I've always had," said Kailar, and despite the burden still hanging around his neck, he pawed the ice as if he could pick it up and carry it in his chest.

"What you have is under threat," Ingavar said calmly, appealing to Avrel as well as to Kailar. "We have walked a long way together. Now is the moment your must hear and understand. You heard me speak some days ago about a race of beings who call themselves the Ix."

"Do they plan to harm us?" Avrel said quickly, standing tall to show his solidarity with Kailar. For all he admired Ingavar's wisdom, he did have some sympathy with the fighting bear's stance.

A gust of wind lifted up a screen of ice spicules. When they had settled, David Rain stood in place of Ingavar again. "Not directly," he said, in the voice of the bear.

Kailar, growing weary of this, set himself down and let the eye of Gawain wriggle free of his neck. Green light fizzed around the place where it landed, but the dragon did not wake and the lid remained closed.

David spoke quietly to Avrel. "I was sent here to

protect you, because of the ice bear's history with dragons. The North is experiencing a period of decline, aided, in part, by the actions of men. The Ix are preying upon this. They are making human beings forget what this region is worth to them and convincing them that nothing can be done to save it. If they succeed, the ice will melt, bears will die out, and the ways of the North will be lost for ever. The auma of the Earth will suffer greatly. Then will come a period of grief and fear. The Ix will harness this mood to ignite dark fire in the hostile dragons they refer to as Darklings. A large flock of these creatures could destroy every living being on this world – or worse, induce them to destroy themselves. This would clear the way for the Ix to mine the resources they need to continue breeding Darklings. Ultimately, they will use this planet as a base to generate something called an *Inversion*. Imagine a permanent polar night with the dark sky gradually closing in, that's the only way I can describe it to you, Avrel. This will happen if we do not act." David put his face to the sky. The spirit arena by now was vast. "The spirits of the North are trying to resist, but alone they cannot hold out or defeat the Ix."

Avrel glanced at the throng of bears. "And why are *they* here? What can they do?"

David walked towards the eye of Gawain. "Nothing."

"*Nothing?*" Avrel felt a sense of panic grip the centre of his chest and then wondered at the back of his mind if Gwilanna's warnings should not have been heeded after all.

David stared into the thoughtful, almond-coloured eyes. "The dragon gave you birth. Now is his time to save you." And he stood beside the eye of Gawain and stretched his arms sideways. The air above him shimmered in four oval patches.

Avrel stood back, snorting in alarm.

Four strange little creatures had just landed safely on David's arms. "Hello, guys," he said. "It's been a long time."

Zanna had never known a gridlock like it. Yet there was no road rage or blaring of horns and everyone seemed in remarkably good spirits. Glancing across to the car at her right, she saw a family of four – a mum and three girls. The youngest girl looked about nine, the eldest maybe fifteen. The middle one nearest to Zanna was clutching a book. David's book, *White Fire*.

Zanna opened her window. "Hey?"

The girl nudged her mother. Their passenger window slid down.

"Do you know what the hold-up is?"

The mother leaned forward. "It's coming. Don't you feel it?"

All Zanna felt was the need for a sandwich. She hadn't eaten since setting off from Blackburn. "I, er, got here a bit late. What did I miss?"

Mother and daughter exchanged a few words. "Haven't you read the book?" The girl tapped the cover.

"Once or twice," Zanna said quietly.

"Then you must feel it?" said the girl.

"A new beginning," said the mother.

Zanna glanced at the youngest child and was about to suggest there must be something weird in the water supply that day when *thunk!* an object landed on the roof of her car. The girl with the book gave a yelp of fear.

"What is it?" Zanna asked. "What the heck hit me?"

Bizarrely, a raven's beak tapped her windscreen.

The girl's window immediately slid up.

The raven hopped sideways and tapped again.

Still struggling to make any sense of all this, Zanna whacked the windscreen with the side of her fist. "Get off. I only just washed this car."

Hrrr, said Gwendolen, risking turning round. She'd been travelling on the shelf again, looking out the back.

"Not a bird? Of course it's a bird," said Zanna.

Gwendolen shook her head. She pointed to the rose petal in the raven's beak then flew to the passenger door and pressed the electric window release. As the window slid down she gave a quick *hrrr*. With a *caark* and an awkward flutter of wings, the raven was suddenly in the car.

"Close the window," it snapped, spitting out the petal.

Zanna recognised the voice immediately. "Oh my God, I don't believe this. I thought you were dead."

"In your family, that's a common mistake," said Gwilanna.

"But you were in the Arctic when Lucy—"

"Yes, yes, yes," the bird squabbled insanely, perching on the swollen leather lip of the seat. "There's no time for all that. Elizabeth has sent me to bring you home."

Hrrr, went Gwendolen, stroking the petal. She confirmed that Liz's auma was indeed on the flower.

Zanna put the car into neutral. Her foot ached, she'd been waiting in first for so long. "As you can see, I'm headed there, but . . ." She gestured at the windscreen. The traffic wasn't moving. And now people were turning off their engines and abandoning their vehicles. What's more, they were humming a harmonic mantra.

"Hurry, we must go," Gwilanna said impatiently.

"How?" said Zanna, gesturing again. "Besides, I'm not going anywhere with you. I wouldn't trust you further than a frog could hop. You don't just turn up out of nowhere making demands. I want some explanations. What the heck is going on?"

"I bring . . . *glad tidings*," Gwilanna said acidly.

Zanna threw her a scorching glare.

"Your boyfriend is alive."

Zanna sat a moment, frozen, not knowing what to say.

Hrrr-rrr, went Gwendolen, humming the mantra.

"I've seen him, girl."

Zanna gritted her teeth.

"Don't you realise, he's the one who's *causing* this."

"That's it. Get out." Zanna grabbed a street atlas from the pocket of the door. She was just about to bat the bird out of the window when a middle-aged man came past the car, bumped the wing mirror and stopped to set it straight. He was carrying a copy of David's book. Zanna checked her anger and looked around. She could see others now, many of them with the book. Some were reading from it as they walked. Some were holding it high like a sign. "No," she said. The rush of denial was unfathomably deep, but her eyes were beginning to glisten and burn.

"Show me your arm," Gwilanna caarked. She hopped

onto the parking brake and pecked at Zanna's sleeve.

"What are you doing, witch?" Zanna slapped her off.

"The mark. I didn't give you the mark for nothing. Haven't you learned to use its powers yet?"

Zanna looked at the three red lines on her arm. The scratch that never healed. The mark of Oomara.

"Hold it and think yourself a bird," said Gwilanna.

"*What?* Why?"

"So we can fly away and reach your daughter quickly."

"Alexa? She's in trouble?"

"In that house, there is always trouble."

Zanna reassessed the traffic. Dead. Every car. No way forward. No way back. She switched off her engine and lowered the window.

"Good. Now, hurry or I'll leave you," said Gwilanna.

Zanna studied her arm again. She slowly curled her fingers round the mark. Several seconds went by and nothing happened.

"Give in to it," Gwilanna said impatiently.

Zanna's hair fell forwards. "It's no good, I can't."

"You're a sibyl! Choose a form and it will—"

Suddenly, the air popped. And then there were two ravens in the car.

"Hurrah," said Gwilanna, blowing away a loose feather.

"I'm glad we got *that* sorted out. Now, concentrate, girl. Hold the spell. It wouldn't do to change again in mid-air, would it?"

"What about Gwendolen? It's too far for her to fly."

Gwilanna fluttered to the window ledge and studied the sky. Grey, but no snow. Minimal wind, despite the moving cloud banks. "You're strong. Carry her on your back if you must."

Zanna signalled Gwendolen to her. In her active form, the dragon was hardly any burden.

Gwilanna prepared to launch.

"Wait," Zanna said.

"What now, girl?"

"If you're lying about any of this, I'll kill you."

Gwilanna clicked her beak. "I believe there's a queue for that privilege," she said. And with a *caark* at a startled passer-by she took off.

Seconds later, Zanna and Gwendolen were with her.

And, Zanna had to confess, it was a *heck* of a way to beat the traffic.

"What breed are they?" asked Avrel, trying to find a memory to describe the new arrivals. He had seen many bird-like creatures before, but never in these shapes or colours or . . . ? It never occurred to him that they might be small dragons.

David replied, "They are my helpers." He turned to his left where a hummock of ice levelled off at waist height. He set the dragons down there.

"Are they spirits?"

"Sometimes," David said, running his hand down Gadzooks' spine. The writing dragon was shaking with emotion. His oval eyes had widened to a pumpkin shape. While David spoke to him calmly in dragontongue, G'reth was excitedly studying the bears. A sea of dark noses and sedentary eyes. All of them held by the song on the wind. The wishing dragon raised his paws to the universe and the spirits sang to him, inviting him in. Gollygosh, meanwhile, was switching his gaze between the eye of Gawain and the eye of the bear that seemed to be protecting it. He blew a smoke ring. It made the bear squint. Golly waved. The bear did not wave back. The healing dragon swished his tail and took a large step nearer to safety, to David. And Groyne sat patiently, soaking up the vastness. As companion once to the shaman, Bergstrom, he was no stranger to this icy wilderness.

With one enormous rattle, Gadzooks settled his scales. He looked warily at Avrel, and decided he preferred to fix his gaze on David. *Why are you here?* he

368

hurred. It was a question loaded with loss.

David took a moment, then answered softly, "Because I can't be at home."

But there is danger there, the dragon said urgently.

David opened his hand. He invited Gadzooks to flutter up on to it. "Tell me," he said.

The Lucy was taken.

David's gaze fell away into the middle distance, a difficult space between caring and heroism. "Tell me all of it," he said, and closed his eyes.

In a physical sense, what happened next did not happen at all, but for the first time in five years the writing dragon *sensed* his pencil moving. Words tore across the pages of his pad. The whole story of Lucy and Tam's disappearance. Blackburn. The mobile phone. The squirrel. The time rift. All that he knew. All that he had heard from Gretel and Liz and the listening dragon. When it was done, David's eyes flashed open. Avrel noted the anger there. The man-bear seemed to utter a slight roar, but it was just a word spoken with guttural intent. "G'reth?"

The wishing dragon turned.

"Can you form a wide link with a listening dragon?"

G'reth tapped his paws together and nodded. *The one in the kitchen?*

"No. Remember Grace?"

Gadzooks rocked back. *He* remembered Grace. The beautiful listener that David's first girlfriend Sophie had taken with her to Africa. Everyone remembered *Grace*.

G'reth raised an eye ridge.

"Send a signal. Make the contact as quickly as you can. Tell me the moment you reach her. Kailar?"

The fighting bear gave a sleepy grunt.

"Break the bag and push the eye of Gawain into the open."

Kailar, never one to be rushed out of tiredness, stood up slowly, his face almost hidden behind his great puffs of breath. "What will happen to the pack?" he asked.

"They will be unified," David said, looking deep into the fighting bear's eyes. "Every son and daughter of the Nine." He opened his jaw and made the barking sound that was used among bears as a mark of sincerity.

Kailar raised his fighting paw. "For Ragnar," he roared, pitching his voice as distantly as he could. He raked his claws into the tough kelp strands and tore them open. Then, using both paws together like a plough, he pushed the eye forward. When he backed away, a ring of sparkling green light was encircling the stone.

The spirits' song became a single '*Ommmmm*'.

David turned to the Teller of Ways. "Avrel, your time has come."

Avrel gulped and stared at the pack. Old stragglers, yearlings, mothers with cubs, not to mention hundreds of belligerent males. All waiting. Looking. Looking to him. "What am I to Tell them?"

"Everything," said David. "Open your mouth, the words will be there."

"But . . . how will they hear me? Most are too far away." From where Avrel was standing the ice curved away in all directions. He could see many bears, but the furthest were little more than a blur.

"Use the fire," said David. "Reach out with it. All you have to do is believe it is possible."

Avrel rolled his shoulders. This was a scene he had dreamt of all his life. Yet, now it had come, he felt strangely disappointed. Perhaps it was the setting? In his memories he had seen great council meetings, where the first nine ruling bears had sat upon pillars of smoking ice, talking of territories and packs and the law. Then there was the Tooth of Ragnar, of course, that most symbolic of islands, with all its mythologies and dramas and wars. And the sacred glacier which men called

Hella, where, it was whispered, Thoran could take any form he chose and had often walked and breathed like a man. Here, there was nothing but a faint green light swimming gaily underneath the surface. Not even a lofty ridge to climb. Nothing grand to mark the place where the ice had begun. Avrel sat down and shuffled his paws. The green dragon light flowed eagerly around them. He extended his claws, letting them find their way into the light. Suddenly, he felt a great surge of inspiration and his thoughts went shooting back to the beginning. Memories of Thoran. Guinevere. Ragnar. All history, there in a breath. He invited the dragon to rise up and take it. And like a glacier making waves as it crashed into the ocean, fire lines streamed away in every direction. They passed swiftly under the first rows of bears, lighting their eyes in dots of green, until all that could be seen was a sea of sparks and all that could be heard was an omnipresent breath of unity and understanding.

There the North paused, as if time itself had frozen.

Avrel and the bears and the spirits were stilled.

This was the End of Days.

At that moment, G'reth gave a gentle hurr to indicate that he and Grace were connected.

Surprisingly, David was slow to respond. He

dropped to one knee and touched the ice. A shadow danced up and connected with his hand. "Alexa?" he whispered. For a moment, he had heard her call to him in fear. For a moment, he had sensed a great swell of darkness. For a moment, the harmonic that was holding the bears had altered its frequency and almost broken.

For a moment.

Then the moment was gone.

David raised himself again. There was frost on his eyebrows, ice in his heart. He called G'reth closer and put out his thumbs. "I'm going to make a wish. When it begins, use the network you've created to scan the Earth for any trail of auma seeking out the eye."

G'reth nodded and raised his paws. David rested his thumbs inside them. The 'nightfire' Avrel loved to watch fractured into ribbons and spread itself freely to every horizon, washing the sky in a halcyon shade of blue. The ice swayed gently. The wind that constantly brushed across its surface settled for a moment and all was calm. The air played host to David's wish. "Gaia," he whispered, "your servants are gathered. Listen to their heart song. Give it your blessing. I wish you to show them your light."

And it was done.

G'reth shuddered and pulled away.

Gollygosh immediately put out a paw and steadied himself against Gadzooks. The green light that had clustered round the eye of Gawain was now flowing through the hummock they were sitting on, too. It was seeking a connection.

Seeking them.

In the dome of the sky the nightfire pulsed, through gradients of blue and pink and violet. The dragonlight called. Gollygosh was the first to answer. He fluttered down and landed on the petrified eye, just beneath the curve of the lower lid. He put down his toolbox. The flaps opened right away and the usual asterisk of light leaped out. He raised an eye ridge at the tool that settled in his hand. It looked very similar to the screwdriver used by the time travelling hero of the dragons' favourite television programme. But it was not that at all. It was a piece of narwhal bone, much like the piece that Groyne could morph into. Groyne, who all this time had been watching patiently, suddenly found his auma very animated indeed. His ears pinged and his tail stood out like a spike. David touched him and whispered to Gollygosh to wait.

G'reth was twitching wildly, as if trying to shake a snowflake out of his ear. *Something was probing the link,* he said. *It felt like . . .*

David took hold of the wishing paws again. He read the signal in a moment and closed G'reth (and Grace) down in a calming trance. "Farlowe," he whispered and closed his eyes, almost as if he was chastising himself for his own stupidity. "Be ready," he said to Groyne. "We're about to travel." He nodded at Gollygosh to proceed.

The healer ran the narwhal bone round the eye. As it moved across the ancient crusted stone, the grey colour softened and the noble green of the olden dragons began to seep into the thick monolayer of rigid scales, lifting them into their familiar pattern. At the same time, the crown of four flared spikes that formed the flap of the primary lid swelled bulbously at the temple side. The small thumb of flesh at the front of the socket soon followed suit. Saline, trapped in the eye's tender sclera, leeched and flowed away in a capillary action to moisturise the stiffened, lower tissues. The eye itself rolled beneath its membranous cover. Yellow lichens slithered off its tented ridge. Then, beginning with the most acute angle of the scalene, the secondary lid slid back and the whole eye blinked. For the first time in centuries, Gawain looked at the polar sky.

Gollygosh felt a sucking motion. Fearing for his tail, he flew away immediately to stand by Gadzooks.

Then from the eye there poured a great light, not upwards, but radially in every direction. It happened at the speed that only light can travel. It surrounded Gadzooks in a strange two-dimensional plane, as though he was standing at the centre of a plate that had negligible thickness. With it came a silence that seemed to bind him to the very centre of the universe, as though he were a star in the eye of Godith. Infinity and the present became one to him then, for it seemed that he was all there was. That all life had been obliterated in one flash. Later he would learn that this was not the case, and that the well of all creation was merely waiting for him to play his part in David's wish. He felt for his pencil. He touched it to his pad. He doodled a moment. The white light pulsed. Then it came. Inspiration. In its purest form. And he wrote down a name. And somehow the name was written across the light. And the name in the light was this:

G'Oreal

* * *

Liz stood up with her hands bunched together across her mouth. "Oh, thank goodness," she whispered, almost too relieved to find the strength to move at first. She said a small prayer, then went hurrying down the garden to greet her daughter.

Lucy stepped silently off the swing.

Alexa did *not* go hurrying down the garden. She was watching Bonnington. The cat had risen high on his feet and was hissing. His ears were pressed back. His spine was arched. A pair of sabre teeth were jutting from his mouth.

"Naunty?" Lexie said.

Too far away to hear, too lost in joy, Liz outstretched her arms to gather Lucy in.

Bonnington's tail whisked back and forth.

Something thumped the window in the Dragon's Den. Alexa looked up. Liz's faithful house dragon, Gwillan, was flapping frantically, steaming up the glass with his urgent hurrs.

"Naunty!" Alexa shouted this time.

Bonnington let out a threatening growl.

Alexa started to run. Liz had her back to her, embracing her daughter. Lucy's arms slid around her mother's waist. She turned her right hand with the skill of a conjuror. The twisted point of a black knife appeared. Lucy aimed its tip at the strip of pale skin between Liz's waistband and her riding-up sweater. Then she scratched a line from one kidney to the other.

Blood trickled like a waveform out of the cut. Liz's head went back with a jerk. She caught her breath once, then fell in a graceless heap on the patio.

Lucy stepped over her to face Alexa.

The child skidded to a halt. She threw a shocked look at Liz, a bewildered one at Lucy. She wrapped one foot behind her ankle. "You're not Lucy," she said.

The Ix:risor controlling Lucy swept her forward to snatch Alexa by the wrist. It bared the child's palm as if it was squeezing a bloated glove. Alexa cried out to Bonnington. But the cat was on his side, aiming rabbit kicks at his thrashing head, as though he was fighting a demon in his ear.

"The feline cannot help you," the risor said. "When I increase the neural suffusion, it and the Fain inside it will die." It raised Lucy's head. "Do you hear that?" The mantra in the Crescent was coming from all directions now, over the gardens as well as the house. "Your father has placed a beacon in the North. He is calling out to humans all over this planet, making them commingle with the auma of the dragon. Listen." It tightened its grip upon Alexa's arm, until she was almost dangling like a doll. The mantra became a single hum. Lucy's lips moved again. "They are together. Any moment now, your father will open the dragon's eye and release The

Fire Eternal. From the collective mind of your race will come a desire, an optimistic plea for the future of this rock. It will succeed – if nothing stops it." The Ix twisted the skin until Alexa squealed. "Call to your father. When he hears you, his control will be broken. When you die, his sadness will multiply in the human collective – and we will turn their fear into fire for the Darkling." Lucy's arm muscles jerked to the risor's command. She raised the knife. "Call!"

"Dad-*dy*!" cried Alexa.

But 'Daddy' didn't answer. With a rush of air so swift that Lucy had no time at all to react, two ravens attacked her. One bird clattered straight into her knife hand, knocking the obsidian into a flower bed. The other sank its claws into the back of her neck. What was human in Lucy gave a cry of pain and she let Alexa go. Without warning, Lucy's knees gave way and she collapsed.

The Ix left her in a moment and chased into Gwilanna. Squawking wildly, the raven plunged to the lawn, knocking over plant pots as it tumbled backwards like a crazy black mop head.

"Lexie! It's Mummy! Hide!" caarked Zanna, swooping past on her way to aid the sibyl.

But the child had other ideas. She dropped to her

knees and tore the twist of hairs from around Lucy's neck. The red of Lucy's ancestor; the white of the ice bear. She ran with it to Bonnington.

Gwilanna, meanwhile, was about to have her life saved by Gwendolen. On their arrival in the garden the little IT dragon had been desperate to fly to Lucy, but under Zanna's command she had reluctantly stayed clear and perched herself on a solar-powered garden light. When Gwilanna came rolling towards her, however, she guessed what was happening and knew that the sibyl faced certain death unless the assassin inside her could be distracted. Gwendolen used her initiative. It was a simple matter to rip open the solar panel on the light, absorb its minimal energy and glow like a Christmas fairy. The result was immediate. The Ix stalled, changed course and came for her instead. She braced herself. Many times she had heard G'reth describe the commingling feeling. So the instant she felt her ear tips tingle, she switched into her solid form. It was a clever move. It confused the Ix and held it up a moment – long enough to bring it out of Gwilanna, into the open, into the invisible.

"Keep flying, girl!" Gwilanna screamed at Zanna. "It has less chance of commingling if you're travelling at speed."

"Baby! Run away!" Zanna called again. Why was Alexa hovering over Bonnington?

Suddenly, all became clear. The cat quadrupled in size and for a second Zanna thought she saw him change into a polar bear – *a polar bear?* – before he settled for his favourite form, a sleek black panther. With a roar that almost blew the garden fence down, he leapt forward flashing his paws. He landed with his claws out, shredding the lawn, then jumped direction with the speed of a flea and shadow-boxed the air several times again.

"He can't see it!" caarked Gwilanna, whooshing past Zanna. "Make it visible to him. Create a spell, girl!"

What happened next was textbook sibyl. Zanna caarked several times and every petal on the rose they had planted for David fluttered off the bush and latched itself to the Ix. Alexa screamed when she saw its form revealed. To her it was a humanoid fiend, with a head like a blunted dragon's snout, two enormous tails and dinosaur spines running down its back.

To Bonnington it was a two-horned mutant, somewhere between a dog and a hog. In an instant, he modified his vibrational energy to match that of the Ix, then with one pounce he took it down. His claws flashed again. Yellow petals scattered. One by one they came spinning back to earth. The last of them fell and the creature was gone.

Lucy stirred. Her vision swam, but her heart filled with hope as she recognised the garden. She saw two ravens on the lawn. They were being shielded by a rose-petalled panther. She listened for the hum in her ear. It wasn't there. Then Alexa entered the picture. She was picking up the hem of her dress and sobbing as if she would never stop. "Lexie?" Lucy muttered, trying to reach out to her.

Gwendolen flew across the garden then and landed beside her mistress's hand. It was she who made Lucy turn her head the other way.

"Mum?"

Liz's body was still on the patio, as grey as the flagstones being wetted by the rain.

At its most basic, the presence of the Ix was a low-level form of mind control, like the feeling of knowing you were inside a dream, but not being able to break the trance. And yet, when the beings invaded Tam Farrell, there was a corner of his mind that he felt had the power to resist or fight back, as though he had some kind of filter there. He saw little in the brethren to indicate the same. Dark marbles planted in a flesh-coloured landscape was the best that could be said of their gawky eyes. The only explanation he had for it was Zanna. That portion of his chest where she had cast her spell had not stopped burning since he'd come through the rift. The mark of Oomara. The sign of the bear. Nothing else set him apart from the monks. A blessing and a curse in equal measure, she had said. He just prayed it would be a blessing to Lucy. A violet star had glinted at the back of her eye when he had pressed her hand to his heart in the tower. *This might be important. A way to defeat them.* The gesture had registered, of that he was certain. But had she been able to act upon it?

Lucy. He felt for the girl. More than he strictly ought to have done. More than common sense and virtue allowed. In the chapel, he had never seen such terror in a human. When her screams had ignited and he'd turned to her to help, the Ix had swarmed his defenceless mind, trying to stall him with his childhood fear of vampires. For a moment, Lucy's mouth was swilling with blood and hung with lurid, sharpened teeth. But then the filter kicked in and Tam knew he was seeing a false vision. He bravely pushed on. In another two seconds he would have reached her. But a weight had struck the back of his head and he'd folded. He'd woken in the tower room, exchanging her kiss.

383

After the anti-dragon Darkling was completed, Lucy had been dragged away unconscious. The figures of Bernard and the spectacled abbot, Hugo, had remained in the tower and stood over Tam a while. In his mind he had sensed them commingling with him, openly 'debating' his worth. He was an irritant, but nevertheless of 'scientific' interest. Had he not withstood them briefly in the chapel? This puzzled them. The human capacity to sustain free will had always varied, but the level demonstrated by this insignificant male seemed well above the norm. Should they kill him? No. For what threat could he be? When the End of Days came, his youthful body strength might prove useful. He could be made Prem:Ix, like the girl. In the meantime, they would upgrade the neural suffusion and apply it unconditionally to every human on the island. He saw both monks shudder as their brains received the 'upgrade'. Their eyes turned a sickly alabaster for a moment. For Tam, in his physically weakened state, it was too much. He passed out with a searing pain in his head. When he came round, in an undisclosed cell, nine tenths of his mind was now answerable to the Ix. The final tenth was not.

Late that afternoon the abbey bells tolled, hooking the monks out of an unnatural sleep. The whole brotherhood of eighteen assembled in the cloisters. Tam fell into line next to Brother Cedric, knowing that at this stage resistance was impossible, rebellion pointless. *Gather. Gather. Gather.* The Ix were sending forceful instructions to their hosts, with an urgency which suggested something significant was about to happen. *March* came the order, and they set off two by two in a schoolboy crocodile, weaving across the open fields. Rain drizzled into their hooded faces. The early moon pricked holes in the cloud. With every trudging step, Farlowe spewed up another small tarn of mud. Squelch. Squelch. Squelch. Turgid and non-stop – until they reached the circle at the centre of the island.

Here the order became more complex. They were to separate, arrange themselves between the stones, and touch them to make an unbroken chain. Where the stones were widest apart it took three men holding hands to achieve this. But Tam placed himself in a narrow gap, kicking away loose shale to get a better stance. He raised his arms like Samson to touch two pillars at once. The pillar to his left was tall and jagged, the other thick and stumpy like an old grey molar. Geology was not his strongest point, but he was pretty sure the pieces were hewn from sandstone, judging by the way they shed small grains when he rubbed his freezing fingertips across them.

Suddenly, the Ix were heavy in his mind. The tinnitus of the left ear became insistent. He watched Abbot Hugo walk into the circle and place the Darkling Lucy had created on a bald, rocky plinth at its centre. The creature's head was facing north.

The hum zinged again and Tam found himself forced into a communal chant. The mantra filled the circle, growing in intensity with every round. The wind stirred, rippling at the hem of his habit. Rain fell in stringy, noiseless splatters. A light mist hung a few feet above the grass. The chanting continued for an indefinite period. Then came a moment when the skyline darkened. As it did, the clouds opened and the moon aimed its full light into the circle. Tam jerked and felt an energy pulse electrify his hands. His nerves recorded no pain, but his body was not his own for a second, just a live conduit between the rocks. The chanting grew louder. The stones began to glow, chasing back the moonlight in fluorescent apple green, staining the mist in smoky patches. That part of Tam still able to resist let him roll his eyes towards the jagged pillar. Symbols were appearing on the surface of the rock. Elaborate, intertwined, highly crafted runes, carved by ancient, reverent hands. Runes of human beings, bears – and dragons.

Suddenly, a wild cry turned his head. It sounded like a bird, but it was bigger, much bigger, coming from lungs that could launch a squeal to burst the ears of a thousand men. The mist flowered upwards, filling out a shape. When it was done, a terrifying echo of the past remained. The ghost of a female dragon had appeared, to hover just a few feet above the Darkling. She was huge, and the Ix had a name for her.

Ghislaine.

Years ago, as a sideline to her college course, Zanna had taken lessons in basic first aid. One instruction she had always remembered was this: in a disaster scene, always tend to the quietest first. Down the garden, Gwilanna was harping about a badly-bruised foot. Alexa was in tears, and Lucy was muzzy but clearly coming round. The one in real danger was Liz.

Zanna transformed herself back into a human, gave Alexa a swift reassuring hug and hurried to the patio. "Liz?" she said, kneeling down beside her, trying to remember the order of it all. A, B, C. *Airway, Breathing, Circulation*. There was nothing in the manual about skin and hands that were graveyard grey. "Liz?" she said more

387

urgently and put her ear against Liz's heart. Nothing. Not even a millimetre rise.

Lucy skidded in, knocking Zanna aside. She forced her arms around her mother's shoulders, and hugged at the limp, unresponsive body. "Mum!" she wailed. "Mum, wake up!"

"You're wasting your time," Gwilanna caarked.

Zanna turned to see the raven hobbling towards them.

"She's been poisoned with obsidian. She's going to die."

"No," said Lucy, in a voice already fracturing with tears.

Gwendolen arrived asking what she could do. "Find Gretel," Zanna said to her. "Bring Arthur, too. He must be in the house." As the dragon whipped away Zanna turned to Gwilanna. "There must be magicks? Or a potion, surely?"

The raven shook its head.

Zanna reached out a hand and drew Alexa to her. "We have sibyls here, daughters of Guinevere and Gwendolen, what amounts to a witch's cat and a host of enchanted people in the Crescent. There must be *something* we can do?"

"Do you think I wouldn't if I could?" snapped

Gwilanna. "It's impossible, girl. It would take Gawain himself to save her."

Zanna rocked back onto her knees. "Then maybe I can help." She stood up quickly and ran to the rosebush, snapping her fingers for Bonnington to follow. "Dig," she said, making the appropriate movements with her hands. She pointed to a spot just behind the bush.

Bonnington dug, furiously and hard. Before long, a strip of red velvet was uncovered. Alexa, who'd been watching, slightly mesmerised by it all, jumped forward and pulled a small bag out of the ground.

"Open it," said Zanna.

Alexa loosened the drawstring.

A piece of dragon scale fell into her palm.

The one advantage, Tam realised, of being semi-possessed by a race of highly-intelligent if arrogant thought forms, was that it was always easy to know what their plans were. The ghost dragon was a clever diversion, designed to disrupt the energy field of what the Ix called the 'human collective'. Put simply, she was a decoy. A means of weakening and confusing David's influence at the point when he opened the dragon's eye. She was there to turn heads – or, more appropriately, minds. As he chanted, her history came through to him. She had died long ago on this very spot, given up her fire tear when the Fain then controlling this primitive planet had taken away the Pri:magon she was to be illumined to. Now the Ix were holding her in her own timeframe, sealed in a dimension made visible above the rift. Tam could feel them playing with her agonised mind, torturing her with disturbing images of the Pri:magon and the Pri:magon's child. The child was of modest interest to them. They knew of her. She was one of the few Premen still extant upon this rock. She called herself Gwilanna. The presence of her spirit, so relatively close on the temporal planes, only made the sourcing of the nightmares easier.

Ghislaine cried out. A dreadful, pitiful barb of pain that should have frayed the hardest heart or diverted the most purposeful mind of every living creature in the universe. The Ix drew their hosts to focus on the Darkling. They were making a beacon of it, trying to create some kind of channel through which dark energy could be transferred. It glowed hideously in the moonlight. To his horror, Tam suddenly grew aware of another link to the Ix:risor controlling Lucy, and knew they were trying to draw negative energy through her as well. The chant became intense, the beacon strong. For a second, all hope for human life seemed lost. But then Tam felt the Ix stall. Ghislaine's cries, they were saying, had gone no further than the arc of the circle and were steadily reverberating back through time. There was something wrong, the circuit was broken. They traced it quickly to a flaw in the Darkling.

It had no heart.

Yes, Tam thought. Lucy had tricked them. His optimism surged and he felt their grip on his neurons ease as they concentrated their energies on an unexpected source of resistance from the north. He immediately turned his head and managed to pull a finger off the stone at his left. Ghislaine cried out and thrashed her tail in anger. She issued fire. It flared in blinding amber-coloured sails, becoming slow and lava-like at the edges of the seal where the energy creating the timeframe absorbed it. The Ix's hold slackened off a little more. Tam felt the sandstone's grit against his skin. His left hand was moving now, lateral to the surface of the pillar. If he could just . . . agh! With a rebel yell that his Celtic forefathers would have been proud of, he pulled away, breaking the circle and the mantra. The Ix rushed to him with a violence that he thought would burst every blood vessel in his brain. But in an instant they deserted him again. Why, Tam could not tell. The monks were dropping and the image of Ghislaine was no longer in the circle, but there did not seem any obvious threat, just a swift, unexpected fall of snow . . .

"This is Gawain's isoscele," Zanna said. She held it tightly and showed it to Gwilanna. The raven's eyes swelled to resemble boiled sweets.

"Rid me of these feathers and give it to me," she said, her voice almost gurgling with pleasure.

"No, tell me what to do," said Zanna.

"It would take too long," the raven caarked. "I'm the only one capable of doing this, girl."

"Please, do as she says," said a voice, and Arthur came staggering down the garden, guided by Gwendolen. He knelt down, feeling for Liz's arm. His upper body shook as he registered the coldness in her hand. Kissing it warmly he whispered, "Forgive me. I was caught in the mantra. I should have been with you." He reached across her body and touched Lucy's shoulder.

"Give it to her," Lucy said to Zanna.

"But first, change me back," Gwilanna insisted.

Lucy and Zanna exchanged a terse glance.

"You'll have to teach me," Zanna said to the sibyl.

In dragontongue, the raven translated a spell.

Zanna spoke it and the woman that was Gwilanna returned, in the skins she'd been wearing in the Arctic when attacked.

"Hmph," she said, fussing with her knotted hair, "inappropriate clothing for this balmy climate, but it will do for now." She extended a hand.

Zanna put the isoscele into it. "Remember what Bonnington just disposed of," she whispered. "Don't try any tricks."

Gwilanna sighed and knelt down. "One day, girl, you will come to understand that I've only ever had your interests at heart." She studied the wound, which was turning black. "This will not be pleasant. It will scar," she said to Lucy.

"Just save her," Lucy said. Her tearful eyes were almost washed of colour.

"Observe," Gwilanna said, "the blood of a dragon." She squeezed the scale. A drop of green ichor bled from the tip. She extended a tongue that looked like it had grown its own mushroom colony, and mixed her saliva into the ichor. Then she leaned forward and plunged the isoscele into the wound.

Alexa gasped. Her mother turned her away.

Gwilanna ripped the scale right across the cut. It opened again with a tearing of flesh. This time, instead of Liz's blood oozing forth, a black acidic froth began to bubble across her back. Gwilanna pursed her lips and spat in several places. Where the fluids mixed, they made a sticky green lather. "The dragon's blood will neutralise the magma core of the obsidian," she said.

"Why the spittle?" Zanna asked.

"I had to dilute it. A pure droplet of ichor would probably have killed her."

"Will she live?" asked Arthur.

Gwilanna rested her hand on Liz's back. "Yes . . ."

". . . but?" said Zanna, sensing one coming.

Gwilanna stood up. She looked at the sky as if she really ought to be somewhere else. "Where is Gretel? This wound will need a poultice."

Right on cue there was a crash of glass and a hole appeared in the window of the Dragon's Den. A jam jar full of pebbles exploded on the patio and through the escape hole it had made came Gretel. She landed in the centre of Liz's back with the disgruntled air of a surgeon who'd been left out of a vital operation – which of course she had.

We were locked in, she hurred, frowning at Lucy.

Lucy started to explain that she wasn't in control of herself at the time, then changed her mind and focused on her mum instead.

"Prepare herbs," said Gwilanna. "Sorrel and fennel, with a measure of thyme. I will assist."

Zanna grabbed her arm. "Not so fast. What were you going to say about Liz?"

Gwilanna looked down. Something softened in the hard lines of her face. "The dragon's blood will do enough to revive her . . ."

"*But?*" repeated Lucy.

Gwilanna looked away.

"What have you done?" Zanna said, and took her by the throat.

"I've saved her life!" screamed the sibyl. "I've done what you asked. The dragon's blood will bring her back. But it might not be enough to save the child she's carrying . . ."

The Darkling was still at the centre of the circle. Though heavily disorientated, Tam struggled to his feet and began to stagger towards the creature. It had to be destroyed, of that he was certain, even if it was imperfect. Ten yards from it he dropped to his knees to lift a large stone from the sodden grass. Snow was falling all around. Yet none seemed to be settling on him. He raised the stone two-handed, well above his head. The creature's black eyes fell under its shadow. Using every last ounce of strength in his body, Tam cried out and brought the stone down – only to see it bounce off the plinth where the Darkling had been. The creature had gone.

"What?" he gasped, and collapsed against the plinth.

Suddenly, he was aware of a presence and rolled over to see a kind of shadow figure stumbling towards him. It was mid-height and slender, with scarecrow fingers and coiled body scales. Its head was being swiftly *eroded* by the snow. He shielded his face and tried to kick away, but the creature was only there for an instant. Then the gathering of snowflakes dispersed in the wind. When Tam focused his eyesight again, they had gone.

Puzzled, he pushed back the cowl of his habit, glad of the drizzling rain on his face. Between the stones, he could see the monks beginning to rise. In a human way. Not controlled by anything alien. Relieved, he stretched his arms so that his hands might feel the comfort of the rain. As he did, two final snowflakes fell. One on his left palm, one on his right.

And then a voice like a wind from another world said, "This is my gift to you. Use it wisely."

Tam looked at his hands. The two flakes were dissolving under his skin.

Both were in the shape of polar bears.

* * *

There was an Inuit prophecy that Zanna remembered from her time in the Arctic. The old shaman, Taliriktug, had once confided to her, "One day the ice will burn." When she had asked him what he meant by this, the old man had said, "You are Qannialaaq, which means falling snow. When the snow falls, you will know what things mean."

Snow was falling gently in the Crescent. The mantra had ceased. The crowds were disbanding. Arthur had carried Liz upstairs, with the dragons and Lucy and Alexa all helping. Leaving Gretel busy making a poultice, Zanna went back outside to stand by Gwilanna. The old woman was cradling Bonnington and staring long at the open sky. She looked ridiculous in her sealskin furs, but this was not the moment for wisecracks about it. Zanna gave a quiet report. "Liz is comfortable. I want to thank you for saving her – and to apologise for attacking you."

Gwilanna's eyes moved in small, shrewd circles.

"This pregnancy—?"

"It's a natural born. They are of no interest to me."

"I was a natural; I still have magicks."

"Without me, you would be nothing."

"Then teach me. This time I'm willing to learn. You

thought me worthy enough to give me the mark. You must have some hope for me?"

"Hmph!" went the sibyl, and threw Bonnington down. He landed mesmerised but completely unhurt. He washed himself once and strolled away.

"You have to guide me, Gwilanna. I want to help Liz deliver this child. You know hospitals are impossible for her. Promise me you'll stay with us, at least till we know the fate of the child."

"It's a boy," Gwilanna muttered, as though the words pained her.

Zanna nodded to herself. "That's unusual, isn't it?"

Gwilanna turned her gaze to the north. "They can be troublesome, especially if they're given too much power . . ."

Zanna walked down the garden a pace. There was one green leaf on a branch of the rose. One leaf. One symbol of hope. "Can I ask you something? Lucy tried to track down David's parents. He gave a home address that was nothing but a time rift. What does that mean? Is he real? Is he human?"

Gwilanna snorted inwardly. "Sometimes," she said, in a voice which suggested she would say nothing more.

Now it was Zanna's turn to find solace in the grey expanse of sky. "Lucy just turned on the TV set.

Apparently, there's some kind of mist in the Arctic, covering the entire ice cap. Alexa says it looks like the ice is on fire." Expecting a comment, she paused a moment. Gwilanna stared silently ahead. "There are reports coming in from all over the world of people assembling like they did in the Crescent. The scientists are saying it's a kind of mass hysteria."

"Scientists," sneered Gwilanna. "What would they know?"

She was about to turn away when Zanna stopped her and showed her the obsidian knife. "How do I dispose of this?"

"Throw it in the dustbin," Gwilanna said tiredly.

"It's not dangerous?"

"Only if you're foolish enough to fall on its point. Its poison was discharged into Elizabeth."

"Where would Lucy get this? It's beautifully made. And quite brilliant the way the light reflects inside it." She held up the knife and twisted it. A grain of light, no larger than a grain of sand, tumbled in a figure of eight at its centre. "That's incredible," she said. "If this didn't have such a stigma attached to it I'd sell it in my shop. People would pay a fortune for it."

Gwilanna poked her face forward and seemed now to show a much greater interest. "Perhaps I should take it after all," she said. "There may be some residual—"

"Erm, no. Nice try." Zanna snatched it away. "This is going straight into the bin."

"No, wait!" cried Gwilanna.

But the lid went up and the knife was dropped.

The sibyl winced as she heard a breakage.

Zanna dropped the lid again and rubbed her hands. "Promise me you'll stay till Liz is safe."

Gwilanna considered it. "Are there mushrooms in your fridge?"

"Sometimes," said Zanna, with a less than smug grin. And she turned away and walked back into the kitchen.

Gwilanna gave a humph and glanced at Bonnington, who was sitting, appropriately, on a stone mushroom. "Well, cat, shall we look?"

Bonnington twitched his nose.

Gwilanna checked the house for prying eyes. Then she opened the bin.

The knife lay in three clean pieces at the bottom. The twisted tip had broken in two, but the thicker body part was still intact. Gwilanna took it out and turned it gently. "Well, well," she whispered, "how did *you* get there?" The dot of light was still present.

She drew the isoscele of Gawain from a pouch in her furs. Hmm. All in all, not a bad day's work. What was that ridiculous human saying? *It's an ill wind . . . ?* She looked at the sky again as if she owned it. Perhaps she did? For now she possessed two of the most powerful weapons in the known universe: the blood of a dragon and . . . no, not the obsidian knife, but what was trapped inside the knife.

The tiniest spark of pure dark fire.

Epilogue

Suzanna Martindale had been a mother for the best part of five years. For much of that time, she had often felt like an understudy to Elizabeth Pennykettle, whom she considered to be just about the perfect parent. She had learned a great deal from Liz, not just about motherhood but the complete dynamics of running a home and family. In the days following the events in the garden, her apprenticeship was put to the test.

With Liz very poorly and likely to be bed-bound for several weeks, Zanna was catapulted into a matriarchal role. She accepted it without complaint or fuss. She hired help in the shop (even employing Henry for two afternoons a week) and stepped full-time into Liz's apron. It wasn't easy. Alexa and the dragons were no trouble at all, and Arthur, although he fretted deeply at first, was soon persuaded to go back to the University and do what he did well: teach and earn a wage. Bonnington was Bonnington; happy with a bowl of *Chunky Chunks* and a tickle behind his ever-changing ears. Even Gwilanna wasn't overly disruptive. She would sweep in and out to great thespian effect, shouting bossy orders (usually to Gretel), and demanding to be waited on, hand, foot and feather (she still had a black one riding in her hair). Alexa, who found her 'aunt' quite fascinating, often trailed in her wake, running errands, and even started up a mushroom colony for her. All of this Zanna managed to tolerate benignly without falling into a single face-off. And though it was obvious to anyone above the age of five that Gwilanna was milking the gravity of the situation, no one could deny that she had saved Liz's life. Liz's scar was healing well, and Gawain's auma, through controlled applications of his blood, was gradually overpowering the poisonous obsidian. One had to be grateful to the sibyl for that. It wasn't easy to live with the obnoxious old witch, but Zanna could have no grounds for putting her out on the street.

On that score, however, there was an extraordinary twist. Henry Bacon, like so many others in the Crescent, had been held in a trance when the omnipresent mantra had drawn the world together in semi-conscious prayer. This explained why he had not gone charging out with a stick to defend his piece of England when the crowds had appeared by his garden gate (though he'd since enquired, with nil success, if the local council would compensate him for the loss of his herbaceous border). But when 'the gathering', as the media were labelling it, was over, he was round within the hour. He and 'Gwyneth' (the name Gwilanna adopted when forced to interact with 'primitive human society') seemed to 'click'. Not even her furs or the waxy smell of raven feathers could put Henry off. After just one cup of Earl Grey tea and an impenetrable discussion of the health-giving properties of Shiitake mushrooms and other spore-bearing fruiting bodies, he invited her to stay at his house. Gwilanna accepted. Zanna's jaw dropped. She tried to find a reason to object, but had none. She just prayed that the sibyl would not turn Henry's guest room into a cave the way she had when she'd lived at number 42, once. Gwilanna, crashing out at Henry's pad: it was far too freaky to think about, but it did at least keep the sibyl out of the way.

And that was important, because of Lucy. After the general domestic workload – the washing, the cooking, the ironing, the paperwork – Lucy was Zanna's greatest challenge. The girl had gone into a shell so deep that she might have been lost for good were it not for the tide of her mother's breathing. She wouldn't talk about what had happened in the garden and refused to do anything around the house unless it was directly helpful to her mum. She sat with Liz all day, every day, sometimes neglecting her personal hygiene, usually dozing off in mid-to-late evening and sleeping overnight in the chair beside the bed. She was becoming a hindrance, especially to Gwilanna, who had twice been on the brink of zapping the girl with magicks for getting in the way when she was checking Liz's progress. Zanna would not allow that. But on those nights when she came to drape a blanket over Lucy and settle the girl's hands and place a kiss on her forehead, she would stand a moment over her, wondering what to do. It was a delicate matter, one she wished she didn't need to address. But in the end, providence lent a hand and the problem resolved itself.

For the first days of her illness, Liz had been fed on herbal infusions prescribed by Gwilanna and wafted into her nostrils by Gretel. Though her eyes had blinked open several times (a dreadful sight to witness for the whites were the greyest shades of death), she had still been far too tired to speak. But as the herbs began their work and Gretel's soothing dragonsong stirred her, she began to have more prolonged wakeful periods, usually early to mid-afternoon. During one of those times, she asked about Gwillan.

Zanna was there. Waiting. Ready.

"Where is he? I haven't seen him," Liz said.

Zanna picked up her hand. "He cried his fire tear," she said. And there it was, done. Evenly and swiftly, the way Arthur had counselled her. No stalling. No sorrys. The hard plain truth. "He saw your body on the patio and thought you were dead."

Liz's face began to drift into agonised despair.

Lucy covered her mouth and ran from the room.

"I should go to her," said Zanna. A tear carved her cheek. She raised Liz's hand and held it to her lips. "He's in the Den, by Guinevere. I'm so, so sorry."

It was horrible, but it was a breakthrough of sorts.

Lucy had not gone far. Her run had come to a halt in a foetal position at the bottom of the stairs. Zanna sat her upright and cradled her closely, using every healing technique she'd ever learned. The girl was crying hysterically.

"Why? Why did you have to *tell her?*"

"Because it would have been worse if I hadn't," Zanna whispered.

And the tears went on. And the guilt poured out. "*It's all my fault. It's all my fault.*"

"No, it isn't," Zanna told her, time after time.

Then the dam broke and Lucy began to blubber frenziedly, finally spilling out what had happened after Blackburn, words about the island, and the Darkling – and Tam.

Zanna pulled back a little so she could see Lucy's eyes.

"You mean Farlowe Island? That's where the time rift took you?" She gave the girl a shake. "Lucy, talk to me. This is important. Tam went after you. No one's heard from him since. Did he reach you on the island? Lucy, what happened?"

"They got him," she said and her head lolled sideways against her shoulder.

Zanna swallowed tightly and looked away. "Is he dead?"

"I don't know." And the tears came again.

"All right," Zanna said, rocking her gently. "Listen, I want you to go to bed. I want you to sleep for as long as you need to. You're exhausted, Luce. You need to lie down and rest."

"Can't. Mum needs me. She—"

Zanna cut her off with a gentle shush. With a palm supporting Lucy's cheek, she said, "Your mum is better left alone right now."

Alexa came into the hall just then, carrying a half-peeled mushroom. She paused, knock-kneed, wondering what was happening.

Zanna said, "Lexie, will you sit upstairs with Lucy? She's tired – but she wants someone to talk to for a while."

Alexa put the mushroom on a step of the stairs. She

called Bonnington, who came trotting on four catty paws down the hall. Alexa picked up Lucy's hand. "Shall we do a story?"

Lucy's bottom lip trembled.

"A story would be perfect," Zanna said. And to her great relief, all three of them went up.

A dark silence gathered at the foot of the stairs. Zanna took out her mobile but didn't dial. She stared at the door and thought about Tam. His quest to find David, his bravado at Blackburn. And how she had cursed him a dozen times since, not because it should have been her on that island, but because she had known that one day she might have to sit like this and deal with the crushing responsibility of the moment.

She called Arthur, seeking advice.

He called back ten minutes later. He had tried to contact Bernard but that line was dead, and the brethren's general communications had only just been restored. There was 'sickness' on the island, he said.

"Sickness?"

"A partial euphemism. They don't want visitors, Zanna."

"Did you ask about Tam?"

"The brother I spoke to claimed he knew nothing. When I pressed him, he was clearly too afraid to speak out. But before he hung up he gave me a clue: he said their row-boat had gone."

Zanna looked at the door again, at the chain bolt dangling free. She walked away from it, down the hall into the kitchen. "Are we in danger?"

"I don't think so. I believe the Ix are defeated – for now. Have you had the television on today? The mist across the Arctic has bulged near the pole. Reconnaissance photographs are showing some kind of developing activity. One of the pilots who witnessed it said it was like 'a child playing underneath a blanket'. An aircraft dropped a probe into the cloud, but all signals were immediately lost."

"And this is good?"

"I don't feel it's bad. Has . . . Alexa said anything?"

Zanna peered at the drawings, still tacked to the kitchen wall. Dragons and polar bears. That fabulous eye. "No, nothing. But Liz knows about Gwillan."

"Shall I come home?"

"If you can. It might help. I've asked Gretel to give her a potion. She's resting now, but when she wakes again the grief is going to come back hard. It would comfort her to know you're around."

There was silence a moment, then Arthur said, "She'll be grateful you told her – you know that, don't you?"

Zanna touched the hollow at the nape of her neck. "I hate myself, Arthur."

And she closed the call.

For the next half hour, Zanna busied herself with the stuff of housekeeping, mainly preparing an early evening meal. She was putting a shepherd's pie into the oven when the doorbell rang.

The listening dragon pricked its ears.

Alexa came thumping down the stairs and as usual reached the door first. As she opened it, Zanna gave a terrified start. It was him. Tam Farrell. Clean shaven. Kind eyes. Heart-melting lowlands accent.

Tam.

"Hello, Zanna." He glanced sweetly at Alexa. A genuine smile. No hint of any threat.

"You're Lucy's friend," said the child.

He gave a splutter of surprise. "Yes. Yes, I am. Is Lucy . . . in?"

"She's sleeping," said Zanna, moving forward. She grasped the edge of the door, making a barricade in front of Alexa.

Tam eased back, sliding his hands into his pockets. There were rain spots staining his black pilot jacket. "I've come a long way, Zanna. Further than Blackburn."

413

She let his gaze sink into her, and hated him briefly for disabling all her doubts.

"Shall I put the kettle on, Mummy?"

Alexa was up, turning sideways on her toes.

Zanna looked at Tam, then let her shoulders fall. "Go through to the kitchen," she said and stood aside.

They had tea. Cake. All the Pennykettle trimmings. Alexa chattered furiously and showed Tam her drawings. He in turn recited poems that made her laugh. Zanna found it all just a little surreal. She was beginning to wonder quite where this was going when Bonnington put in a moody appearance. He was trying to escape from Gwilanna, who entered via the back door just as Tam was offering to juggle apples for Alexa.

He rose politely instead.

"Who is this?" Gwilanna snapped, every bit as austere as the grey two-piece suit she was wearing.

"A friend," Zanna said.

Tam proffered a hand.

The sibyl refused it and quickly passed her right hand in front of his face. Zanna saw it was a hex, a mild form of hypnosis, and was about to utter sharp words of rebuke when she realised Tam Farrell hadn't flinched.

Gwilanna breathed in sharply. With a voice that

might have driven forth a blizzard she said, "He has the mark of Oomara upon him." She gave a disgusted sniff. "And he smells of *bears*."

"I like bears," said Alexa.

"Be quiet, child." Gwilanna narrowed her gaze. "Who are you? Why are you here?"

He sat down calmly, slipping his fingers through the handle of the mug he'd just emptied of tea. "My name is Tam Farrell. I've come to fulfil a promise to Lucy. I said I would help her to . . . protect the environment."

"He's a journalist," said Zanna.

"*Is* he," said Gwilanna, but it was not a question. She ran an overgrown fingernail under Tam's eye, digging down slightly to lower the lid. "You've commingled," she whispered, reading his retina with the telescope of her witchery. "You—" She stopped speaking and pulled away sharply. "You and I have met before. How can that be?"

"Tam tells poems," Alexa said gaily.

"And stories," he added, turning the handle of his mug towards Gwilanna.

The sibyl, slightly startled, jutted her chin. "How is Elizabeth?" she snapped at Zanna.

"Talking. I had to tell her about—"

"Good." The sibyl opened the door again.

415

"Hey, slow down. Aren't you going up to see her?"

"Tomorrow, perhaps. Gretel knows what to do." And glancing warily at Tam, the old woman swept out as quickly as she'd come in.

Zanna threw up her hands.

Alexa said, "Hhh! She didn't take her mushrooms."

"Good, cos I'd be tempted to—" 'poison them' Zanna was about to say, but checked herself when she realised that here was her chance to be alone at last with Tam. "Yes, well you'd better run after her, then. Stay a while if you want to."

Alexa grabbed a punnet. "Will you juggle apples for me when I come back?"

"Four," said Tam. "And an orange, too."

Alexa's eyes grew as large as a Cox's Pippin. She set her shoulders straight and whizzed away.

"She's cute," he said, as Zanna set the door to.

"She's none of your business. All right, talk."

"I would *like* to see Lucy."

"She's asleep. You talk to me."

"You still hate me?"

"Not if you tell me the truth."

He put a hand to his heart. "You saved my life, Zanna. Lucy's too. Why would I want to lie to you?" And he told her all that he remembered from the island.

416

Everything about the Ix, the Darkling, and how he had escaped. "At the end, I couldn't be sure whether the Ix had left the monks completely, so I stowed away in the boat house and rowed off the island the next day when the water was calm. I'll go back at an appropriate time and tell the brothers what I know."

By now, he was onto his second mug of tea. Zanna opened a fresh pack of biscuits. "That creature you mentioned, the one that disappeared. What do you think happened to it?"

"The Darkling was on a time rift. Something either cloaked it – or moved it for safekeeping."

"The Ix?"

He shook his head. "No, don't think so. Not unless it was an emergency measure. They appeared to be defeated by then, anyway. I think it was the same source that sent the snow."

She raised a pencil-thin eyebrow. It made her look quirkily beautiful, he thought.

"Snow is a natural phenomenon, Tam. It's not sent, it falls."

"Not in the shape of polar bears, it doesn't."

She snapped a biscuit in two and laughed.

"They weren't *snow* flakes, Zanna. They were bear flakes. A small pack of them, come to battle the Ix." He

417

leaned back in his chair. His foot tapped the floor. "Two of them landed on my hands. Since then I've remembered things about the Arctic – stuff I shouldn't know, legends I can't know – coupled with a crushing desire to protect you and Lucy."

Zanna put her biscuit down on a plate. She dropped her hands into her lap and glanced at Gauge, who was sitting on the windowsill just behind Tam. The timing dragon made a five past the hour pose. Five minutes before the pie came out of the oven. "I'm afraid I'll have to ask you to leave now," she said. "In any other circumstance I'd invite you to stay for dinner. But things have been difficult. Your presence won't make it easier."

She lifted his car keys out of a wicker bowl and put them down on the table in front of him. "It's still in Blackburn, I'm afraid." He gave a nod of understanding and rose to leave.

"One thing," she asked, as he repositioned his chair, "why would Lucy's . . . aunt think she'd met you before?"

He glanced at the drawings Alexa had made. "Must be that scent of polar bear," he said. "By the way, are you familiar with the word 'Nanukapik'?"

"I might be. What of it?"

"There is a great bear in the Arctic – but he travels,

I think. Tell Lucy I called."

He leaned forward and kissed her cheek. Zanna averted her eyes. Her gaze was still fixed on Bonnington's cat flap when she heard the front door close. "Question," she said to the listener, in dragontongue. "What colour were his eyes?"

"Brown," it replied.

Zanna swallowed and felt a sudden weakness in her back. When she'd first met Tam, she'd remembered them as blue.

It was like a viral sickness. A condition that didn't quite bring you down but which you carried every day, in every fibre of your being, wondering if it was ever going to come to an end.

So many signs were pointing to David.

So many times, Zanna felt so alone.

She made Alexa promise not to talk about Tam and told Lucy of his visit herself the next morning. Lucy was in her dressing gown, eating breakfast. Her mouth stayed open for a full ten seconds. She was not a pretty sight, with rings of tiredness darkening her eyes, her hair unbrushed and like a squirrel's nest, and milky cornflakes swilling round her teeth.

Strangely, the expected tantrum didn't happen. Lucy,

though shocked and clearly disappointed, seemed to understand. "Will he come back? Do you think I should call him?"

Zanna recalled his remark about protecting them. "He'll come back."

Lucy put her bowl down. "I'm scared," she wailed. "I have dreams about the Darkling hunting for us, hurting Mum, killing the dragons."

On the fridge top, the listener rattled its scales.

"It won't come," Zanna said, stroking the brilliant red hair. "Tam told me how you fooled the Ix by making the Darkling without a heart. That was pretty smart."

"What did you do with it?"

"With what?"

"The heart."

Zanna frowned and shook her head. "I don't understand."

"Don't be dumb. Course you *do*. They made me use it on Mum. You knocked it from my hand. It must still be in the garden. I'm going out to look."

"Wo!" Zanna caught her as she tried to stand. "That knife was the Darkling's heart?"

"*Yes!*"

And Gwilanna must have known it, Zanna decided. That was why she didn't want to see it binned. Tough.

The thing was in pieces now. "It's in the dustbin, wrecked. When the bin men come tomorrow it'll be nothing
but dust."

"It's evil," said Lucy, meeting Zanna's eyes.

"It's dust," Zanna told her, and clinked the cereal bowl, indicating Lucy should get on with her breakfast.

That afternoon, Zanna had a visitor. Henry Bacon dropped round looking thwarted. "Gwyneth," he grumbled, spread-eagling himself on Bonnington's favourite chair (and just about filling half the kitchen).

Zanna was ironing. "Yeah, I've got some issues with her myself. What's the scheming old crone been up to now – apart from abandoning Liz to me and Gretel?"

"Gone," said Henry.

Zanna lifted the iron. "What, you mean she's left?"

"Just took off."

"Not—?" No, ravens were best left out of this.

"Can't understand it," Henry muttered. "One minute she was grateful for the use of the room, then she disappears without a word of goodbye. All very odd."

And deeply suspicious, Zanna thought. She and the iron both blew a little steam.

"Perfectly within her rights, of course. I mean, there

was no . . . affiliation," Henry coughed.

"I should think not!" Zanna said sternly, feeling as if she'd morphed into a Victorian governess. "You listen to me Henry, Gwil— 'Gwyneth' is just about the most selfish woman I've ever met. You don't know her. I do. You're far better off without her. Trust me."

He pursed his lips and frowned. "Talked about a holiday."

"*What?* No! Out of the question. What are you thinking of? You've only known her a week!"

"Her suggestion," he said.

Zanna straightened a collar. "*Her* suggestion?"

"Mmm. I was flattered. Showed her brochures – for cruises . . ."

"Good grief," Zanna muttered. "This is getting worse." The thought of it: Gwilanna and Henry, doing cocktails in the Caribbean. Weird.

". . . but she wanted something cheaper, more domestic."

"Oh, right. Like Eastbourne?"

Henry shook his head. "Further north. Scottish Islands."

"What?" said Zanna. A sudden chill gripped her heart. "Where in the Islands?"

Henry opened his hands. "Never discussed it. Gone

before you could shake a kilt."

"Mummy!" Alexa dashed in from the hall.

"What, darling?"

"Lucy says you've got to come and look at the tellingvision."

"Television, Lexie, how many times? In a minute, I'm talking to Henry."

"But there's snow, going upwards!"

"Not technically possible," said Henry. "Gravity wouldn't allow it, child."

"Zanna?!" Lucy's voice shouted through from the front.

Zanna switched off the iron. She aimed a finger between Henry's eyes. "Stay away from that woman. She's . . . well, just do as I say, OK? Go on," she said to Lexie, and followed her into the lounge.

On the screen were aerial pictures of the Arctic. To Zanna's amazement, Alexa's description was accurate. The northern sky was filled with an upward-moving blizzard. But at ocean-level, it was still impossible to see any ice or any structure resembling ice.

"Awesome," said Lucy. She was on the edge of the sofa, clutching a cushion. Gretel and Gwendolen were with her, holding paws.

"What are the scientists saying?" Zanna asked.

Lucy gave a snort of derision. "That it's a vortex, a kind of tornado, caused by a freak combination of ocean currents and atmospheric doo-dahs. They're wrong, of course. It's Gaia. It's—"

Suddenly, both Lucy and Zanna became aware that the dragons were humming. It was the same mantra they had heard from the congregation in the Crescent. Zanna glanced at Henry. His face was a picture of bliss and his mouth, though silent, was clearly following the cadence of the hymn. Zanna passed a hand in front of his eyes. He was completely transfixed.

"What do you think?" Lucy said.

Zanna glanced at the television. "I guess we keep watching," she said.

Meanwhile, upstairs, Elizabeth Pennykettle was dreaming – perhaps. She was feverish but she could clearly hear dragonsong and it was making her think of her beloved Gwillan. "Lucy?" she whispered. "Lucy, are you there?"

Eyes closed, she laid her hand across the bed.

A strong but gentle hand came to cover it.

"Arthur? Are you home?"

Like a wind from another world a voice said, "Dream it."

Liz rolled her head against her pillow, and there was

David, sitting holding Gwillan.

Her mouth trembled and she said, "Is this it? Am I dying?"

"No," he replied.

"You look . . . Are you *real*?"

He stroked her fingers. "Sometimes," he said.

She gazed at Gwillan, drained of colour, solid. "Can you help him?"

"I'm here to help you all."

Liz's face was a sea of questions.

"His tear is not lost, that's all I can tell you. Will you give Zanna a message for me?"

"She's just downstairs. She—"

He held a finger to his lips. "Tell her to go to the library gardens."

He stood up then and let her hand slip back onto the bed.

"David? Don't leave me. I've missed you so much."

He leaned over and kissed the centre of her forehead. "Gawain is with you. Be at peace. Sleep."

The television stayed on into the evening. It was rather like watching an old moon landing, long and laborious but strangely compelling. Twice Zanna went upstairs and found Liz sleeping. Before her third visit she reminded herself that even if the world was on the brink of a major ecological change a household didn't run itself. So she did a few chores. One was to take the kitchen rubbish to the bin. Although it was dark, she hesitated before dropping in the polythene sack. She put it to one side and tilted the bin. Her heart beat double when she didn't hear a sizeable chunk of obsidian go rolling across the bottom. Gwilanna. The thieving . . .

Something was wrong here. Very, very wrong. Gwilanna wanting the knife in the first place, then a holiday in the Scottish Islands. Her strange suggestion that she'd met Tam before and the even stranger suspicion that she was running away from him. The light inside the rock that wasn't a knife but was really a heart. Why did that make Zanna's blood run cold? Why did it make her think fearfully of Gwillan?

She went upstairs to check on him. He was there, in the Den, on the table where she'd left him, but he appeared to have moved slightly. She didn't remember him facing the window. Maybe one of the others had turned him? She would have asked but, like Henry, the dragons were transfixed. All of them were looking at the sky. Everyone, it seemed, was looking at the sky.

She went in to see Elizabeth. "Oh, hi, you're awake. How are you feeling? Have you been crying?

You look so sad."

Liz was sitting up, her red hair falling in waves across her pillows. "I'm OK. In fact I feel a little better."

"Could have fooled me."

Liz shook her head. "Come and sit down. You're a treasure, do you know that?"

"I do my best," Zanna shrugged. "Everything's shipshape. Cat fed. Shirts ironed. Daughter(s) occupied. Physics genius solving equations somewhere."

"And what about you? What about Suzanna?"

"Learning. Steeply. But then I have had a very good teacher."

Liz glanced at the night sky. "Something's happening, isn't it?"

Zanna shrugged again. "Funny weather in the Arctic."

Liz smiled, long and deeply. "How's the shop?"

"Shop? Good question. Haven't been in for a couple of days. I really ought to pop down there, I suppose."

"Go tonight."

"What? At this time? No. There's far too much to do here. I'll find a slot tomorrow. There's nothing that won't—"

"Go tonight," Liz insisted. "Go and visit the library gardens. They're beautiful in the moonlight. Take Alexa with you."

It was the oddest of suggestions, but Zanna nevertheless warmed to it. Leaving Lucy and Henry glued to the television, she buttoned Alexa into her coat and drove her down to a deserted Scrubbley High Street.

An odd sense of déjà-vu started to grip her as they stood by the shop window and Alexa waved at Gruffen (who'd gone back some weeks before). The candle had burned down, right to a stub, but the Valentine card was still there beside it, still giving out its message of love.

Hrrr, went Alexa and knocked the window.

Gruffen looked out for prying eyes. Finding none, he hurred on the candle and re-lit the wick.

Alexa reached up and gripped her mother's hand. "Can we go to the gardens, Mummy?"

Liz was right about the gardens. But it wasn't just the moonlight. The glow from the amber lamps that David had described so beautifully in *Snigger and the Nutbeast* was creating a stunning collage of shadows, all across the paths, right down to the duck pond.

"I want to say hello to Conker," said Alexa.

She meant the grave under the tree, where a squirrel of that name had been buried long ago.

"Be careful," said Zanna, as they parted hands. "Don't

run, Lexie. If you trip on something—"

"Hhh!" went the girl.

Zanna saw her freeze, a little way along the path. "Lexie?"

Then the child was running again.

"Lexie?" Zanna shouted. "Lexie, come back. There won't be squirrels at this time of night."

And that was true. But as Zanna quickened her pace and took a twist of the path she saw Alexa running towards the silhouette of a man. He was standing where the path levelled out, waiting.

Alexa was slightly above him when she took off. She almost flew through the air, landing in his arms and squealing, "Daddy!"

Zanna stopped walking. There was a hand rail beside her which she reached for and gripped, but only to stop her body collapsing. She sat down on the path.

"Hello, Zanna," he said.

Zanna let go of the hand rail and wept.

Above their heads, the sky was suddenly lit by a brilliant all-encompassing sweep of violet.

Alexa looked up and gasped, "What is it?"

"A kind of angel," said David.

For there was a great light in the North.

And dragons had returned to the Earth once more.

About the author

Chris d'Lacey originally wanted to be
a songwriter, and only started writing books
when a friend suggested he enter a competition to
write a children's story. Since then Chris has had
over twenty books published, including
Fly, Cherokee, Fly, which was
Highly Commended for the Carnegie Medal.

In July 2002 Chris was awarded an honorary
doctorate by the University of Leicester (where he
worked until recently as a scientist of sorts) for his
services to children's literature. Chris is married
and lives in Leicester, England. You can read more
about him by visiting his website:
www.icefire.co.uk

Have you read the other books in the *Fire* series?

The Fire Within	Chris d'Lacey	978 1 84121 533 4
Icefire	Chris d'Lacey	978 1 84362 134 8
Fire Star	Chris d'Lacey	978 1 84362 522 3
Dark Fire	Chris d'Lacey	978 1 84616 955 7 **

Other Orchard books you might enjoy

Fly, Cherokee, Fly	Chris d'Lacey	978 1 84616 606 8
Shrinking Ralph Perfect	Chris d'Lacey	978 1 84362 660 2*
The Salt Pirates of Skegness	Chris d'Lacey	978 1 84121 539 6*
The Howling Tower	Michael Coleman	978 1 84362 938 2
The Fighting Pit	Michael Coleman	978 1 84616 214 5
The Hunting Forest	Michael Coleman	978 1 84616 044 8
A Crack in the Line	Michael Lawrence	978 1 84616 283 1
Small Eternities	Michael Lawrence	978 1 84362 870 5
The Underwood See	Michael Lawrence	978 1 84121 170 1

All prices at £5.99, apart from those marked * which are £4.99,
and those marked ** which are £6.99.

Orchard books are available from all good bookshops, or can be ordered
direct from the publisher: Orchard Books, PO BOX 29, Douglas IM99 1BQ
Credit card orders please telephone 01624 836000 or fax 01624 837033
or visit our website: www.orchardbooks.co.uk or
email: bookshop@enterprise.net for details.

To order please quote title, author and ISBN and your full name and address.
Cheques and postal orders should be made payable to 'Bookpost plc.'
Postage and packing is FREE within the UK
(overseas customers should add £1.00 per book).
Prices and availability are subject to change.